Hunted by Vampires

Joy Mosby

Hunted by Vampires

Editor: A Fading Street

Cover By: Anelia Savova AKA Ann RS

Ruby Gulch Enterprises LLC
P.O. Box 64
Craig, CO 81626

For Leah,
You had faith in me when I had none.

Chapter 1

Alex

Alex stood at the dock, watching the ferry pull away.

Fuck, he thought to himself. *I am so screwed.*

The whole reason for this mission was floating away. The ferry had a long trip back to Athens, he could get on his plane and meet it there, but there was no way of knowing whether Katie would go to Athens or get off on one of the islands the ferry would stop at on its way there. He pulled his phone out of his pocket and dialed a number.

"She's on the ferry, scheduled to arrive at eight-thirty, be there and find her." He hit the end button on his phone and sent Jared a picture of Katie. He got back in the Land Rover he had stashed near Theron's the day before, and drove back to the compound to pick up his men. He had grown to hate the island just as much as he hated her. He could not wait to leave. At least Vince was dead, Katie would have a hard go of it without him to help her.

Alex wanted to be in the air already, but his men were making sure there were no survivors. As he approached the compound he saw the fire department was already on scene which meant his men would be at the rendezvous point waiting for their ride back to the airport. He clicked his radio. "ETA two minutes. Be ready. We need to bug out." A few miles past the compound, he pulled over and honked his horn once.

Six men emerged from the surrounding shrubs and piled into the SUV. Everything had gone as smoothly as they had rehearsed the night before. The only thing not panning out was Katie.

1

"Where's the girl?" Todd asked, looking in the cargo area of the SUV.

"On a ferry on her way to Athens." Alex's voice was tight with annoyance. "Jared is going to meet her at the dock then meet us at the airport. We will get more money with her alive. It will all work out." He had to stay positive. His men didn't need to know about his doubts. Katie wasn't as dumb as he initially thought she was.

He drove to the airport following the speed limit. There was no need to attract the attention of the police. If they were pulled over they would spend the rest of their lives in a jail cell.

"Do you think Jared can take her?" Berry asked, sitting on the center console. "Last I checked the only way he could hurt someone was by freezing their bank account."

"I hope so, otherwise she will probably disappear and we will never see the money," Alex said, trying not to think of what would happen if they didn't catch Katie at the port.

Everyone in the car groaned at the thought of missing out on the payday they were anticipating. Alex understood, but he was more worried about what Lolita would do to him when she found out he didn't get Katie as he promised. They would get to Athens before Katie, but they would land over an hour away from the ferry landing. He should have anticipated her getting away; he could have chartered a helicopter to take him from the airport to the bay, but it was too late now.

Everything would work out, he thought to himself. No matter where she went he would be able to find her. Even if she had plastic surgery on the ferry he would recognize her body and the way she used it, he wasn't sure Jared could. Alex had spent all summer drooling over her. He cursed himself for the missed opportunity, if he had found out about the bounty sooner he could have kidnapped her and kept all the money for himself.

He pulled up to the airfield and blew out a breath. *At least something was going right*, he thought, looking at plane's open door waiting for them. They jumped out of the Land Rover and moved quickly to board. The pilot greeted the men as they stepped through the doorway.

"Why aren't you getting ready to take off? I thought I made my instructions clear. We needed to be in the air ten minutes ago." Alex wanted to punch the man.

"I'm sorry, sir, but we cannot take off until we get the all clear from the tower. They shut down all flights on and off the island until they catch the terrorists. If we take off without their permission, we will be asking for trouble. We have to wait it out."

"Fuck," Alex yelled, walking to the back of the small plane, and throwing his bag into the overhead compartment. He took a deep breath, pulled his phone out, and dialed Jared.

"Sir?" He sounded panicked. "Is everything all right?"

"You are going to be on your own at the dock. We aren't going to be able to take off until they lift the no-fly zone. Can you handle it?"

"No problem, sir. How hard will it be to find her and make her come with me?"

"She can kick my ass, Jared. Are you sure you can handle it?"

"Yes, sir I picked up a Taser. If she gives me any problems, I'll zap her."

"Good. I'll call you when we land." Alex hit end on his phone and looked around. "He bought a Taser."

The men chuckled as he sat down, leaned his seat back to wait, and prayed that Jared would be able to take her.

Chapter 2
Miguel

As soon as the sun set, Miguel was in his boat racing across the water toward Theron's compound. He no longer cared if Vince killed him on sight. They had been attacked, and no matter how many times he called Theron's cell phone no one picked up. Was Katie OK? She was the only thing that mattered. Without Katie, he wasn't sure life was worth living.

He beached the boat and ran up the hillside calling out, praying he would get a reply. He had never been to Theron's compound before, and he had no idea where to start looking for survivors. He ran to where the mansion had once stood and started digging through rubble. He found ashes, lots and lots of ashes left by Theron's vampires. They must have fried in the sun after the mansion blew up. He didn't know what the Cretan authorities had found but since they were gone, they must not have found any human remains.

He assumed Theron had tunnels connecting the homes and other structures on the property, but since he had never been there, he had no idea how to access them. The sun would be up soon, and he would need to find a dark place to hide if he didn't want to join those who had already perished. After clearing more than half the debris off the foundation of the mansion and not finding a tunnel entrance he started to walk the property looking for a place to wait out the sun.

He was about to give up and dig a hole when he found a random door in the side of the hill. He broke the lock and went inside. He could smell her. Katie had been there. It was an old smell, days old, but what if she was hiding in the three? He could save her and maybe get the forgiveness he craved. He moved deeper into the labyrinth following the path Katie had taken a few days before. When he entered the room where she had fought Ben, he fell to his knees and prayed she was safe. Most of the blood wasn't hers, it was a vampire's, but that meant nothing. The vampire could have drunk all her blood and left no trace. He wandered through the rest of the labyrinth finding no sign of Katie.

Chapter 3

Katie

I woke up the morning after the attack on Theron's compound, my heart was racing, and my body was covered in a cold sweat. I sat up, panicked, and looked around the room like it was the first time I had seen it. *So much for the last twenty-four hours being a dream*, I thought to myself, getting out of the hard hotel bed, and making my way to the bathroom clicking on the television on as I walked by.

"Early reports have confirmed that the explosions were part of a mob hit aimed at the head of the Cretan Mob, known locally as The Syndicate. Local authorities believe there were no survivors and are attempting to recover bodies for family members at this point. In other news—" I clicked the remote off when I came out of the bathroom and said a silent prayer to my mother. How could the only people in the world who I trusted be dead? Now instead of one enemy I had two, and to make matters worse they were working together.

Everyone was gone; dead as far as I could tell. I had not heard from Theron, Helen, or Vince since Vince told me to run when the bombs started going off. Their thoughts and presence in my mind just blinked out after a bomb blew the mansion to pieces. I was trying hard not to think about the grief Alex had caused me, trying to keep the fear, fury, and, most of all, the black hole of loss from taking hold.

I wasn't safe yet. I needed to get out of the country and off-grid as soon as possible. I had a plan. I had plane tickets, and I had a house set up. All I needed to do was go shopping for the few things I needed and sit tight until the plane was scheduled to leave. Then I could start over, again. I shook my head starting over was becoming a bad habit.

I couldn't go shopping with my go bag and my katana, so I left them in my room and put the 'do not disturb' sign on the door. I had no one left to trust so I protected what I had the only way I could. I hid the katana along the top of the drape rod and shoved my go bag into the safe.

After I cleaned up and ate breakfast in the hotel, I caught a cab to the mall. I stocked up on everything I would need in the Bahamas. It would cheaper in Athens than it would be on the small island I planned to regroup on. I wanted to go home, but I wasn't going to risk Alex or Lolita following me to the states where my parents would be easy targets. I just needed some time to come up with a plan to find and kill Lolita.

Shopping wasn't fun this time around. It was the last thing I wanted to do. What I wanted to do was curl into a ball and cry until the memory of Vince's lips on mine disappeared. I didn't have the luxury of wallowing in my loss though, I had to find somewhere safe to lay low, then I would allow myself to mourn.

I didn't notice the tail until I was almost done shopping. Two men were keeping me in their line of sight. They were good, they looked like locals, but whenever I stole a glance their way they would quickly look in another direction. I thought of Alex, he would have resources and ways to track me that Lolita would never think of using. It didn't matter who they were. I needed to lose them, but how? Vince taught me how to fight, but I wasn't a spy. I had no idea how to lose a tail when I was on foot, and in a mall of all places.

I went into a computer store and approached a bored looking clerk. "Can you please help me? There are two men following me and I need a safe place to hide." I darted my eyes to the men waiting outside the store. They were looking to their left and smiling. Crap, someone was walking up to him.

"I can call the police for you," the man said, eyeing the men.

"Please, they are trying to kill me." My eyes filled with tears, and I struggled to keep them from falling. If he called the police, I would be in even more trouble since I was traveling with a fake passport.

Something in my voice must have won him over because he said under his breath, "When I start yelling, run for the back room. As soon as you turn the corner there is a fake wall on your right. Push on it hard and it will open to a saferoom."

I nodded hoping my luck would hold and this guy would help me and not give me to Alex.

"Get the hell out of my store, you whore," he yelled, pointing at the front door. I took a step back, looked at the front door, then bolted for the back room. I found the wall as soon as I was inside and pushed it hard. There was a quiet click, and the door swung toward me. I went inside and pulled the handle back, closing the door. It was dark in the room, and I felt along the walls until I hit the back corner. I sat down, pulled my knees to my chest, and closed my eyes, praying that I could trust the salesman.

Chapter 4

Alex

"I waited around looking for her for three hours, but I never saw anyone who looked even a little like her." Jared held his hands up in surrender.

It was one in the morning, and Alex and his men had just got back to the safe house. When he got off the plane and called Jared, he could tell by the sound of Jared's voice that he didn't have Katie. As soon as he walked in the house Jared was waiting to explain. *Never send an IT guy to make a snatch,* Alex thought to himself. He punched the wall, putting a fist size hole through the drywall. It was possible she got off the boat at one of the other stops, but he doubted it. Katie would want to get as far away as possible, as soon as possible.

"I uploaded the photo you gave me into the facial recognition software and it's running a search now."

At least the man had done something right. "How long will it take to get a match?"

"It depends, it's searching cameras in Athens right now, and the immigration database. If she used a passport to enter the country, we will at least have her real first name. Now we just have to wait until she walks by a camera."

"Let me know as soon as you have a hit. I'm going to shower. Will you order some food?" Alex walked to the stairs of the narrow, three-story house they were using for their headquarters.

"On it," Jared said, going back to his workstation.

After Alex showered, he dressed in loose-fitting black pants and a gray long-sleeve shirt before he went back down stairs following the smell of food. He hadn't eaten since the MREs they had on the beach early that morning.

Everyone was lounging around the room eating gyros and staring at the television. He walked past them into the kitchen, he pulled a beer out of the fridge and opened it on the side of the counter. He went to the takeout boxes piled on the table and grabbed one before heading back into the living room to hang out with his men. He took a seat at the back and watched the footage of the attack on Theron's compound. The guys were laughing and admiring their handy work. It wasn't very often they got to see the aftermath of an operation of this size. They were typically on a plane flying far away when the news covered it.

Jared jumped out of his seat. "We have a hit," he said, looking to Alex.

Alex stood and walked over to the computer and looked down at it. There was a picture of Katie's passport, only the name associated with it was Mary Sims, not Katie. He forced himself to breathe through the betrayal he felt. She hadn't even given him her real name? "Where is she?"

"I don't know yet, but at least we found her real name. This is a better picture too, so the software will be able to come up with hits easier now. If she walks by any camera wired to the net, we will get an alert. I can start a financial search for her as well. If she uses a credit or ATM card with her name on it, we will be able to pinpoint her location."

Alex walked back to his seat and forced himself to eat. She wasn't going to be able to leave Greece without going through Athens. They would get a hit, then he would find her, and take her to Lolita.

He finished his food and threw the take-out box in the trash.

"I'm going to get some sleep. Wake me up if you find anything."

The following day Alex woke up to the smell of coffee. Almost before he opened his eyes, he was putting a shirt on to go in search of it. Jared was sound asleep at the table with his computer still on. Alex smacked him on the back of the head as he walked by. Jared jerked awake and looked around, forgetting where he was for a minute.

"What have you got for me?" Alex asked, getting a coffee mug out of the cabinet, and filling it with the coffee.

"Sorry, I fell asleep. Let me see if we got any hits last night." He clicked his computer mouse, and multiple windows popped up, then disappeared.

Alex stood behind him sipping his coffee and watching him work. They had to find her before she left the country.

Leaving Greece would be on the top of Katie's to-do list, Alex thought.

"OK, looks like we have four possible hits. They range from a fifty percent likeness to seventy-three percent." Jared hit a few buttons and brought the four grainy images on screen.

Alex moved closer and Jared looked over his shoulder. He squinted, looking for something to stand out about the four women, but the images were so grainy and taken at such a distance there was no way to be sure which one was Katie. "Can you clean them up any?"

"I wish. This country is so broke, the last thing they have money to spend on is better quality cameras."

"Go wake everyone up, we need to come up with a plan." Alex took Jared's chair when he left and stared at the pictures on the screen. The first one had a fifty-percent match; it looked like the woman had blond hair, but she had a big hat on. She was wearing leggings and tennis shoes with a plain white T-shirt. It didn't feel right to him.

The next photo was of a woman wearing a baseball hat with her hair tucked up into the cap. She was wearing shorts and a work out shirt. It could have been Katie, she had a fifty-five percent match.

He moved to the next photo, it was of a woman with brown hair cut in a bob walking down the street with shopping bags in her hands, she was looking over her shoulder in the photo and had large lensed sunglasses on. It had a sixty-nine percent match. That was her, he had no doubt in his mind.

He looked at the last match, but it wasn't her. The woman was in a business suit walking with a briefcase and high heels. There was no way Katie would be caught dead wearing something so professional.

The pounding of feet coming down the stairs alerted him to his men joining him. He spun his chair around and glanced at them to make sure they were all in the room.

"We have four possible sightings of the mark. We are going to break into teams and check out each one of these women. Jared will stay here and keep us appraised of their locations."

After he broke them into teams, they left the house to track down the women assigned to them. Todd, Berry, and Alex were going after the one in workout clothes while the others went to check out the others.

They found the woman running down a street lined with closed stores. They pulled up behind her and Alex jumped out to jog next to her for a minute. When the woman looked at him he knew it wasn't Katie-Mary, whatever her name was. There was no recognition in her eyes and she was much older than Katie. He stopped and went back to the van.

"Not her?" Todd asked, as Alex got into the passenger seat, and put his seatbelt on.

"No." He picked up his phone from the center console and called Jared. "We have a negative on our mark. What is the status of the other teams?"

"Team four has a negative. The woman works in a law office,

has her picture on the wall. Team two is trying to get closer to the mark. Team one is trying to find theirs."

"Send me the location of team two and we will help them out." He hit end on the phone then waited for the address of team two to come through. When it did he entered the information into the GPS, and they started across the city.

Alex stared out the window as Todd drove. He really thought the woman running was Katie, but maybe it was only because he had spent so much time with her running. He had to find her. If he didn't he was going to have to tell Lolita he failed, and he was afraid what she might do to him if he did.

Twenty minutes later they pulled up to the address Team Two was watching when his phone vibrated. He clicked the answer button. "What?"

"Sir, I think we found her. She is at the mall, shopping. She dyed her hair blond."

"Berry, check on team two," Alex said, moving the phone away from his mouth, then bringing it back. "How do you know it's her?"

"It looks like she has heavy makeup on covering bruising and she is buying summer clothes, in the fall."

"Send me your location and don't lose her." He looked over to Todd. "We are going to the mall; it looks like she dyed her hair. Tell Berry to catch a ride with Team Two." He looked back at his phone then put the address in the GPS, and they were off to the mall.

"Sir, I think she knew we were following her. She just ran through a computer store and out the backdoor."

"Shit, I'm on my way. Stay where you are in case she's hiding in there." Alex ran, meeting his men outside the store. "Where is she?"

"She hasn't come out and the clerk seems really mad."

"I'll talk to him. Have Jared see if he can access the mall's cameras and track her." He walked into the store, looking around in case she was hiding behind one of the displays.

"Hi, do you speak English?" Alex asked, when he reached the counter.

"A little," the man behind the counter said, taking a step back. "How can I help you?"

"My girlfriend just ran in here. I need to find her, we are supposed to fly home in a few hours."

"Why did she run away from you?"

"We got into an argument about how much stuff she was buying. My friend out there said he saw her run into your backroom."

"Oh, the crazy girl? She ran through the backroom and out the backdoor. I don't know where she went."

"Would you mind if I checked your backroom just to make sure she isn't hiding in there? She can be sneaky."

"I'm not supposed to let anyone back there, but if you think she might be hiding in there go ahead." He came out from behind the counter and led Alex to the back. The clerk stood by the door keeping one eye on the front and the other on Alex in the back.

Alex looked in the bathroom, behind shelves, and under the desk before he went to the backdoor. "Well, she's not here. I'm going to try and follow her from here. Thank you for your help."

"Good luck," he said, and let out a breath when the door closed.

Alex pulled his phone out and called Jared. "Where did she go?"

"I hacked the system, but they don't have any cameras in the back. I have no idea where she would have come out. I'm trying to get the blueprints of the mall. They don't show the back hallways on the main map. I'm working on it."

Alex went to the left from the backdoor of the computer store. "Don't bother. Run her name through the credit card system, find out where she's staying. Send Team Two to the airport, and

Team One to the train station. She's probably not leaving the country today but just in case she is, I want to catch her before she leaves." He pushed through a fire door and squinted in the late-afternoon light. "We have to get her." He hit the end button on his phone and sent a text to Team One, telling them to meet him in the parking lot. He had lost her again. He slammed the palm of his hand into the concrete wall; she could not have gone far, for all he knew she was still in the mall somewhere.

They re-grouped in the van and got some fast-food to tide them over while waiting to hear back from Jared on the results of the credit card report. He sucked the last of his water out of the straw when his phone rang.

"What did you find?" he asked, putting his empty cup in the trash bag.

"She is staying at a hotel about five minutes from the mall. She bought a plane ticket yesterday for the Bahamas. Her plane leaves tomorrow morning at six a.m."

"Send me the address of the hotel. Call Team Two and have them meet us there. I want all the exits covered as well as the parking lot." He hit the end button on the phone and entered the coordinates into the GPS.

"Hope you guys are ready for a stakeout," he said as they left the mall.

Alex had half his team in the van in the parking lot logging all the cars that came in and out while the rest of them covered the exits of the hotel. Alex played the part of a concerned older brother while talking to the hotel manager, explaining that his sister had run away the night before and he thought she was staying there. The manager confirmed that Marry Ann Sims was a guest of the hotel, and she had not yet checked out, but Alex couldn't convince him to give up her room number, instead he had Jared find it for him.

As he sat on a sofa in the lobby waiting for Jared to send him Katie's room number, he watched the front door and fantasized about waiting for Katie in her room. There was no way she was going to get away.

It took Jared longer than it should have to hack the system, which meant Alex didn't get the room number until almost midnight.

He skirted around the manager and snuck into the elevator taking it to the fourth floor. He walked with purpose down the hallway until he reached the door. He slid his universal key card out of his wallet and unlocked the door.

He inhaled and cursed himself for savoring the smell of Katie. He hit the light switch and found an unmade bed, and towels on the floor. He went into the bathroom and found nothing but used complimentary bath products. He checked the closet, the safe, even behind the curtains. There was nothing to prove Katie had ever been in the room other than her scent.

He shoved the door open and marched down the hall punching buttons on his cell phone as he stopped in front of the elevator. "Find the surveillance tape, I want it ready for me to review when we get back to the house," he told Jared as he stepped into the elevator.

"She's gone?" Jared asked, over the clicking of keys being typed in the background.

"There is nothing in her room. I want to know who fucked up and didn't see her come in and out of the hotel." Alex hit the end button on his phone and tapped his foot while the elevator slowly descended to the ground floor. She could've moved before she went to the mall, for all he knew. Damn, he just needed to find her.

He was out before the elevator doors fully opened. "We are out of here," he said to his men, not waiting for them as he stomped out the door to the van.

They drove back to the safe house in silence. Alex was too mad to speak, and the others knew if they said anything, he would take it the wrong way. Alex was out of the van almost before it came to a complete stop at the house and ran inside.

"What have you found?" he asked Jared, storming over to his command center.

"Alex, I'm sorry man. They found the backdoor I used to access her room number and reinforced their entire system before I could get back in. They are monitoring everything happening with the network right now. I can't get in."

"What the fuck? I thought you were the best of the best. That's why we hired you. A crappy little hotel computer system kicked your ass? Is that what you are telling me?" Alex's hand balled into a fist, he needed to hit something.

"It is not a crappy little hotel system. It's connected to Weston hotels, they found the breach two minutes after I accessed it. It would be pure stupidity to even try and break back in for at least a month." Jared pushed away from the computer and got to his feet. "I'm done for the night." He pushed past Alex and went upstairs to his room.

"Fuck," Alex screamed to the empty room. If he didn't find Katie soon he would forfeit his life.

He was just about to lay down for the night when his phone lit up with an incoming call. He looked at the caller ID, Lolita. *Fuck*, he thought to himself. He wasn't ready for this conversation.

"Lolita," he said, after pushing the connect button on his phone.

"You put on quite a show in Crete. Is she dead?" her sultry voice asked.

He didn't want to answer. He wanted to lie and tell her the bitch was dead, but if she found out Katie was still alive, and he had no doubt she would, he would be dead. "Not yet, she escaped."

"What?" she screamed into the phone, her sultry voice replaced by a banshee. "This wasn't part of the agreement."

"I know, I'm sorry. She hasn't left Greece and she won't unless it's with me."

"What about the rest of the vampires on the compound?" She was still screaming at him.

"We didn't find any survivors other than Katie. You shouldn't have

19

to worry about Theron or Vince ever again." At least he had some good news for her. "I watched them be buried alive."

"Find her. I am giving you six months, if you do not bring her to me alive or with her head in a bag you will learn a new meaning for the word suffering."

"Yes, ma'am," Alex said, but she had already ended the call. "I'm so fucked."

Chapter 5

Katie

After what felt like hours there was a soft knock on the door. I tensed. I had no idea who was going to be on the other side of it. The computer guy or Alex and his mercenaries. I stood and blew out a breath. If I was going to go down, I was going to go down fighting. I wasn't going to run anymore, damn it. I pushed the door open ready to beat the crap out of any bad guy on the other side.

The computer guy stood there with his hands up in surrender. "They're gone. You're safe."

I slumped and rubbed my eyes. "Thank you." Now what was I going to do? There was no way I could go back to my hotel; if they found me here they probably knew where I was staying.

"Here I brought you some water. You can call me Ramstein," he said, offering me an unopened bottle. "Was that guy your boyfriend?"

I choked on the water I just swallowed. "Boyfriend?" I asked, coughing. "No, he was a friend for a while. Now he wants to kidnap me and take me to a woman who wants to kill me." I didn't want to tell this stranger what was going on with me, but what other choice did I have? I could not go back to the hotel and I had a feeling I was going to need to stop using Vince's credit cards. If Alex found out what name I was using, he could easily hack Vince's accounts and figure out where I was. I was going to have to take a leap of faith and trust this guy. "That guy, he's a mercenary who was hired to collect a bounty on me. Is Ramstein your real name?"

He blinked, and his eyes widened for a second before he shook his head and backed out of the room. I followed close behind, I didn't want him to lock me in there and find Alex to get a finder's fee. "You're not joking, are you? No, it is my code name." He walked deeper into the backroom and started hitting buttons on a desk top computer dominating a small desk.

"I am deadly serious. I have no idea what I'm going to do. If he found me here he probably knows where I'm staying and what name I am traveling under. Which means he can tag and track my credit cards. I have one hundred euros in my pocket and the things I bought today. I can't even go back to the hotel to get my stuff." I held back the tears threatening to fall. My katana and my laptop were the only things I really needed. The katana because Theron had given it to me, and my laptop because it was the only thing that made me feel like I had a way out.

"Listen, I know some people who will help." Ramstein got up from the desk and started turning off light switches. "I have to set the alarm on the store in the next ten minutes or my boss will think I am up to no good. Would you mind waiting in the hall while I close up? Then I will help you get your stuff back and take you to my friends, if you want."

"Why are you so willing to help me? You don't even know me. Why should I trust you?"

"I can't make you trust me but what other choice do you have? From what you said, not many. You could go to the police, but without any evidence, the police aren't going to do anything about it."

I closed my eyes. I did not have any other options unless I wanted to spend the night on the streets, jumping at every shadow thinking Alex had found me. "OK, I'll wait for you in the hall."

I stood in the back hall of the mall waiting. I had never been in the back of a mall before. It was creepy. There was a long hallway, the walls and the floor were all made of concrete and while the ceiling was finished with drywall and paint, it looked like it had been years since they had a fresh coat. There was no place to run. If Alex came through the heavy door at one end of the hallway I would be a sitting duck. There were other doors scattered randomly down the hall but if they were anything like the door to the computer store, they automatically locked, and were heavy fire doors, I would not be able to force my way in.

I closed my eyes and used my ears to alert me of any threats. My eyes snapped open when the door in front of me opened and Ramstein came out. I automatically fell into my fighting stance before I realized he was a friend, not a foe and relaxed. He jumped back like I was going to attack him anyway. I let my arms fall to my sides and moved my legs into a neutral position. "Sorry, I'm a little on edge right now." I gave him a half-smile.

He nodded his head, pulled the door closed behind him, and checked to make sure it was locked. "I would probably be the same way if I were going through what you are." He led the way down the hallway to the door leading to the parking lot. He opened it, stepped out, and held it open for me. I hesitated before walking out; I didn't want Alex to sneak up on me.

"Don't worry I made sure they left. You're safe." Ramstein held his arm out, trying to get me out of the building.

With no choice I exited, and took in my surroundings looking for anything out of place. There was a video camera over the door and it dawned on me. "Come on let's go," I said, almost running away from the door, hoping I didn't look at the camera long enough for it to get a good picture of me.

"What are you worried about?" he asked, trailing after me. "My car is over there." He pointed to a lone car in the parking lot.

I adjusted my course and moved toward it. "I think I know how he found me."

"How?" Ramstein caught up to me and matched my rapid gait.

"He probably has access to photo recognition software, if that camera got a good shot of me we are both screwed." I kicked myself for not thinking of it before. Alex had deep pockets and the bounty Lolita had on me would be worth spending money on top-of-the-line equipment to track me

23

down. There was no way I would be able to sneak into the hotel and get my stuff.

"I put the camera on a loop before we left." He pushed a button on his key chain, and his VW beeped. "Get in, let's go."

I got into the car and put my seat belt on, while he got in on the driver's side. "You know how to do stuff like that?" I didn't know why I was surprised, he did work in a computer store.

"Yeah, and a lot of other stuff too. What hotel are you staying at?" He started the car and drove to the nearest intersection.

I told him where it was, and he turned the car in that direction. "I don't think I will be able to get in there without one of Alex's goons waiting for me, or being spotted by one of the cameras."

"I'll get your stuff for you," Ramstein offered, without looking at me. "Then I can take you to my friends, with some incentive, they will help you."

"Why are you helping me?" I didn't know this guy and he didn't know me. From my experience, strangers would not help me unless they wanted something in return. I was done doing things in return for people, as I always ended up with the short end of the deal. Well, except for Vince, but I couldn't think about him or I would lose it, make a stupid mistake, and get caught.

"My brother, Marathon, and I are part of a group who help people. You need help, so I am giving it to you." We pulled into the parking lot of the hotel and parked as far away from the lights as possible.

"OK," I took out my room key and gave it to him. I didn't trust him, but I wanted my katana back. "It's room 419. My bag is in the safe. The combo to the safe is 010502, and on top of the curtain rod there is a katana in a scabbard. I could care less about everything but the sword, it was a gift."

He looked at me like he was expecting me to be joking about the sword, when I didn't follow up my statement he let out a nervous laugh. "I'll be back as quickly as I can. In the meantime, keep your head down and the doors locked." He got out of the car and shut the door. I listened to his footsteps fade away before he locked the car with his key fob. The double beep almost had me jumping out of my skin.

It felt like hours before he came back, I heard lots of steps and people talking, but none of them were Ramstein. Why wasn't I trying to fight Alex? He wouldn't be stupid enough pull a gun on me in a populated place. I could take him, I thought about getting out of the car and walking into the lobby with my katana and killing Alex and all his men, but I didn't have my katana and he had at least three other guys with him. I didn't think I could do it without some kind of a weapon. I looked at my watch, it had only been ten minutes, but it seemed too long. I was starting to panic, if he wasn't back in another ten minutes I would leave and find a somewhere else to stay for the night, but then what? Hitchhike out of the country?

The car beeped twice, and I heard the trunk pop open. I heard Ramstein put something in the trunk, close the lid, then he came around to the driver's side and opened the door. "Good thing you didn't go inside." He sat on the driver's seat and put his seatbelt on. "The lobby was crawling with guys acting like security guards. They wouldn't let me in until I showed them my key card."

"I'm so sorry I put you in danger." I sat up and rested my elbow on the door, then rested my head in my hand. "The sword is really important, but I should've just left everything." Alex was going to be a bigger pain in the ass then Lolita ever was.

"It's OK. I got in and out without anything bad happening, but it took me a while to find the sword." He started the car and took off at a normal speed out of the parking lot. "Do you want me to take you to my friends?"

"I don't think I have a choice. I can't travel by air, probably not by train. I could buy a car, but I don't want to use my current passport, plus he would know I bought a car," I said, thinking aloud. I was so screwed.

"You can lay low with my friends. They are in a small village in the mountains. No one will be able to find you there. They might even be able to help you acquire a new passport, and access your money without being traced."

It sounded too good to be true. "What's the catch?" There was no way these people would hide me and help me without something in return.

"Well, you will probably have to win them over. They don't like outsiders." I looked out the window at the lights of Athens. This guy could be a serial killer for all I knew. Maybe he wanted to take me to his mountain torture chamber, where no one could hear me scream. I thought for a moment; I could take care of myself now. Vince made sure of it. He would always be with me when I had to fight. I fought back the tears for the hundredth time. It still wasn't time to breakdown and mourn him like he deserved. I was far from safe. "I don't have any better options at this point. Will you take me there?"

"Yeah, I was going to head there after work anyway. Don't worry about it. Lay back and get some rest, it will be while." He moved the car into the right turn lane and took off down the highway.

I was being dumb, but my adrenalin was spent, and sleep sounded like the best thing in the world. I closed my eyes, let my mind drift to the sounds of the car and was asleep in minutes.

"Where are you going?" my mother asked, from her seat on the dais of her temple.

"Somewhere Alex and Lolita won't be able to find me." I walked toward her from the back of the room.

"You need to go to Delos, they will protect you there." She folded her hands across her lap.

"I have no way of getting there without alerting Alex." I was tired, and I wasn't in the mood to deal with her. "He's using technology to track me. Until I figure out a way to move under the cameras and credit card monitoring, I can't take public transportation, and I can't buy a boat to get there." Not that I would if I could, I had no idea how to maneuver a boat.

"This unacceptable, you must kill him." She stood and met me half way. "You are strong enough, you have the skills that Vince taught you. Kill him so we can get back to business." She grabbed me with both her arms and shook me lightly.

"It's not that easy, Mom." I pried her hands off me and took a step back. "He has a small army and guns. I know nothing about guns." I wanted to kill Alex almost more than I wanted to kill Lolita. He had taken Vince from me. I let out a sob and she pulled me into a hug.

"Vince will be missed," she said quietly into my ear.

I allowed her to comfort me while the tears started to fall down my checks. "Is he dead?"

"I do not know. I cannot feel him anymore, so most likely. His work was complete. He trained you very well."

I pulled away from her. "I loved him. How can you say that he served his purpose?" I turned away from her, wanting to rage at her.

"Sweetheart, you know what the prophecy says:

'Those of my begotten who have forgotten me will be made
to heal by a woman bearing my mark.

She will be found on the east shores of the great ocean
beyond the Pillars of Hercules, in a protected bay.

None will be able to deceive her, as she will be able to listen
to what is in the hearts of my creation.

Her powers will manifest as her knowledge of her kind
grows.

Those who try to enslave her will reap the recompense of her
exasperation.

The one who mentors her will be endowed with an accolade
from the chosen one.

The one who changes her will suffer putrefaction in Tartarus for all days.

She will bring my creation back into the fold.'

"There is nothing about love, a queen should only love her subjects. You do not need him. Get over it."

"I don't want to be queen," I yelled, walking toward the exit. "I wanted Vince and now he's gone. Just leave me alone." I walked through the door and jolted awake. Ramstein had turned the engine off. "Where are we?

"Just stopping for fuel. Do you want something to eat or drink?" Ramstein asked.

It had been a while since I ate, and my throat was powder dry. "Yes, can you get it for me? I don't want to be seen on any cameras."

"Yes, I'll be right back." He got out of the car, started fueling it, then went inside the store.

I looked around trying to figure out where we were, but there was no moonlight, and the gas station seemed to be in the middle of nowhere A few minutes later he came back to the car with a plastic bag full of goodies. He opened the door and handed it across to me.

"Here take this." I took it from him, glancing inside.

He got in, closed the door, and fastened his seat belt. He started the car and moved to park on the side of the road where there were no lights.

"If you want to eat, do it now, I am going to have to blindfold you for the rest of the trip." He took the bag from me and pulled out a candy bar.

"Why do you have to blindfold me?" I was taken aback. I thought we were trying to trust each other.

"Listen, you have no idea how paranoid my friends are. If I don't blindfold you, I don't know what they will do to us."

"OK, I'll wear the blindfold. Give me back the bag." I had a bad feeling about this, but there did not seem to be any other option. At least I would be closer to the border if I needed to leave the country using my thumb. I took the bag from him and pulled out some chips and chocolate covered peanuts. I opened them and started eating. I took a water bottle out of the bag, and sipped on it between mouthfuls. "So why is this place such a big secret?" I asked, around a mouthful of chips.

"Because we do a lot of things to bad people and they would love to know where our headquarters is."

"How long have you been part of it?" I asked, I needed to keep my mind off the black hole of loss trying to swallow my mind.

"Since I was a kid. My parents were part of it." He looked at me quickly then out the window.

"Oh, I'm sorry. Did they pass away?"

"Yeah, they sacrificed themselves for the safety of the town. I was ten and my brother, Marathon, was twelve. The residents ended up raising us after they were gone."

"Sorry I brought it up," I said, crumpling the empty bags, and putting them back in the grocery bag.

"You ready?" he asked, pulling a knitted face mask out from under his seat and handing it to me. "Put this on backwards please."

"Yeah." I took it from him then took one last look around. "I have no idea where we are now, there is no way I will be able to find my way back here," I vented, but pulled the mask on and leaned back in my seat. He started the car and took off down the road. We rode in silence for a while before thoughts of Vince started to drive me crazy.

"What have these guys done? Were they the ones who released all those names from the Ashley Madison website?"

He laughed. "No, but I know the group who did. That was a great hack. Remember when all those emails about the oil companies from your vice president were leaked?"

"Yeah," it had been a huge scandal and the VP was now in jail for the next ten years.

"We did that."

"Wow it was some major hacking from what I remember the news saying." I was impressed, if he was telling the truth.

"We have done a lot more in Europe. Most of it doesn't hit the news in the States. We do other stuff too."

"Really like what?" I had nothing to do but listen, and feel the change in the road as we went from pavement to dirt.

"We help when no one else will. We have helped free hostages from terrorists demanding ransom from individuals. If the government won't step in, and we can, we will get them out without paying the ransom."

"How do you fund it? It doesn't sound like you run a for-profit business."

"We have a few obscenely wealthy benefactors."

That had my mind jumping to vampires. "Can you tell me their names? How long have you known them?" The last thing I wanted to do was hang out with vampires I didn't know, especially since all the ones I trusted were dead.

"No, I'm sorry they are anonymous. They won't be there if you are worried about it."

"Sorry, I'm paranoid." I let out a breath. I didn't want to deal with any more vampires.

"After what I saw tonight it looks like you have a right to be."

"How much farther do we have to go?" I was nervous, this might have been a huge mistake.

"Not long, when we get there let me do the talking."

After what felt like hours the car finally came to a stop and Ramstein let out an audible breath making me think he was nervous too. "You can take the mask off now. We're here."

I pulled the mask off and looked out the windshield. It was dark, but it looked like we were in the center of a small town. The buildings along the street were three stories tall, but the windows only went as far as the second story. The streets were cobblestone and narrow. There were no sidewalks.

"What do you call this place?"

"Kevó," he said, opening the door.

"Why is it called that?" I asked, getting out of the car, and walking around to join him. Kevó meant Void, in Greek. It was an eccentric name for a village.

"Our founder stumbled on the location a long time ago. He suffers from a mental illness and it is the only place he has been able to find peace."

We walked to a brightly lit building with boisterous voices bubbling out of it. He held the door for me. As I stepped inside, the room went silent. Ramstein followed me in and put a hand on my shoulder to steady me.

There were about twenty people in the room, mostly men with a few women scattered here and there. Most of them had shot glasses or beers in their hands. Everyone had turned to stare at me except for one, who kept his back toward me. He was a vampire, I felt him, I tried to a step backwards but Ramstein blocked my path.

"What the hell, Ramstein, who is this?" A man who looked a lot like Ramstein slammed his beer down, stood, and stomped over to us, it must have been Marathon.

"She needs our help." His hand tightened on my shoulder. "Isn't that what we do? Help people."

"Yes, but we don't bring them here." He stopped in front of us and crossed his arms over his chest.

"Let me tell you what's going on and you'll understand why I had to bring her here."

I wanted to stick up for myself, but I didn't think it would help my cause. I let the brothers argue while I stared at the vampire sitting at the bar like nothing was going on. I found his mind and tried to break in, but he didn't have just a wall around his mind, it was a foot-thick steel barrier. It would take me hours to break in. He looked over his shoulder and gave me a quizzical look before turning back to the bar.

I was glad, the last thing I wanted to do was talk to a vampire. I turned back to Ramstein and his brother. "I don't want to be a problem. I'll go if you could point me to the closest town maybe I can hitchhike out of the country."

Marathon turned to look at me. "Is it really that bad?"

I didn't want to get into it, but I didn't have a choice, I needed help. "Did you see the attack on Crete?" I asked, keeping the vampire in my field of vision to see how he would react. "I'm the only one who made it out of there alive, and unfortunately they know I survived."

"Were you followed?" A young woman who was sitting nearby asked.

"No, they thought she ran away at the mall. When I went to her hotel to get her belongings there were guys everywhere, but they didn't give me a second glance, we are safe."

"This is a huge risk. What are we supposed to do with her?"

I was getting tired of them talking like I wasn't in the room. "Look all I need is a new passport, and someone to show me how to access my money, without it being traced. Then I will get out of your hair. Believe me I don't want anyone else to get hurt because of me."

"Do you know who's after you?" Marathon said, finally turning to look at me.

"Only their first names. The one who tried to kill me on Crete is named Alex, he's a mercenary. The one who put a bounty on my head is named Lolita."

"Fuck, if it was Alex Jorgensen, you're screwed. He never lets a job go. What did you do to piss this Lolita person off?"

I was dumbstruck; these guys knew who Alex was? More importantly what was I going to tell them about Lolita? I couldn't tell them the truth. "Well, it's complicated..." I trailed off trying to come up with a lie they would believe.

"She can stay," a voice boomed through the room, and everyone turned to the vampire sitting at the bar. He turned and locked eyes with me.

"Thank you." I prayed that saying her name wouldn't bring her here. *Please let this vampire be on my side*, I thought to myself.

"Come, I will show you where you can stay." The vampire stood and made his way to me. Everyone in the room took a few steps away from him, giving him a direct path to me.

"Can I get my things out of Ramstein's car?" I asked, as he walked by me out the door and I turned to hurry after him.

"After I show you to your apartment," he said in a clipped voice that did not invite any other questions.

He walked down the road so quickly I almost had to jog to keep up with him. He veered off the main road and down a narrow alley that could only be traversed by foot. Halfway down he stopped and opened a door to my right. He held his hand out inviting me to enter first. I walked in and felt around for a light switch. I heard him move behind me and fearing he was going to attack, I tucked and rolled away from him.

"Good," he said, before switching a light on. "If you bring any other of my kind here I will kill you," he said, turning to leave.

"I won't bring them here on purpose. All the vampires I counted as friends died on Crete." My voice cracked as I choked back tears. I told myself to toughen up. "As long as none of your people tell anyone I'm here, we shouldn't have a problem."

"Then we are in agreement. Fear not, I will not bother you as long you do no harm to me and mine." He turned and closed the door on his way out.

I bent over and put my head between my knees. From what Ramstein said, I thought vampires might be funding the town, but I wasn't expecting one to live here. He didn't seem to care that I knew what he was, but I didn't trust him to leave me alone. Most of the vampires I had met couldn't help themselves, but I believed him when he said he would not tell anyone where I was.

33

After I found my breath, I looked around the small apartment. There was a small living room with a couch in hues of orange, very 1970s, against one wall. On the other were drawers built into the wall. There was an old beat-up coffee table in front of the couch and a bookshelf along one wall with tattered paperbacks on it.

There were only two doors in the place, the front door and one on the opposite side of it. I went through it and found a small bedroom with a single bed, a small wardrobe, an even smaller dresser, and a nightstand with a lamp on it. The walls were white with faint outlines where wall-hangings were once hung. There was one small window on the wall, I doubted I would could fit through it if I needed to escape.

I opened the only other door in the room to find a tiny bathroom. There was a shower, sink and toilet. I could probably brush my teeth at the sink, take a shower and pee all at once. It was small, but it was better than the alternative.

I turned silently when I heard the front door open. I hated that there was no way of escape. I moved to the open bedroom door and looked out through the crack between the door and jamb. Ramstein was standing there looking around with his arms loaded with my bags.

I came around the door. "Thank you for bringing my stuff. Is that everything?"

"No problem, the only thing left is your sword. I thought you might like to get it. Where do you want me to put everything?" he asked, looking around.

"On the couch is fine. Yeah, I'll get my sword. Did you leave the trunk open?" I asked, as he set my shopping bags down.

"No, I'll walk back with you, then I have to get some sleep. It's been a long day."

We walked out the front door and I turned to close it. "Is

there a way to lock the door?" I asked, seeing a lock on the knob but no key.

"The key should be on the coffee table. If it's not, I'll get one for you tomorrow."

"I hope I didn't start a fight between you and your brother." We walked down the alley back to his car.

"We'll be fine. It was my decision to bring you here. It's not your fault."

"Who was the guy who said I could stay? He never told me his name."

"He is our founder, we call him Tad, but I don't think it is his real name." He hit a button on his key fob and the trunk opened.

I looked in and found my katana resting in the middle with its scabbard in place. I reached in with two hands and pulled it out. I brought the grip to my face and let it rest against my forehead for a second. "You will never know how grateful I am for what you did."

"No problem. Look I'm going to bed. I'll come by around eight tomorrow, and show you how everything works around here."

"See you then." I turned and went back to my new home with a lighter heart. I always felt better when I had a sword in my hand.

Chapter 6

Miguel

Miguel spent the day wandering around the labyrinth wondering if anyone was still alive. When the sun finally set, he went out and continued his search for the tunnels.

He started at what was left of one of the smaller houses this time, thinking that finding an access point to the tunnel system in one of the smaller houses would be easier than the mansion. Connecting the buildings by tunnel was the only way to get things done during the day when they could not go outside.

He dug through the broken slabs of concrete for half the night before he found the entrance. Once he was in the tunnel he ran, hoping to find someone alive. Theron's tunnel system was complex and better built than the ones he had at home, it seemed like he was spending more time trying to find his way than he was looking for survivors. He needed to remember it when he got back to San Sebastian. His tunnel system was adequate, but Theron's made his look like a four-year-old built it out of blankets. He always started by taking the tunnel to the left, and when it led to the surface he would go back and take the next one. If the tunnel had caved in, he would dig until he came out on the other side.

He worked for hours trying to find any sign of life. He was starting to tire. He was going to have get something to eat before long. He was about to give up when he came to another blockage, he did not know if he had the energy to get through it. He looked at his watch, it was only midnight. He could get through one more before he needed to eat.

He made it a few feet in when he felt it, something that wasn't a rock but not a chunk of dirt either. Excitement surging through him. He worked quickly, moving the debris away hoping to find a vampire, and hoping whoever it was, wasn't dead. After digging around the form, he pulled it out and laid him on the ground. He had no idea who the dirt-encrusted vampire was, but he wasn't dead, only unconscious.

He continued to dig, hoping he would find other survivors. He was hungry and tired, but after finding one survivor, he strengthened his resolve and continued to dig. He was ready to give up when he found another hard-soft spot. He cried out in relief as he pulled a female vampire out and laid her next to the first one he found. His strength was almost gone, but where there were two there was likely more. He dug, wishing he had someone to help him, but he didn't have to dig long before he found another male vampire. After pulling him out of the dirt he fell back, he could do no more, he needed rest.

They needed blood. He looked at his watch, he had an hour before the bars would begin to close, he had enough time. He took off to find donors for the unconscious vampires and grab something for himself. They were damaged and broken but they had their heads and their hearts, all they needed was blood and time.

An hour later he pulled up to the only opening to the tunnel he had been able to access and escorted the four people he had been able to compel, into the tunnels. He brought them to the vampires who desperately needed their blood.

Feeding the unconscious vampires directly from the source was easier said than done. He had to compel the humans to stay still while he cut open their wrist and hold it over the vampire's mouth while somehow keeping the Vampires mouth open. Once it was done and he had eaten as well, he dismissed the humans and compelled them to forget what they had done for him. He leaned against the wall and closed his eyes wondering where Katie was, and why the humans attacked Theron in the first place. He wouldn't know until he nursed the vampires on the ground back to consciousness. It was going to take a while for them to recover enough to be able to take care of themselves, so he got to his feet, and kept digging, wanting to believe there were more than three survivors.

Chapter 7

Lolita

Lolita hit the end button on her phone. She wanted to throw it across the room, Alex failed to kill Katie. He created an international incident and he still had not completed his mission. Katie was still out there alive, but she was on her own. At least Alex had been able to kill Vince and the rest of the vampires helping her. If Vince had survived, she would have killed Alex without a thought.

Katie was a liability, but there was no need to stop building her army. Lolita was going to take over Europe one way or another and it was moving day. Once she was at her new home, she would not have to worry about anyone finding her army. Her new island was finally ready to move too, and besides Paris's head vampire from wasn't very happy with her. Too many people were missing or turning up dead drained of blood.

"Ilhami, let's get the soldiers loaded." Lolita opened the cargo hold on the train car she leased to move her army to Venice. Ilhami opened the door to the catacombs and the filthy, half-starved, hoard followed the smell of blood into the train car. They were going to need to get cleaned up before she started her attack. They looked like something out of a zombie movie as they were.

With one car loaded, Ilhami and Louise closed the door and moved the train forward to load the next group. It was taking longer than Lolita thought, if they didn't hurry they would have to leave some behind.

"Pier, hurry we have to have them all loaded before the sun comes up. If you need me I will be in my car." Lolita turned and walked up the line of cars until she reached the luxury car she leased for herself. Soldiers, were soldiers, they could ride as steerage, but she needed her space and her things.

She sat down on the sofa and got her phone out. What was she going to do about Alex and his failure? He was smart and knew how to track people down, hell he had found Katie when no else could. She typed out a text message to remind him what she expected from him.

You have six months, if you do not have her by then, your life is forfeit.

Chapter 8

Katie

I woke up in the morning feeling refreshed and the best I had felt in the past two days. I didn't feel anywhere close to myself, but better than the day before. I got cleaned up and looked at my watch. It was seven forty-five, Ramstein was going to meet me at eight. I went over to the bookshelf and looked at the titles of the books. They were almost all in Greek. Theron and Helen had helped me learn how to speak Greek, but I could barely read it. I was about to go into my room to pick up the book I bought the previous day when there was a knock on the door.

I picked up the key I found the night before, and put it in my pocket. I looked at my katana sitting on the table. I would feel safer taking it with me, but it might not send the right message to my new community. I left it sitting on the table and went to the door.

"Good morning," Ramstein said, taking a step back. I exited my apartment and closed the door behind me, making sure it was locked.

"Good morning." I pasted a fake smile on my face and waited for him to show me where we were going. He turned and started up the alley. I looked around as we walked. Everything was white stucco, as I expected but there was something odd about the roofs. They weren't symmetrical, it was a very unusual style I had never seen before. "Where are we going?" I asked, as we came to the mouth of the alley.

"Breakfast of course. Your apartment doesn't have a kitchen, so you will need to eat in the cafeteria. You can always get food there and take it back, but it's a pain because then you have to bring your dishes back. Most of us eat there all the time."

We walked down Main Street until we came to a set of glass double doors. We went inside, and everyone stopped talking. These people weren't happy I was there. I wasn't happy about it either, but I wasn't going to leave unless they made me.

"Follow me," Ramstein said, walking to the back of the room where a door stood open.

I followed him, reminding myself I had permission to be there, so I pulled my shoulders back and held my head up. Through the doorway there was a buffet with eggs, meat, pancakes, donuts, and cereal. I hadn't had much of an appetite since the attack in Crete, but I forced myself to put enough food on my plate not to be rude and at the same time little enough I could eat it without being wasteful.

We exited the buffet area into the main dining room to find it almost empty. "They cleared out fast," I said, following Ramstein to a clean table.

"We are a shy bunch, but they'll get used to you. Give them time." He sat down at a table, and I sat down across from him.

"What do I need to know about this place?" I asked, forking up some eggs, and eating.

"Try not to get into anyone's business and they will stay out of yours. Breakfast is from six 'til nine, lunch is from noon 'til two, dinner is from seven 'til ten. If you need something in the meantime, there are usually some snacks and fruit on the table by the door. There are two kinds of people here, hackers and mercenaries. Don't worry, they have all been here for years, they won't bother you."

The word mercenaries made me cough and choke on the sausage I had just eaten. "How am I going to get them to help me?"

"I'm a coder, but I don't know how to do the things you need. You are going to want to talk to Hound, Barkley, and Copperhead, they can show you everything you want to do. I wish I could tell you how to win them over but it's going to take time. I have seen it take years for these people to trust someone."

"What should I do in the meantime? I want to earn my keep." I was desperate to keep the black hole of loss hovering in the back of my mind at bay.

"We all take turns with kitchen duty. You could help clean and get ready for meals until you find something else to do. We all hate it. If you lightened the load it won't go unnoticed." He continued eating, while I mulled it over.

"Anything would be better than sitting around with my own thoughts," I said, going back to my food, and forcing myself to eat what was left.

"Good, here are the other things you need to be aware of. No one goes by their real name to protect their identity; your phone will only be able to send and receive text messages. There is a satellite phone in headquarters, but you need permission from Tad to use it. This is our secret hideout, you have to swear you won't tell anyone about it when you leave."

"OK." I put my napkin on my plate. "But wait what name should I go by?"

He looked at me for a long moment assessing me. "I think you should go by Karate Kid, since you're obsessed with your katana, but you can choose any name you want as long as it's not your real name."

I thought about it, Karate Kid was kind of corny, but I could not think of anything else. "OK, you can call me Karate Kid then. Should I go ahead and get started cleaning this place up?" I looked around at the trays, sitting on the tables, with half eaten food on them.

"No, I want to give you the rest of the tour before I leave. I have to get back to Athens and work tonight." He got up with his tray, and I followed him.

"You're leaving?" I asked, bummed out, as he was the only one who wanted me here in the first place.

"Yeah, but I will back before you know it. He flipped his tray over a trashcan then put it on a table next to it. I did the same and followed him out the door. I had no idea how I was going to deal with this place on my own.

"Across the street is the laundromat." He pointed at the building across the street, the glass on the windows covered in steam. "The buildings on either side of it are apartments." He started walking away from the cafeteria and up the street. "You know where the bar is." He pointed. "Over there is the general store. They only take cash. If there is anything you can't get there let me know and I'll pick up for you in Athens."

"I'm going to need some warmer clothes, but I don't have enough money to pay you," I said, as we walked by the store.

"You can pay me back, I know you are good for it." He bumped my shoulder with his. "Over there is the gym, no membership required."

I looked across the street. I saw a few exercise machines through a dusty window, it did not look very appealing. "Does it get used?"

"Not very often, the soldiers use it when the weather is too bad to work out outside." He laughed.

"Who are the soldiers?" I asked as we stopped in front of the tallest building on the street.

"They're mercenaries who only work for us. You could almost call them our army. This is headquarters, everyone has an office here even if most of us work from our apartments."

"Over there," he pointed to the other side of the street, "is the post office and the bank. There's a park down that alley, and there are some trails you can check out. We are so far from civilization you won't be able to figure out where you are."

"That's a happy thought," I said, looking around the village, glad I could work in the kitchen, otherwise I would go insane.

He looked at his watch. "I have to go. Walk me back to my

46

car?"

"Sure, I have nothing else to do," I said as we turned and walked back down the street. "Do you have time to introduce me to the cook before you go?"

"Yeah, crap, I forgot." We hurried back to the now empty cafeteria and made our way to the kitchen. "Lucy, are you back here?"

"Right here," she called, and we went behind the buffet table weaving our way around the industrial kitchen.

"Lucy, I want you to meet someone, this is Karate Kid. Karate Kid, this is Lucy, our cook."

I pasted a smile on my face and extended a hand. "Hi, it's nice to meet you."

"Welcome to our little place in the world." She took my hand and shook it lightly. She was short with a white chef's coat and zebra striped pants on. Her hair was up under a hat, but I thought it must have been brown with a little gray based on the wrinkles on her face. I guessed she was in her late fifties.

"Thanks, Ramstein said you might need some help around here. I'm not a very good cook but I can clean, or something if you need the help." I looked around at the pile of dishes from breakfast.

"When can you start?"

"As soon as I say goodbye to Ramstein." I turned to look at him.

"Walk me to my car?"

"Sure."

"I can't thank you enough for all your help," I said, once we were at his car in the underground garage.

"Like I said it's what we do. Oh, I wanted to get your phone number." He pulled his phone out of his pocket.

"I don't have one," I cringed as I thought back to fleeing Crete. "I ran it over; I didn't want Alex to track me through it."

"I'll bring one back for you then. Stay out of trouble and try to make some friends." He got in his car and I watched him drive away.

I blew out a breath and I turned to go back to the cafeteria. At least I was in a safe place even if no one wanted me there. Plus, I had something to do to keep me busy at least part of the time, then I could train until I was too tired to walk. Maybe with some luck I would be able to sleep without any nightmares.

"Do you want me to start on the dishes?" I asked, once I was back in the kitchen watching Lucy stir her pot.

"Yes, the buffoon who had kitchen duty hasn't shown up yet. There are aprons hanging over there." She pointed with the wooden spoon she was using to stir the pot. "Do you know how to use an industrial dishwasher?"

"No, I've never used one." I went over to the stack of towels and aprons, grabbing an apron, slung it over my neck and tied it behind my back.

"Come on, I'll show you." Lucy led me back to the dishwashing area.

Five minutes later, I was elbow deep in dishwater wishing I had my MP3 player, so I could at least listen to music while I worked. It didn't take as long as I thought it would to get through the plates, and a half hour later I was scrubbing pans when someone tapped on my shoulder. I whirled around ready to attack when he held his hands up. I should have heard him coming, what was wrong with me?

"What are you doing here?" he asked. He was about five-foot-ten with wavy light brown hair ending just above his shoulders. He had hard, brown, almost black, eyes and bushy eyebrows. He was probably in his early forties.

"Doing the dishes what does it look like?" I was trying to make friends, but I was tired of washing dishes.

"Why are you doing them? I pulled kitchen duty this week." He crossed his arms over his chest. "If you think this is going to make people like you, you're wrong."

I closed my eyes and found my center. With the way I was feeling, I could have cared less about making them trust me. "Look, I have nothing else to do so I thought I would help out. You should check with Lucy, but as far as I am concerned you are off the hook. I got this for the foreseeable future."

"Lucy," the man yelled, and I covered my ears.

"What Mordor?" she asked, walking over to us with her hands on her hips. She looked at her watch and raised her eyebrows. "Finally, here, I see. You were supposed to be here at nine o'clock."

"Yeah, well I had real work to do. What is she doing here?" He pointed an accusing finger at me.

"It looks like she is doing your job. What are you complaining about?"

"No one here knows her. She could poison us when you aren't looking. What if she's a spy?"

"She is washing dishes nothing more. If you want her to leave she can, and you can do the dishes for the rest of the day."

"I'm going to talk to Tad about this." He stomped out through the backdoor, slamming it on his way out.

"OK," I said, just staring at the door. "Did that really just happen?"

"Mordor is an asshole, excuse my language. Unless an idea came from him and it works, he hates it. If his idea doesn't work, he blames it on someone else." Lucy turned and went back to the stove. "Don't let him get to you, honey. You'll be fine."

I went back to the pans and after an hour of scrubbing I finished the last one. "I'm all caught up on the dishes. Do you need me to help with anything else?" I asked Lucy, after hunting for her in the labyrinth of the kitchen.

"Not right now, if you want to come back around three there will be more dishes to do."

"I'll see you then." I went back to my room and lay down on the bed. All I wanted to do was sleep. I wasn't sure if I was still recovering from my test and the attack on Crete, or if it was something else. I didn't matter all I wanted to do was not think about all that I had lost.

Lucy was surprised to see me back a few hours later ready to continue my work. There weren't as many dishes to wash this time, and Lucy chased me out of the kitchen when I pestered her for something else to do.

I walked down the road and found the park Ramstein told me about. There was a jungle gym for kids, and a few covered picnic tables, surrounded by a lawn. I sat down at one of the tables to take in the landscape. In front of me was Mount Olympus, already covered in a fine layer of snow. The Olympus Range reminded me of the Rocky Mountains back home, they weren't as tall, but they were just as rocky with jagged rocks and sharp peaks. I had a feeling the warm day I was enjoying wasn't going to last, as I watched dark clouds formed above the peaks.

I went back to my apartment, I changed into my workout gear and went for a run. My body was still sore from my test and fighting Ben. The bruises on my face and body were still there and they hurt, but I ran through the pain. When I got back to town there were a few people on the street. When they saw me, they stopped and stared, like they forgot I was there. I didn't know how I was going to deal with being shunned, but I didn't have anywhere else to go.

With nothing else to do I went back to the park to work on my martial arts. There were a few people already there enjoying the sun or playing with their kids on the jungle gym. I found a quiet space with no one around and started working through the katas Vince had taught me. It was all right at first; I concentrated on the moves and being exact, but then I started thinking about when Vince showed me the kata. How I followed him through his mind and the intimate feelings we shared as we practiced together. I forced myself to continue and not let the black hole of loss hovering in my mind take over, but when I was done I was exhausted and on the verge of tears.

The people who had been minding their own business when I began were now staring at me. I could not tell if it was in astonishment or condemnation, but I wasn't going to wait around to find out. I bowed and ran back to my apartment. I was going to fall apart, and I did not need an audience for it.

Chapter 9

Alex

Alex paced back and forth in front of his computer with his men standing behind him. He ran his hand through his hair before he stopped and faced them.

"Where did she go?" he asked.

"We don't know. The last time we saw her was when she went into the computer store," Thomas said, looking around to the other men. He didn't understand why this was their fault. They did what Alex asked them to do.

"Why hasn't she shown up anywhere since then?" Alex asked them, like they were hiding her location from him.

"We don't know. Maybe she changed her appearance again. Look Alex, I know you have to find her, but if we are not going to get paid for this job we have another one that will put us back in the black," Thomas said, holding a paper with the details out to him.

"I can't do anything until I find her. You don't understand who I am dealing with, Lolita fronted me some of the money for this hit, and since we failed she is going to expect payment for what I borrowed plus interest." He batted the paper away and ran his hand through his hair again.

"Come and do this job with us and you'll be able to pay her back." Thomas obviously had no idea. If Alex failed, he would be lucky if Lolita let him keep his life.

"No, you guys go. I'm not going to give up." He turned, sat down at the computer, and started to add alerts to the program to track Katie.

"If you change your mind, give us a call." The men turned, picked up their bags, and left Alex alone.

Part of him wished he could leave with them and write off the last three months of his life. Forget about ever meeting Katie and falling in love with her. Well, he thought it was love. He had never truly been in love before, but he thought he could have loved Katie. She was strong, determined, funny, and yet she was gentle, and she acted like she cared about him. He pushed back from the desk looking for something to hit.

She had played him. She had talked him into helping her, train with her, protect her from the crazy bitch who wanted to kill her. Then she rejected him, and it was all Vince's fault. Those two were fucking behind his back while she batted her eyes at him to get him to do things for her. She had made a fool out of him. Katie probably went home after their workouts and had a good laugh with Vince about how she had him wrapped around her finger.

Katie was more than a hit, it was personal. He should not let his feelings affect him, but he could not help the way he was feeling about Katie. He had to find her.

Maybe she found her way to the Bahamas since she was going to go there before he found her. He didn't think she would be that stupid, and he was sure her passport photo would have been tagged by his system. Nonetheless, he had tagged all the cameras he could find on the islands just to be on the safe side.

He pulled up the video feed of the airport. She could leave the country in many ways, but the airport would be the easiest. There was no money trail though, knowing the devious bitch, she probably had another bank account and was using it instead of the one he had tagged. She could not hide forever though. He would have to wait, find some patience. She would pop up, then he would find her and take her to Lolita. There was no other choice.

Chapter 10

Katie

I woke up in the middle of the night cold, remembering that I wasn't in Crete and that Vince wasn't in the next room if I had a bad dream. I would never see him again, how was I going to go on without him? The man I had barely trusted three months ago had become the most important person in my life and I lost him. The black hole opened, and I let it take me. I was safe at least for the moment.

I sobbed into my pillow. I told Vince that I loved him in the voice message I left him on my way to the ferry in Crete, but he would never get to hear me say it. He took such good care of me, took an average American college girl, and turned her into a finely tuned warrior.

I let out a sob thinking of all the pain he had forced me to work through. The pushups, punching the board, the punching bag, swimming in the sea with cracked and bleeding knuckles. The arduous work turned me into the warrior I needed to be if I was going to survive. I had already defeated my first vampire, Ben was dead at my hand, and I had more to kill. I didn't know if I could do it without Vince.

I thought about the massage room and how Vince would dispassionately work all my muscles until I was so relaxed I could barely walk. I sobbed again, thinking he wasn't impassionate, he was holding himself back. All the times he would touch me only to pull away. He had been in love with me, maybe since the beginning, but he followed the rules. He didn't want to be romantically involved with me until he was done training me. It hurt us both, but his training made me so much stronger, mentally, and physically, it centered me, I was so much better than I was before. I had to believe he did the right thing.

But then I thought about all we lost by not acting on our feelings while we were together. We got one kiss, that was it. Now I would never know what it would be like to make love to him or what it would feel like to wake up in his arms.

I went into the bathroom and pulled a wad of toilet paper off the roll and blew my nose. It would've never been fucking with Vince, no matter how hard, or dirty, or where it would have been. It would have been making love. I went back to my bed and threw myself onto it. Falling asleep thinking of Vince, as tears continued to leak from my eyes.

I did not wake up until noon the next day. I dragged myself out of bed and forced myself to take a shower and put clean clothes on. I went to the kitchen and waved to Lucy before I started washing the dishes. When I was done I went back to my room and slept.

I wasn't hungry, I just wanted to sleep. I slept until nine that night then went back to the kitchen and washed the dishes. On my way back to my apartment I passed the bar and stopped to look in the window. Everyone was laughing and talking. A few couples were dancing, they all looked so happy. I didn't know if I would ever be happy again. The tears started to come back, and I quickened my pace, not wanting the strangers to see me cry.

I went back to bed and slept. It was the only escape I had from the pain in my chest. It became my new routine: sleep, washed dishes, sleep, and do it all over again. I didn't talk to anyone or even smile. I had to force myself to take a shower, somehow the pain was always worse when I was in the shower.

My face healed, the bruises faded, and I had nothing to remind me of my final days in Crete, and it hurt. I never took off the necklace they gave me. It was all I had left of them other than my katana. Every time I saw the necklace around my neck pain, shot through me, it felt like it was stabbing me, burrowing through my skin trying to find a way to pierce my heart and end it all, but I couldn't bring myself to take it off.

I spent my first week in Kevó being consumed by the black hole of my grief. I could not bring myself to do anything except the necessities. I had never been more tired in my life. Drowning in the memories of Vince, Theron, and Helen was all I could think about. I thought about the dream I had when I entered Vince's mind and the kata we had done before making out. We would never get the chance to do it as we had in my dream. Entering his mind and having him lead me through the kata was one of the best memories I had. The love I had felt from him, how I thought it had been for someone else, when it had been for me.

I was lying in bed staring at the peeling paint on the ceiling, a week after I arrived in Kevó and started to think about Alex. All I had wanted was to be his friend, but he couldn't do it. He had to have all of me or nothing. The bastard. I wished he had never shown up on Crete, I would still have Vince and the rest of Theron's vampires if not for him. My allies were gone. Anyone who could help me kill Lolita was gone, all because of Alex. It was more than that though. I was stuck. I had nowhere to go. I could not access my or Vince's money, and I could not show my face anywhere without Alex finding me. He would not give up. He was determined to ruin my life because I didn't want him the same way he wanted me.

Once I started thinking about Alex, I started to get mad. It was all his fault, it was Lolita's too, but Vince was dead because of Alex. I was going to kill him, and I couldn't kill him if I was sleeping all the time and barely eating. I needed to get my ass out of bed and start to plan. Figure out how to kill both of them, I didn't care if I lived through it or not, but they both had to pay.

Chapter 11

The Turk

"Leydim, do you have minute you can spare?" The Turk asked, poking his head into Lolita's train car.

"Ilhami, of course, please come in." She put down the magazine she had been reading. They were still hours from their new home and The Turk was always a good diversion. He bowed then took the seat across from her. "What can I do for you?" she asked, folding one leg over the other.

"My contract with you is up today." He was terrified; she could feel it.

"Is it? Where has the time gone?" She looked at her nails. "I'm sorry that your contract wasn't up in time for you to enact your revenge."

"What do you mean?" He leaned forward in his chair, and rested his hand on his knees.

"Did I forget to tell you what happened on Crete? I'm so sorry. Theron's whole compound was bombed, in the middle of the day. There is nothing left, and from all reports there were no survivors."

"Who did it? Why? Why didn't you tell me? I have been waiting a lifetime to get back at him and now he's dead." He wanted to cry. His whole life's purpose was gone, and he had not been there to watch.

"A mercenary was trying to collect the bounty on some girl who was staying at the compound. I'm sorry I didn't tell you, it must have slipped my mind." She put a hand on his leg. "Of course, you are free to go, if you want to go back to Crete and see what is left, you can."

"I do not know what I want to do. I have only had one goal for so long that I have no idea what to do with myself now that I cannot accomplish it."

"Well, Theron did run the island, it is likely in chaos without a leader. You could get even with all those who opposed your family, and take over the island."

He straightened in his chair. "That would help me fulfill the promise I made to my family. Would you mind if I went?"

"Of course not, but I hope you will remember all of the things I have done for you in the past. If I need you, and you are able, will you come back to me and give me aid?" It was taking everything she had to let him go, but Crete was and always would be a valuable location. If he stayed loyal to her and ruled Crete, he could help with the coming war.

"Yes, of course, you know I believe in your vision. I will leave after we get the army settled on the island."

Chapter 12

Miguel

Miguel sat on the dirt floor of what was left of the tunnel system Theron had created, with three unconscious vampires propped up against the wall. He wanted to get some water and clean them up. He still had no idea who they were, they were so covered in mud and dust it was impossible to tell. He hoped one of them would wake up soon.

He was bored sitting in the dark, but he had nowhere else to go. He could not even safely look for more survivors until the sun went down. He brought his phone out, but the battery had died hours before. He needed to solve some basic needs problems when the sun went down. He needed to get more blood for the unconscious vampires, charge his phone, get some water, maybe find a house nearby to stay in. If he went out looking for more blood covered in dirt and smelling like he did, it was going to be harder than it needed to be to compel humans to follow him.

As soon as the sun went down he went out in search of a more permanent place to stay. There was a house across from the compound that had escaped damage from the attack. It was an older home with small windows he could easily paint over. The lights were on, so he approached and knocked on the door. An ancient looking woman answered with a surprised gasp at his appearance. He quickly grabbed hold of her mind and forced her to invite him inside. When he had both, the old woman, and her husband, under this compulsion he told them to take an extended holiday to see their children. They packed and left within the hour.

With the couple gone he moved the vampires from the tunnel into the house, took a shower and put on some clean clothes. They weren't his clothes, but they would work until he could get to a store and buy something better. Dressed, he took his car and went to the nearest town. He bought black paint for the windows, a pick, a shovel, and clothes for himself, and the rest of the vampires in his charge.

He was loading the trunk of the car with the items he bought when a car pulled in next to him. Four people started to get out, but he caught their minds and compelled them to follow him back to the house. After he fed the unconscious vampires and dismissed the humans he went back to the tunnels and continued looking for more survivors.

Finding none he went back to the house a few minutes before dawn. He was beginning to think he found the only vampires who survived the attack.

With the sun up, he took each vampire into the shower, and cleaned them up. This first one he washed was Theron, or he was pretty sure it was Theron. The woman was Helen, the one who had come to talk to him on the island when he first arrived. He shook his head when he washed the dirt and grime off the last face. Part of him was elated, the other part of him was terrified of what would happen when the vampire woke up.

Chapter 13

Katie

I had just gotten back from my run and was getting ready to strip down and take a shower, when someone started pounding on my door. I snuck as quietly as I could to the door and looked out the peephole. There was no escape from the room but at least I had a peephole to see who wanted to kill me.

The girl on the other side of the door looked left then right and crossed her arms over her chest. She had long bright pink hair up in a ponytail, she was bone thin with high cheek bones, bowtie lips, and big blue eyes. She looked harmless, but I kept my katana in my hand as I opened the door a crack.

"Yes?" I asked; my voice cracked and sounded deeper than normal.

"Karate Kid? Tad wants to see you," the girl said. She looked no more than fifteen.

I blinked, trying to remember who Tad was for a second. *Crap, the vampire wanted to see me.* "Let me get some shoes, do you want to come in?"

"Sure." She followed me inside, while I sat down and started to put my shoes back on.

"What do you go by?" I asked, trying to be polite.

"Uni." She looked down her shirt.

"Short for Unicorn?" I asked, smiling at the unicorn on her shirt.

"Is there something wrong with it?" she asked as she crunched her face up in anger.

"No, I think unicorns are cool. I've always thought they would be way better than regular horses. They have a weapon on their head."

"Way cooler than horses, but not just because of the horn. Are you ready to go?" She looked down at my shoe-clad feet.

"I guess. What else makes them cool beside their horns?" I asked, trying to think of anything else that made them different from horses.

"They just are. You can't take your sword." She looked at the katana I picked up from where I set it down to put my shoes on.

"Why not?" I felt naked without it.

"He doesn't trust you, actually, almost nobody here trusts you." She opened the door for me and we exited. When she shut the door, I pulled the key out of my pocket and locked it.

"That's better than I thought." I put the key back in my pocket.

"How so?" Her brows pulled together, trying to understand.

"Well I thought nobody here trusted me. Things are starting to look up if almost nobody does."

"It takes a long time for anybody here to trust a new person."

"It's OK, I don't trust very many people either. Do you know what Tad wants to see me about?"

"No, I was just told to bring you to him at headquarters." We started to walk up the alley to Main Street. "Hey, are you OK? It looks like you've been crying."

"What?" I instinctively wiped at my eyes, even though it had been at least an hour since I had cried. "I'll be fine. I lost my friends a few days ago, and I'm feeling a little lost."

"I'm sorry. I'll be your friend." She grabbed my hand and swung it back and forth with hers.

"Thanks, you're really nice. What can I do to earn their trust?" I asked, smiling, despite how much I hurt inside as we walked down the alley.

"I wish I knew. They are all paranoid you're going to rat them out. I know you won't." We turned and walked up Main Street. There were a few other people walking toward us, but when they saw me they moved to the other side of the street.

"I'm not going to rat anyone out. Thanks for trusting me." We stopped outside the three-story building and I looked up at it.

"Sure, look when go you inside there's a staircase on the right going down to the basement. Tad will be waiting for you down there. I have to get back to work."

"Uni, how old you are?" I was stalling. I didn't want to go into the basement unarmed with a vampire waiting for me.

She laughed. "Everyone does. I'm eighteen, I'm one of the coders."

"Well, it was nice to meet you. Maybe we could hang out sometime." I was desperate for anything to keep my mind off the friends I had lost.

"Yeah, meet me for dinner at eight thirty?"

"Sounds good." I watched her walk away and went up the steps into Headquarters to find my way to the basement.

Chapter 14

The Turk

The Turk smiled as he left the airport and breathed the air he was born in for the first time as a vampire. When he left fifty years before, Theron had scared him enough not to venture back until he had been turned. Now he wasn't only a vampire, but he had the backing of one of the most powerful vampires in the world. He wasn't going to throw her name around though, and he would not call her for help unless there was no other way to win the island on his own. He wanted to prove to her that he could be just as powerful and ruthless as she was.

He hailed a cab to take him to the house he rented. It wasn't going to have any of the things he would need, but it was only temporary. He would have a villa with UV protected windows and servants to cater to his every need soon. In the meantime, the rental had a fully furnished basement and would work until he had control of the island.

The taxi stopped outside the house in the middle of Heraklion. He paid the driver and got out with his one bag. He unlocked the door and went inside. It was nice, with white walls and marble floors. There were two bedrooms on the main floor with a kitchen and a dining room. He found the stairs to the basement and found another bedroom and an entertainment room. He put his things away and looked at the clock. He had just enough time to get to his meeting.

Ilhami knew they would be meeting the night he arrived. There would be a lot to discuss. Their leader was dead, and a new head of The

Cretan Syndicate must be appointed. Otherwise a turf war would start, and the island would be thrown into chaos. Ilhami was going to be the new head of The Syndicate, there was no other option.

He walked to the meeting stopping a few hundred yards from the bar. Security would be tight, and he didn't want to kill anyone yet. It would give them the wrong idea and he might need to kill them later to prove a point. Instead, he used stealth to sneak past the guards.

All the lights in the bar were off except for one, hanging over a long table where five men were seated. He could smell their cigar smoke and a hint of ouzo coming from their glasses as soon as he entered the room. They were all talking quietly to each other with solemn expressions on their faces. He thought it was interesting that the meeting had not started yet. He noticed there was one empty chair with a full glass of ouzo in front of it and he wondered if it was a place of honor for their lost member, or if they were waiting for someone else to join them. He moved away from the door silently and stood in the corner of the room waiting to see how things would unfold before he made himself known.

"OK everyone, let us have one last toast to our fallen brethren. To Theron, may he dwell in whatever heaven he believed in," the man at the far end of the table said, holding up his full shot glass of ouzo.

"Opa." Everyone called then downed their shot.

Ilhami came out of the shadows, took the glass meant for Theron and held it up. "To Theron the man who killed my family and exiled me from this island. May he rot in hell, where he belongs." He threw the shot glass at the wall, and glass exploded around the room. Two of the men at the table shot to their feet, their hands at the waistbands of the pants looking for weapons that were not there. The other three sat up straighter in their chairs, their eyes open wide with shock.

"Who are you?" The man who made the toast snarled, putting his hands on his hips.

"I'm Theron's replacement of course. You did not think that one of you would take his place, did you?" Ilhami sat down in the vacant chair and pulled out a notebook.

"Why do you think we would follow you? We do not even know you." The man folded his hands together and rested them on the table.

"Because you need a strong impartial leader who wants nothing but the best for Crete." Ilhami did not look up from the notebook he was flipping through. "Here we are, you must be Takis, head of the drug trade, next to you is Agapios, who oversees entertainment. At the end of the table we have Leonidas, in charge of imports and exports, then we have Serafeim, in charge of arms deals, and Evangelos, head of protection and general racketeering. I am Ilhami Tilki, you may call me The Turk." He closed his notebook and crossed one leg over the other.

"How do you know who we are?" Leonidas asked, his eyes darting around the table, it was obvious he wasn't used to being in a situation like this.

"I have done my research; it does not take much to figure out who oversees what with today's technology."

"You are going to threaten us to follow you? Is that your plan?" Serafeim asked, remaining calm and unperturbed.

"I do not wish to threaten you, but look how you have welcomed me." He looked around the room. "No welcome home, no 'it's great to see you'. How should I handle this when you all look like you are going to kill me if I turn my back on you?"

"You have not instilled any trust with us." Leonidas returned to his seat and placed his hands on the table. "How do we know you aren't the one who killed Theron?"

"Would that it had been me, believe me." Ilhami grinned, making eye contact with all of the members. "But no, it wasn't me."

"Maybe, if you tell us your plans for the island we can begin to build a relationship." He was trying to be level-headed, but his heart rate betrayed him. The only calm ones in the room were Takis and Serafeim. They must be used to tense situations.

"I will not sit here and listen to his plans when Theron is not even cold in the ground." Evangelos's face turned red.

"Decisions must be made if we are to continue," Takis said. "We cannot wait until the mourning period is over before we chose a new leader. If we wait, things will start to fall apart. We have a good partnership, and we need someone to make sure it will continue."

"Why would we choose a dirty Turk?" Evangelos spat the last word. "They have never done anything but treat us as less than human."

"What choice do we have? None of us know him, so he will be impartial." Serafeim leaned back in his chair. "He snuck past our guards, which means he is cunning. He says he was born here. If he was, he is a Cretan."

"How do we know he will put the good of the island before all else?" Leonidas asked. He was sitting with his hands on the armrest of his chair, ready to bolt for the door at the first opportunity.

"We ask him." Serafeim turned to Ilhami. "To be the head of the Cretan Syndicate you must take an oath."

"I would like to hear it before I agree to it." Ilhami was surprised; they were criminals, yet they had an oath. He would never understand the Greeks.

"Very well." Serafeim nodded his head to Evangelos. "Read him the oath."

"You must swear to put Crete above all else in this world, whether it is money or family. If you become part of The Syndicate your family will be all of Crete.

"Swear that you will not harm any civilians in your role.

"Swear that you will not turn in any of The Syndicate for a

reduced sentence if you are ever arrested.

"Swear to be a life member, once you are in you can never leave."

"I cannot travel?" Ilhami asked, looking confused.

"Of course, you can, but you will always be part of The Syndicate, if we call for aid, you must come," Takis said half-laughing.

"Is that it?" Ilhami asked, looking around. He no issues with any of it, and besides as the head, he could change the rules however he wanted.

"Yes, but there is the matter of the buy-in," Agapios said, his eyes going bright.

"How much is the buy in?" Ilhami asked, scanning the room.

"You have two options: you can pay us three million euros each," Serafeim said, looking around the room to make sure everyone understood what he was doing. "Or, you can avenge Theron, by killing the man who killed him."

It took everything Ilhami had to keep his anger under control. He was about to compel them all to just accept him, but unless he made them his slaves, the compulsion would not last longer than a few hours. He did the math quickly in his head, he had nowhere near fifteen million euros, and the last thing he wanted to do was kill the one who orchestrated the death of the man he hated. Hell, he wanted to buy the man a beer. He could ask Lolita for the money, but he did not want to depend on her. He wanted to show her he could rule in his own right. If the war she wanted was going to happen he wanted to be on his own, in his own little bubble.

"I will avenge Theron or raise the money which ever I can do quicker." He stood from the table but left his hands resting on it. "Do you wish me to take the oath now?"

There were grins all around. "No, you cannot take the oath until you have completed the initiation processes," Takis said, relaxing back in his chair. "But you still must abide by it if you wish us to accept you into our numbers."

"What can you tell me about who did this?" Ilhami asked.

"We know nothing more than he had a team of men, and they acted quickly. They did not set foot on the island until they were already engaged." Serafeim filled his shot glass with ouzo. "He did not buy his firepower from me, and he used stuff I have never seen before."

"I better get started then." Ilhami pushed away from the table. "Gentlemen, I will see you all very soon to take my oath."

"Very well, in the meantime stay out of our business," Takis said.

Ilhami walked the streets hungry for blood. He had not eaten since they had left Paris and it was getting to a critical level. He found a bar and went inside. It was late- almost empty. He found a man sitting alone in a booth at the back. He sat down next to the man, and when the man looked up in outrage Ilhami grabbed ahold of his mind before the man could get a word out.

"You are tired and ready to go home. Pay your bill and meet me outside." Ilhami got up and left the bar before anyone noticed him. He waited outside and a few minutes later the man exited looking dazed. "Over here," he called, and the man followed him into a dark alley.

Ilhami stopped and let the darkness blanket them before he bit into the man's neck and let the warm blood flow into his mouth. When he was done he sat the now unconscious man against the wall and strolled away. He needed to plan. These men thought they could take advantage of him. He would show them.

He went back to the house he rented and went straight to the basement. He pulled his laptop out and looked at all the information he had gathered on them. Turning Takis and Serafeim into his slaves first would be the best course of action. The others were already afraid of him. If he had the ones who could not be rattled on his side he would be able to take over the island within a month, without putting too much effort into finding out who killed Theron or raising fifteen million euros.

Both men kept odd schedules, there was no way to know where they would be from one night to the next and it was going to be hard to get them alone. He picked up his phone and dialed the only number for member of his family he kept in touch with.

Chapter 15

Katie

The inside of headquarters looked like an office building anywhere in the world. There was a reception area with hallways off to the left and right of the desk. The walls were white and blank, which was unusual. I walked up to the desk and smiled at the woman sitting behind it. She ignored me and continued typing on her keyboard.

"Hi, I was wondering how I got to the basement? Tad asked to see me," I said in my sweetest voice.

The woman looked up quickly then back down and pointed to the doorway on the right. "Go through there, the stairs are right around the corner."

"Thanks for your help." I walked through the doorway, not waiting for her to respond. I was getting tired of people treating me like I was invisible. Around the corner I found a set of stairs that were not as creepy as I expected them to be. They were concrete, four feet across with a handrail. I had been envisioning a rickety set of spiral stairs leading to a dungeon.

When I reached the bottom of the stairs, a closed heavy steel door stood, blocking the way. It was gray with nothing written on it. If I did not know where I was going, I would think it just led to a storage area. I tried the handle, but it was locked so I knocked on it.

"Who is there?" a voice on the other side asked.

"Katie, I mean Karate Kid." It was going to be hard to remember my new nickname.

A second passed before I heard a deadbolt being pulled and the door opening. Tad was already walking back to his desk when I entered. "Please close and bolt the door behind you," he called over his shoulder without stopping.

My heart rate picked up, he wanted me to lock us in together with no escape route. *Trust goes both ways*, I thought to myself. I pushed the heavy door back into place and slid the bolt home.

I was expecting a dank, moldy-smelling dungeon, but I found myself in a clean well-appointed room. There were knickknacks everywhere, from beaded necklaces hanging inside cases, to Spartan helmets and spears. The walls were white, and the floor was black concrete covered in rugs. I had a feeling everything in the room except for the desk and the computers were hundreds or even thousands of years older than I was.

I walked to the desk trying not to step on the rugs and stood before it, waiting to find out what Tad wanted. He looked at me then back at his computer monitor for a moment. "You are Katie Hunter, you were reported as a missing person in San Sebastian, Spain three months ago, shortly before half the city was burned to the ground. Miguel, the leader of the vampires there, and has not been seen since. Then you tell me you were at Theron's on Crete when it was decimated, and everyone on the compound is dead. Are you trying to destroy vampires?"

His question caught me completely off guard. I never thought about it from his angle before. "I've only killed one vampire and it was in self-defense."

"Who was it?"

"Theron's third in command. There's a bounty on my head and he tried to collect it. He failed." I would never be sorry for killing Ben.

"I watched you train this afternoon. Who taught you?"

"Vince, the gladiator." I had no idea what Vince's last name was, but it sounded good. "Theron and Helen helped."

76

"Why would they spend their time training you?" He leveled his gaze upon me.

"Are you familiar with Asteria's Prophecy?" I sat down in the chair, praying I was making the right decision by telling him.

He stopped looking at his computer and pushed his chair back.

Has the Goddess finally found me?

"No, but I'm her daughter, 'The One'." Whoever Tad really was, he didn't want the Goddess to find him.

"Can you read minds?" He cocked one eyebrow.

What am I going to do if the Goddess found me? He was freaking out on the inside even as his face remained calm and neutral.

"Only vampires, and unless you project to me I have to break into your mind do it. You were just projecting. I don't think I could break into your mind without a lot of work." I was trying to set his mind as ease, but I only seemed to be agitating him more.

"When did you try and break into my mind?" He demanded, slamming his hand down on his desk.

"The night I met you. Please understand I meant no harm, but I have been screwed over by a few of your kind, and I don't trust as easily as I once did."

"Did she send you here to find me?" He changed the subject abruptly.

"I don't know who you are other than a vampire, but if you mean Asteria, she did not send me. She wanted me to go back to Delos."

He let out a breath and pulled his chair back to the desk. "Do you know why we call this place Kevó?"

"No." But I had wondered why. 'Void' seemed like a depressing name for such a picturesque town.

"There is void here, the gods cannot see what happens in this valley. It is why I settled here two thousand years ago, I needed to get away from Asteria's eye."

"Why? What did she do to you?" I asked, thinking back to how demanding she had been in my last dream.

"I am the first vampire, Tadeas." He stared into my eyes and I felt for a lie, but found none.

"You have heard the story of my creation I am guessing?" he asked, leaning back in his chair.

"Yes, Vince told me you fell off the roof and died on Delos. Asteria created you as the first vampire. He told me you left the island for years but came back and built her a temple. She manipulated her magic, so you could die and not spend your after life on Tartarus. I don't know what happened after she changed her magic." I leaned back in the chair I was sitting in.

"I worshipped her for a long time on Delos. I turned a few humans in the beginning. Only the ones who came to worship at her temple though, none of the others. I spent many years there before I grew bored and left the temple to explore the world. My goal was to create more vampires and spread the word of the Goddess throughout the world, so she could keep, or even gain, power. Everywhere I settled I would create a new vampire and spend a decade or so training them in the ways of Asteria and pass on the magic she gave me. I traveled the world over and when I got back to Delos the vampires I had left there had created their own prodigies.

"Time went on and everything was fine, we kept the temple in perfect shape and let the people who worshipped other gods come and go as they wanted. I began having dreams of Asteria where she asked me to create more vampires, and to make sure they worshipped her. She was fighting with Zeus and needed more power. I did as she asked for a few decades but as time went by none of the vampires I created believed the story, instead choosing to believe in other deities. She began to torment my sleep every day, demanding I create more of us and force them to worship her. I have no idea what her grand plan was but after spending every dream for a hundred years chained to a wall listening to her tell me what to do,

I had to find peace. I searched for decades before I found this valley.

"You have to understand, I made a deal with her and I did my best to keep it but when my children's children began to turn people, I lost my hold on them. They stopped listening." Tad leaned forward in his chair and gave me a pleading look.

"You don't have to explain yourself. I think everyone should be able to believe in whatever they want." His story was giving me an idea of who my mother truly was, and it was starting to frighten me. "She has never brought your name up. I only know your story because Vince told me. I won't tell her; you can live your life however you wish. If you do not mess with me, I won't mess with you."

He stared into my eyes for a long moment trying gauge whether I was lying. He finally blinked, satisfied he could trust me. "Tell me what happened on Crete."

I swallowed hard trying to keep the tears from coming once again. "I would have to start with Miguel and Lolita. I didn't find out who I was until I visited San Sebastian. Miguel and Vince found me at almost the same time. I went with Miguel at first and he tried to make me his slave. Then Lolita showed up, and it went downhill from there. I left San Sebastian with Vince's help after Lolita tried to kill me. I don't know if she believes in the prophecy or not, but she does not want me around anymore."

"What about Miguel?" Tad folded his hands together and rested them on his stomach.

"Miguel followed us but stayed on a nearby island. I have no idea where he is or what he's doing now. He is the one who started the fire in San Sebastian. I was already in Greece when it happened. Anyway, Vince met me in Greece and took me to Theron's where I trained. Theron had a mercenary named Alex staying on the property while I was there. We were friends for a while, until I rejected his sexual advances. I don't know when Lolita took out the hit on me, but she did, and Alex tried to fill it." I wiped my fingers under my eyes to get rid of the tears. "Instead of capturing me, he killed all the vampires on Crete, and he's still after me. Ramstein saved my life when he helped me."

"If we help you get a new passport and access to your money what are you going to do?" He leaned back in his chair and crossed his legs.

"Track down Lolita, kill her, then do the same to Alex and Miguel." I sat up straight in my chair, wishing I had been able to bring my katana with me. I didn't know if he would be all right with me threatening other vampires.

"Lolita is playing a long game. Do you know why she wants you dead?" He raised his eyebrows.

"Not really, but I think it's fear that if I am turned, I will be more powerful then she will ever be. When she and Miguel tried to turn me into his slave she thought she would be able to manipulate me through Miguel to do his bidding. When I broke the bond, and ran away with Vince she flipped out."

"She must be desperate to kill you if she put a bounty on your head. She normally does her own dirty work."

"Vince said, Miguel wouldn't tell her where we were, and we didn't know where she was."

"You have a lot to learn before you are ready to get back to the real world then. The people here can show you everything you need to know." He rested his hands on the table and leveled his eyes on me.

"I would be so grateful if they would." I blinked back tears and sniffed.

"I can't make the people here teach you, but if you prove your loyalty to the group, they will. You have nothing but time. Use it to your advantage."

It was dark when I left headquarters, but I felt lighter. I didn't understand what Tad's deal was, but at least I could trust him not to turn me over to Lolita. I looked at my watch. I had fifteen minutes before I needed to be at the cafeteria to meet Uni for dinner. I shivered. The fall evening was cooling down, so I went back to my apartment and got the only hoodie I had. I hoped Ramstein would buy me some clothes appropriate for this climate. My island wear wasn't going to cut it for long.

I walked back to the cafeteria and saw Uni waiting for me. "Hi," I said, as I approached her.

"How was your meeting with Tad?" she asked, turning to the door, and leading the way inside.

"Enlightening, I guess would be the best word for it." The room went silent when we entered as it had at breakfast and lunch. We walked to the back where the buffet was set up.

"He's kind of weird, I think he is an old soul. It's the only word I have been able to come up with to describe him." Uni picked up a tray, then a plate, and got in line.

I wasn't super hungry but if I was going to get out of the funk I had been in for the past week I was going to need to start eating right. I picked up a tray and plate, then followed her through the line filling it. "He's going to let me stay, which is all I can ask for right now."

When we entered the main dining room again, all conversation stopped, and I felt every person in the place staring at me, so I ignored them and followed Uni to an empty table. I tried to act like the silence was no big deal, but it was. How was I going to get these people to trust me enough to teach me when they were afraid to talk around me? I cut a piece of my steak and brought it up to my mouth feeling every eye on me.

"This is ridiculous," Uni said, before standing. "Hey, why are you guys being so rude? You were all the new kid once, stop acting like Karate Kid is a pariah. Go back to your conversations. She's not going to run to tell the bad guys what you are saying." She slammed back down in her chair. "I'm the youngest one here, but the way they are acting you would think I was the oldest."

"It's fine, I'm not a very trusting person. I'll find a way to win them over." I ate a piece of my steak. "Did they treat you the same way when you came here?"

"Me? No, but that is because my dad worked here for a long time." She lowered her eyes and pushed her food around on her plate.

"I'm sorry if I brought up a touchy subject." Something bad had happened to her dad from the way she was acting.

"He died of cancer last year." She looked up at me with tears in her eyes. "I really miss him. We were only here for a month before he had to go back to Athens to have treatments."

"I'm sorry." I put my hand on her arm. "I'm sure he is watching over you now."

"Oh, I know he is. He told me in a dream that I should be friends with you."

"Really?" She must have interesting dreams especially after Tad told me about this being a place where gods could not see.

"Yeah, I have weird dreams when I'm in Athens. It's nice up here though, I never dream."

"When did you dream this Uni?" I asked, butterflies starting to erupt in my belly.

"Last month, when I was home visiting my mom. My dad came to me in a dream and said someone important was coming to stay in Kevó. He said I needed to help her. You are the only new person we have had in ages so I'm guessing he meant you." She put her head down and started eating again.

I wondered who her father was, and if he was somehow connected to Asteria, or someone else. A month ago, I was still on Crete, training. I finished eating and noticed that at some point, while we were eating, people started talking again. I didn't recognize all the languages they were speaking but there was a lot of Greek, English, and German. Maybe they were getting used to me.

"What are you doing now?" Uni asked, leaning back in her chair, and drinking the rest of her cola.

"I was going to head into the kitchen and start doing the dishes."

"Why would you want to do that? You aren't even on the rotation yet."

"I want to help out, earn my keep. It seemed like the best way to do it. What are you doing?"

"I'm working on some code for a hack we're working on. I have to get back to it." She stood with her tray in her hand.

"I'll see you tomorrow?" I asked, getting up with her.

"Yeah, I skip breakfast, but I normally have lunch around one if you want to meet here again."

I smiled, I wasn't totally alone for a change. "I'll be here."

"Great, have fun on kitchen duty."

"Have fun staring at a computer screen."

Chapter 16

Miguel

Miguel spent a week finding humans to feed the vampires, and looking for survivors. The sun had just gone down, and Miguel was watching the vampires he had saved sleep. He was starting to wonder if any of the vampires would ever wake up when Theron sat bolt upright and looked around. "What happened?" he shouted then slumped back on the bed.

"You were buried alive during the attack." Miguel jumped up and ran to Theron's bed then smiled down at the vampire. "I'm Miguel, I was able to save you and those two. I have not been able to find any more survivors."

"Alex, I remember now." He shook his head, then tried to get off the bed, but he didn't have the strength. "Miguel, I told you not to set foot on my island. Where's Katie?"

"I tried to warn you about the attack. I left you a message on your cell phone. I came after I heard the bombs going off. I don't know what happened to her. There was no sign of her when I arrived."

Theron let out a breath, he didn't know why he was worried. If she had been there when Miguel showed up she would have killed him without thinking. Vince told her to take a car and run, he hoped that was what she did.

Theron slowly sat up and leaned against the wall. He looked at the other bodies in the room. "They're alive?" he asked in a whisper, as if it hurt to talk.

"Yes, they are healing slowly." Miguel leaned back in his chair.

"Have you found any other survivors?" Theron asked, blinking his eyes quickly.

"No, I have been spending as much time as I can, digging out your tunnels looking for anyone else who might have survived but I have found no one."

"Is there anything left?" He rested his head against the wall and looked up at the ceiling.

"Buildings? No, they were all leveled. The labyrinth is still in one piece and most of your tunnels are good. Only the tunnels near the mansion caved in."

"You can stop looking for survivors then, everyone was in the mansion except for us. We were trying to get to Katie when they blew up the house." A red tinged tear spilled down his cheek.

"I'm sorry for your loss." Miguel said quietly.

"Thank you for saving us." Theron wiped away the tear and looked at Helen and Vince. "I hope Katie made it to safety."

"Me too." Miguel said quietly. "Do you think he is going to kill me when he wakes up?" He looked over at Vince.

"I don't think he will have the strength to." Theron rolled his head toward Vince then back to Miguel.

"Tell me what you know about what happened here," Theron said, lying back down.

Miguel told him what he knew; about the men on the island, the voice message he left with Theron, the bombs, what was left of the compound.

"I will track down Alex, and torture him before I kill him. Double crossing mercenary, I should have known better than to let him stay so long." He thumped his head against the wall.

"The sun is down if you want to go and survey the damage. I'm going to get a new round of donors." Miguel stood and made to leave.

"I would go with you but I'm not at my full strength and I can't be seen until I am back to myself. I am not going to lose my island over this," Theron said, staring at the ceiling.

"Don't worry, I can handle it. Is there anything else you need?"

"Not right now, but I will make a list for you later."

Miguel left, relieved that Theron was wake. He was starting to get lonely and he was worried about what Vince would do when he woke up. At least Theron would be there to try and talk some sense into him. He went to a bar and waited for a group of people to leave. When they reached their car, he approached them, compelled them into his car and drove them to the house.

He fed the vampires, then sent the people on their way. After Theron ate they walked over to see what was left of the compound.

When they got back to the house Miguel was sat in the chair between the lifeless forms of Helen and Vince. "I'm sorry, I should have ignored your warning and come to tell you about them instead of calling."

"I would have killed you, and they still would have come. Don't blame yourself, I allowed Alex to stay with me, he would have never met Katie if it wasn't for me. This is my fault not yours."

"What are you going to do?" Miguel asked.

"I'm going to rebuild of course. This is my home. I'm not going to give it up because of one mercenary who will not be long for this earth. It will take time, but what else do I have besides time?"

"True, my city is in the middle of rebuilding, and I should be there, but something is telling me that I am needed here to see this through. Even if it means Vince kills me when he wakes up." Miguel rested his elbows on his knees and buried his face in his hands.

"I won't let him kill you. You saved us all." Theron leaned against the door frame. "I hate that I am stuck in this house during the day. There are things I need to be doing. Do you have a computer?"

"No, but I will get one tomorrow. What else do you need?"

"I need a cell phone and a pad of paper. I need to make a list of what I need to get done."

"I will get everything you need tomorrow. You can use my phone if you would like until I get you one." Miguel sat up and started to pull it out of his pocket.

"No, that's OK. Everything I need to do needs to come from my number. Everyone thinks I'm dead, I need to make a statement when I reveal I'm alive."

"I understand. I will get one for you tomorrow night. Did you have a blood delivery service?"

"Yes, I will get it set up as soon as I have a phone. Then we can hook up an IV to Vince and Helen, maybe it will help them heal quicker.

Chapter 17

Katie

When the dishes were done Lucy asked me to take the trash out to the truck waiting behind the building. I hauled the bags out and was about to throw them in when I heard a noise. It was almost like a whimpering.

"Hello?" I said into the trash, and the whining got louder. It sounded like a puppy. I climbed into the back of the truck and started moving trash bags around trying to find the source of the whining. I moved a box out of the way and found a brown and black puppy lying in a box full of shredded newspaper chewing a bone as big as he was. "Hey, little guy, are you OK?" I knelt and put my hand out to him. He sniffed it, then dropped his bone, and licked me before starting to whine again. I picked him up and gave him his bone back. I grabbed the box with the shredded paper in my other hand and got out of the truck trying not to hurt the puppy in the process.

I put the box next to the back door and put the puppy back in while I reloaded all the trash bags I had thrown out to find the little guy. When I was done I looked in the box and found him fast asleep with the bone between his teeth. Not wanting to wake him I took the box inside to find Lucy.

She was cleaning the griddle when I found her. "Lucy, do you know who the truck belongs to? I found this little guy in the bed and I want to make sure he gets taken care of."

She glanced in the box and a small smile curved her lips. "What a cute little guy. You better keep him. Jim hates dogs, he would probably just dump him somewhere."

"Keep him?" I looked down at the sleeping ball of fur. I could barely take care of myself. How was I going to take care of a puppy? "He'll dump him? How could anyone want to dump this cute little guy?"

"Jim was attacked by a dog when he was a kid. He never got over his fear of them. You take him." She turned back to her work, dismissing me without a word.

"You can stay with me until I find a good home for you. Lucy do you mind if I take some milk for him?"

"Help yourself," she called.

I put the box down and went to the fridge. I found an empty water bottle and filled it up with milk. I took a bowl and put it all in the box next to the fur ball. I went back to my apartment and realized we both smelled like rotten food.

I filled the sink in the bathroom with warm water and woke the little guy up. "I know you are not going to like this, but we both need a bath." I put him in the water, and he yelped like it was too hot. I held him with one hand while cupping a handful of water, and dumping it over his fur. "It's not too hot. It's just water." He looked at me and growled the cutest puppy growl I had ever heard. "No," I said, shaking my finger at him. I poured some shampoo on his fur and started to work it all over his body. He stood there straight-legged and miserable while I washed, then rinsed him off. I pulled the plug on the drain, and before I could get a towel around him he shook, covering the entire bathroom in water. I shrieked when the cool water hit me, and he whined. "Come here, let's get you dried off." I wrapped a towel around him, and rubbed him down, trying to soak up as much water as I could. I put him in his box with the shredded paper which did not smell as bad as I thought it would, then got in the shower.

Thirty minutes later I had a clean puppy, happily licking milk from the bowl, and I was clean, wearing shorts, and a T-shirt. I wasn't sure what I was going to do with him, but it was nice to not be alone.

When he was done drinking his milk I took him outside and tried to get him to pee while I froze my butt off. After he finished we went back inside and I put him in the box in the living room. I went into my room, got into bed, and turned off the light. I was almost asleep when he started whining. I hadn't had a dog since I was a kid, but I remembered my dad telling me that you have to let puppies whine themselves out. I lay there staring at the ceiling thinking that I needed to find the little guy a home. There was no way I was going to be able to take care of a dog.

After fifteen minutes of whining I couldn't take it anymore. I went into the living room and brought the box into my room. I set the box next to the bed and scratched his ears until he settled down. I smiled thankful and rolled over hoping to sleep. I was almost there when he started whining again. I rolled over to see him with his paws on the side of the box looking at me like he was going to die unless I let him sleep with me. Letting out a breath, I picked him up and put him at the foot of the bed. He cuddled up against my feet and we both finally fell asleep.

Something was licking my face, I didn't know what it was, but it had sweet, skunky breath. I opened my eyes to see my fur ball's nose inches from mine. "Good morning, how are you?" I asked, and he grunted and nipped at my nose. "I bet you need to go outside and pee." I got up, threw on some clothes, and ran out the door with him.

It was cold outside, everything was covered in a layer of frost and I ran in place to try to stay warm while he sniffed around to find a good place to go. "Come on little monster I have to pee too."

When he was finally finished we went back inside and I gave him some more milk before I went into the bathroom and got ready for my run. What was I going to do with the fur ball while I went running? He was too little to keep up with me, but I didn't want to leave him alone in my room. I ended up using the backpack I bought at the mall. When he got tired I put him in the bag while I kept running.

When I got back to town I went straight to the cafeteria and put the puppy down while I started on the morning dishes. Marathon, Ramstein's brother, came in a few minutes later. "What are you doing here?"

"The dishes, what does it look like?" I asked, scrubbing a plate with something hard dried on it.

"I have kitchen duty today."

"You're off the hook, I'll take care of it."

"Are you trying to make friends by doing their work for them?" he accused me, folding his arms across his chest.

"No, I am trying to earn my keep. Tad is letting me stay here free of charge. Besides what else do I have to do?" I asked, shifting my foot, and a squeak came from the fur ball sleeping on my foot.

"Sounds like you could do karate all day and no one would mind. What was that?" He looked around.

"I want to help, and I have nothing else to do. Don't worry about it. Oh, I found a puppy in the trash truck last night. Lucy said Jim would dump him if I left him there. I want to find him a good home." I stepped back and bent down to pick him up.

"He is a cute one." Marathon scratched behind his ear. "What's his name?"

"I haven't given him one yet." I pulled him to my chest and ran my hand through his fur.

"He needs a collar; you can probably get one at the General Store." Marathon backed up a step. "My brother wants to know if you need anything else from town."

I thought for a second. "Just warmer clothes, all I have is beach wear. He said he was going to bring me some when he came back." I wasn't sure I wanted to trust a man I barely knew to buy me clothes, but I didn't have a choice.

"It was cold this morning. What size do you need, and I will tell him?"

I gave Marathon my size information. "Thank you for helping me."

"Hey, you are helping me too. I hate doing dishes." He turned and left me with the dishes, and I got back to work.

When I was done with the breakfast dishes, the puppy and I left the cafeteria, and started walking up the street. He stuck right by my side the whole time, without a leash. Outside the General Store I stopped and looked down at him. "You're a good boy, but I had better pick you up. There is no telling what kind of trouble you would find in here."

I bent and scooped him into my arms. He whined but stopped when I scratched behind his ear. I opened the door and went inside. The place was jam-packed with stuff. I felt like I walked into an entire superstore stuffed into a boutique. Along one wall a counter stretched from the front to the back of the store, and behind the counter there were rows and rows of candy bars and snacks. Under the counter was more food. There was a man standing behind a cash register with his arms crossed in front of his chest and a frown on his face.

Great, someone else who doesn't want me here, I thought to myself, before walking over to the man.

"Hi, I was wondering if you had a dog collar and leash I could buy?" I asked in Greek.

"You speak Greek?" he asked, and his frown disappeared for a second.

"Yes, I speak it fluently, but I can't read it very well," I said, rubbing the puppy's fur to keep me calm.

"You speak it very well, let me show you what we have." He came out from behind the counter, and I followed him down the second row of shelves to the back of the room. "There are not very many dogs here, but I always try to keep a few things on hand." He stopped in front of a rack of dog collars and toys.

"Which one do you like?" I asked the puppy in Greek, trying to get the clerk on my good side. I held up a black one and the puppy sniffed it before biting it.

"You break it, you buy it," the man said.

"I guess we will get this one then." I picked out a matching leash, and a three pack of tennis balls. "Do you have any puppy food?"

"Let me check in the back. I'll meet you at the counter." He turned and went into the backroom.

I slowly made my way up to the cash register. I put the collar and the leash on the counter then went over to look at the clothes. I found a hoody I thought would be nice. It was my size and would keep me warm until Ramstein brought me more clothes. I put it on the counter as the man came out of the back with a small bag of dog food in his hand.

"This is all I have but I'll order you some more. It will be here next week."

"Thank you. How much do I owe you?" I asked digging my wallet out of my pocket.

He rang everything up in the cash register. "Fifty-two euros."

My jaw dropped open, it was over half the money I had. "How much was the hoodie?" I didn't remember seeing a price tag on it.

"Twenty-five."

"Ok, I'm going to put it back then. I need to make sure I can buy him food. I won't get too cold." I put the sweatshirt back on the rack and paid the man for the other things.

I went home carrying the puppy, he was the only reason why I hadn't started crying. I had no idea how I was going to live with less than a hundred euros to my name. When we got home I put the puppy down and sat down on the couch. I put my head between my knees and tried not to cry, but I could not help it. I was so screwed. Unless someone helped me access my bank account or Vince's I wasn't going to make it.

I could always call my parents, but I had a feeling Lolita and Alex had tapped their phones. I had to do this on my own; they didn't need to get involved with my problems. The puppy's barking had me looking up to see him tearing at the bag with his new toys and food.

I smiled and got up. "No, you can't play with the bag." I took it away from him, and put some food in the bowl I had given him milk in the night before. "Sit," I said to the fur ball. He cocked his head and stared at me with his tail wagging a million miles a minute. I leaned over and tapped his rump. "Sit." I applied a little bit of pressure and he sat down. "Good boy." I put the food down in front of him and went to unpack the rest of the stuff I bought. By the time he was done I had collar and leash ready to go and the balls were sitting on the coffee table. I took one, put it in my pocket, picked up my katana from the table and put the leash on the puppy.

"Let's go to the park." We played fetch with the tennis ball until he was tired out, then I tied his leash to a tree, and pulled out my katana.

The last time I used it, I cut Ben's head off. Theron had told me at the beginning of my training with the sword that the more battles a person was in with their katana, the more the blade bonded to the person. Killing Ben with it began the bonding between me and the blade. It also held one of my last memories of the friends I had lost on Crete. Theron had given it to me as a gift for completing my training. It felt like it had been a long time since I used it, and I wondered if I would remember everything Theron had taught me.

I stepped away from the tree and found my breath. I thought about the form I wanted to start with, I moved through each step in my mind before I began with the sword. I hadn't forgotten and as I worked through the forms I felt more myself than I had since the day on Crete when everything changed.

When I was finished I heard people clapping. I looked around to find ten people watching me. I bowed and quickly went over to the dog embarrassed. I put my sword on the table and sat down in the grass to stretch out. The puppy watched me with inquisitive eyes.

"I guess I'm going to have to give you a name little guy. I can't keep calling you puppy, can I?" He came over to me and started to chew on my fingers with his sharp teeth. "How about Vinny? I think it's a good name for a puppy who will grow up to be a big strong dog."

Vince's eyes popped into my mind and I blinked back the tears that were threatening. "Yes, Vinny the mighty protector of 'The One'."

We worked on a little bit of training and too much playing until it was time to meet Uni for lunch. She fell in love with Vinny at first sight. "Do you want him?" I asked. I really couldn't take care of a dog, even though he had already wormed his way into my heart.

"I wish, but no. They need exercise and someone to clean up after them and it's just not my thing. I will play with him though and if you need me to watch him for you, I can." She rolled him over on his belly and gave it a good rub.

"I might take you up on that." I dug into my food. "How is work?"

"Oh, pretty good. I am almost done with my part of the program, then I will hand it off to the next person, so they can add their part." She took a bite out of the chicken leg she was eating.

"What do you do when you finish a project? Do you have another one waiting or what?" I asked, taking a bite of my apple, and crunching on it.

"It depends, sometimes there is another project waiting for me, if there isn't I usually go into Athens for a few days to get the shopping done that I can't do here. Hey, do you want to come with me when I go?"

I wanted to cry, I would have loved to go shopping with Uni, have a girl's weekend. "I wish. I would love to, but I was tagged on a facial recognition software. I can't go anywhere without worrying about being found."

"That sucks, well do you want me to pick up anything for you?" she asked, before sticking the entire drumstick in her mouth, and sucking the meat off it.

"I have less than a hundred bucks to my name, I'm going to have to save it for Vinny's food, but thanks." My life sucked. I was stuck in a tiny town where only one person liked me, I had no money and I couldn't leave unless I wanted to be caught by Lolita and Alex.

"I'm sorry, give everyone some time and they will show you how to access your money. I would help you if I knew how." She put her hand on my shoulder. "I've got to get back to it. I'll see you later OK."

"Yeah, have fun. Leave your tray I'm headed back that way anyway."

"Thanks." She put her jacket on and was out the door a minute later.

"Come on Vinny, the dishes await us."

I gave him a tennis ball to play with while I did the dishes and he happily chewed on it while I scrubbed. When I was done, we went back to our apartment and I jumped in the shower to get rid of the smell of the kitchen. Wrapped in a towel I opened the door to the bedroom and found Vinny with my running shoe, my very expensive, running shoe, between his paws.

"Vinny, no," I yelled at him and picked the shoe up. Luckily, there were only a few teeth marks on it. I let out a breath. I had no idea what I would do if he ruined my running shoes. He backed away with his head down and whined. "You can't eat my running shoes, where is your ball?" I asked, looking around, but not finding it. "Let me get some clothes on and we will find it all right?"

After I was dressed, I found the ball under the bed and Vinny was happily chewing on it while I finished in the bathroom. It was four in the evening and I had nothing to do. I looked at Vinny, if he was going to be my protector I was going to have to train him. Puppies did not come out as guard dogs. I spent the rest of the night teaching him to sit, and we were getting to 'stay' when we both fell asleep on the couch.

I was reading my book on the couch late Friday night when someone knocked on my door. No one had knocked on my door since I had found Vinny and he barked up a storm, running back and forth between me and the door.

"Vinny sit," I said, going to the door but waiting to open it. He sat down but his butt and his tail were still wagging back and forth. "Good boy, stay." I looked through the peephole at Ramstein standing outside, shivering, with a bunch of bags in his hands. I opened the door. "Hi, come in. Hurry, it's cold out there."

"Did I just hear a dog?" he asked, coming in, and closing the door. Vinny whined, looking at me with puppy-dog eyes begging me to release him from his 'stay' command. Ramstein looked dumbstruck when he turned around and saw Vinny sitting on the floor with his tail swooshing back and forth.

"Yes, this is Vinny. Vinny this is Ramstein." I patted my leg, and Vinny ran over to him.

"I'm gone for almost a month and you found a dog?"

"He was in the back of the trash truck. I had to save him." I moved out of the way, and he dumped the bags on the couch.

"Hi, you're a good boy, aren't you?" Ramstein scratched behind his ears. "Besides finding this guy, how has everything been?"

"Good, Uni and I have been hanging out, and everyone loves to watch me train in the park." I went and sat on the sofa.

"No one's offered to help you yet?" He sat down on the far end of the couch.

"No, but your brother was glad I took his kitchen duty from him. He even talked to me."

"He hates kitchen duty, you just made his week."

"It's going to take time, but I think I'll be able to win people over. I just hate sitting here waiting."

"Well, why don't you change into some warm clothes and

we can go get a drink. It will help for them to see you act like a normal person."

I shrugged and took the bags of clothes into my room and closed the door. I dumped the bags out and found a pair of jeans and form fitting cable-knit sweater. It wasn't what I would have picked but it was warmer than what I had. I quickly changed and put my chucks on, I was going to need some better shoes if I was going to stay here very long. When I came out of my room Vinny sat on my feet and whined.

"Well, where's your leash? You can't come without it," I said to him and he ran around the room until he found his leash, then brought it over to me. "Good boy." I clicked it on and looked over at Ramstein who was standing staring at me with a coat in his hands.

"You must be a dog whisperer, you have had him less than a month and he does everything you tell him." He handed me the only light coat I had, and I shrugged it on.

"I have a lot of free time." I went to the door and opened it with Vinny at my heels.

"Smart dog too," Ramstein said, going out the door first. I followed, closing the door behind me and locking it.

"I think he's a German Shepherd, but we will have to wait and see how he grows up." We walked down the alley to the main drag then turned toward the bar.

When we entered the bar, everyone stopped talking as usual. I ignored them and found an empty table to sit at. I told Vinny to lay down and he found a comfortable spot on top of my feet.

"What do you want to drink? I'll go get it," Ramstein said, taking off his coat, and hanging it on the back of the chair.

"Vodka on the rocks," I said, pulling my arms out of my coat, and hanging it on the back of my chair. Slowly, people got back to their conversations and when Ramstein got back with our drinks everyone was acting normal.

"How's work?" I asked, taking a sip, and almost choking. It was the worst vodka I had ever had.

"Good, the same guy came in asking about you though."

I gripped the edges of the table so hard my knuckles turned white. "What did he want to know?"

"What happened to you after you ran through the store and out the backdoor."

"Crap, I'm sorry I put you in this position. What did you tell him?"

"It wasn't the first time I have had to deal with people like him. I told him you ran straight through, I even showed him the backroom again, not the saferoom but everything else."

"Is he going to leave you alone?" I rolled my glass between my palms.

"I think so, I showed him the doctored security tape as well."

"Thank you, Ramstein."

"You're safe, that's all that matters now."

"Can you show me how to hack into a security system?" I asked, thinking it might come in handy down the line.

"You want to learn?" He looked skeptical.

"Yes, with my luck I'm going to need it." I didn't want to beg but I wasn't above it either.

"OK, we will start tomorrow after you finish your kitchen duty. You have a computer, right?"

"Yes, I haven't turned it on in a while but it's in my room."

"Don't turn it on until I can look at it." He took a sip of his beer.

"OK, why?" I had almost forgot I had it.

"I want to make sure there aren't any tracking devices on it. You trusted this Alex guy for a while, right?"

"Yeah, I did. Good idea, I don't want anyone to be able to track me."

"Does your watch have a GPS on it?" He looked at the fitness watch around my wrist.

"Yeah, do you think someone could track me with it?"

"If they knew where to look they could," Ramstein held his hand out and I quickly took it off.

"I've been using it when I run. What if Alex knows where I am?" I asked, giving it to him.

"You have been using it all month, right?"

"Yeah, I am so stupid." I rested my elbows on the table and buried my face in my hands.

"I doubt he tried to track you by it or he would've already have found you. I'll fix it, so you can use the GPS, and no one will be able to find you."

"Thank you again. It seems like all I ever do is thank you."

"I'm here to help remember?" He gave me a smile and finished his beer. "Do you want another drink?"

"Yes, but not this, the vodka is horrible. I would love a beer."

"I'll be right back." He got up and went to the bar.

I sat back and looked around the room, people were talking in quiet voices. Occasionally someone would make eye contact with me before quickly looking away and whispering to whoever they were sitting with.

"What are you doing in here?" Mordor asked, standing in front of my table, and Vinny growled from underneath.

"Having a drink with a friend." I was starting not to like this guy. First, he was mad because I took his job in the kitchen, that he did not want anyway, now he was questioning my right to be in the bar.

"When are you going to get it through your head that no one wants you here?" He put his hands on the back of the chair and leaned toward me.

"I know no one wants me here, but that does not mean I'm leaving." I leaned forward to get in his face. "Tad said I could stay, so I am going to stay until it is safe for me to leave."

"Mordor, stop being an asshole," Ramstein said, sitting down, and giving me a beer.

"I still can't believe you brought her here." He leaned over to get in

Ramstein's face.

"She needed help, isn't that what we are supposed to be doing here? Helping people who need it?" He took a swig of his beer.

I looked around, all talk had stopped, and everyone was staring at our table. I wanted to slide under it and disappear.

"We do, but you don't bring them here." He pointed a finger in my face. "You need to leave."

"Please do not point at me," I said, feeling my anger rise. I had done nothing to this man. I wasn't going to take him belittling me.

"I will do what I want. I belong here," he shoved his finger in my chest. I snatched it before he could pull away. "Let go."

"My dad isn't a violent man, but he has one rule when it comes to fighting: Don't ever throw the first punch. I have lived by the rule for my entire life. You just touched me, which means I am justified to retaliate." I cocked my head to the side. "Tell me Mordor, do you need this finger to type?" I started to bend it backwards, and he tried to pull away.

"Let go of me you bitch." I rose to my feet as he took another step backwards.

"You didn't answer my question." I continued to bend his finger almost to breaking point. "Do you need this finger to do your job?"

"Yes," he yelled, his eyes going wide with pain. "Please, let me go."

"Leave me alone and I will leave you alone. Understand?"

"Yes, please. . ." he trailed off and I let go of his finger. He stumbled back a step, turned bright red, and left the bar.

I let out a breath and took a long sip of my beer. I looked under the table. "Are you all right Vinny?" He gave a sharp bark, turned in a circle, and lay down.

"Are you? I'm sorry, he is such a dick."

"I'm fine. Is he always so difficult?" I asked, chugging more of my beer. Everyone had gone back to their conversations, and I didn't want to let Mordor win by running away, but I was ready to leave.

"Yeah, he keeps thinking Tad is going to give everything to him when he retires, he does not understand that Tad isn't planning on retiring anytime soon. He thinks by being an asshole people will respect him more."

"Good luck with that." I finished my beer and pushed my chair back. Everyone stopped what they were doing to watch me again. I felt like an animal in a zoo, every time I did anything everyone wanted to watch. I ducked under the table and picked Vinny up.

"What time do you want to get started tomorrow?" he asked, finishing his beer too.

"Well, I have to do the dishes after breakfast, I usually get done around ten, then I'll need a shower. How does eleven sound?"

"That will work, I will meet you at your apartment at eleven."

"See you then." I left the bar and went back to my apartment, making sure Mordor was nowhere in sight.

Over the next few days Ramstein taught me how to break into secure servers and hack video feeds. I was starting to form a plan to track down Lolita. I wasn't giving up on my goal of ending her. I was being smart and not calling her out when she could ambush me. I needed to learn everything I could about her. Where she was, what her habits were, what she was doing. Once I had her figured out I would go after her.

Uni came back the day Ramstein had to go back to Athens. We were having lunch before he left when Uni ran inside, out of breath. "There you are Karate Kid; I have been looking everywhere for you."

"What's wrong?" I asked, pulling my eyebrows together.

"I need your help unloading my car. Hey, where's Vinny?" She looked around on the floor then under the table. "Hey little man, I missed you." She crawled under the table, cooing to the dog.

I looked at Ramstein, rolled my eyes, and shook my head trying not to laugh. "I'm glad you and Uni are friends," he said, getting to his feet. "Try to stay out of Mordor's hair for a while."

"I will, and don't forget to give me the receipts for the clothes. As soon as I can access my money I'm paying you back."

"I'll see if I can find them. In the meantime, take care of yourself." He put his coat on and walked to the door.

"Drive safe," I called as he waved and walked toward the parking garage.

Uni popped her head up a second later. "Wasn't Ramstein sitting here a second ago?" she asked, pulling up a chair, and sitting down.

"Yeah, he had to go back to Athens." I picked up a French fry and popped it in my mouth. "Did you have a good time?"

"It was OK, but I wish you could have gone with me." She stole a fry from my plate.

"Me too, maybe when all my drama is resolved we can meet for a girl's weekend."

"Promise?"

"I don't make promises, but we will try."

"Perfect, so tell me what I missed while I was gone." She gave me a knowing smile.

"Why? It looks like you already know."

"I want to hear it from the horse's mouth is all."

I caught her up on everything that had happened at the bar, and how Ramstein was helping me learn how to hack security systems. After I finished eating we left the cafeteria, and were walking to her car when the sky opened up and sheets of icy rain began to fall.

"Let's just grab everything and take it to my place. When it stops raining we can move it to yours," I yelled over the sound of the rain hitting the street.

"OK," Uni said, opening the hatch of her Mini Cooper.

We grabbed everything and made a dash for my apartment.

"What did you buy?" I asked, falling back on the couch, surrounded by bags.

"A little of this and a little of that." She started to go through the bags. "I got this for Vinny." She pulled out a huge dog bed that took up an entire bag and threw it on the floor. "Come here Vinny check it out."

Vinny poked his head out from the bedroom then walked in and started sniffing the bags.

"Vinny, come here." Vinny finally made his way over to her, walking around the bed. "This is for you." She patted the bed, he sniffed it, and sat down on the floor.

I was trying my hardest not to start laughing when she picked him up and put it on the bed, he sniffed it and ran to hide between my legs.

"He hates it," she looked up at me with tears in her eyes.

"He doesn't hate it; it just doesn't smell like him or me. I'll put a T-shirt in there tonight and make him stay there for a while. He will love it before you know it." I kissed Vinny on the nose and put him back on the floor.

"Are you sure?" she sniffled.

"Yes, thank you for spoiling my dog." I wondered what else she had bought.

"That is not spoiled. This is," she dumped a pile of dog toys on the floor, and Vinny whined, and went over to check them out. He picked up a stuffed gorilla, and took it into the bedroom.

"Oh my gosh, he isn't going to know what to do with all this stuff. You really did spoil him."

"I know, but he's cute." Uni stood and started looking in bags. "I had all this stuff organized before I left but now I have no idea what is in what bag."

"What are you looking for?" I asked, bringing my eyebrows together.

"Nothing," she said, opening a bag, looking inside of it, and quickly closing it.

"What's in the bag?" I asked, raising my eyebrows, she was acting very peculiar.

"I got you something I thought you might need." She looked like she was about to start crying again. "But you will probably hate it."

"I am sure I will love it and when I have access to my money I will pay you back." I held out my arms for the bag and she walked it over to me.

I took the bag from her thinking it was heavier than I thought it should have been. I opened the bag and looked inside confused. All I could see was leather and Sherpa. I stuck my hand in and pulled the pile of treated animal skin out. It was a jacket, a beautiful brown leather bomber jacket with a detachable Sherpa lining. "Oh Uni." I held it up to my face and breathed in the smell of leather. "It's beautiful." I stood and put it on.

"You like it?" she asked, her eyes were bright with tears and excitement.

"Yes, I love it." I zipped it up and was immediately wrapped in warmth. I walked into the bathroom and looked in the mirror. It fit perfectly, snug but not too tight. I came out of the bedroom and gave her a hug. "This wasn't cheap. I have to pay you back for it."

"Fine, but not until you have your money back."

"Deal." I unzipped the coat and hung it on the hook by the door. It was going to be nice to have a coat that would actually keep me warm.

"Same goes for the rest of the clothes I bought you."

"Why did you buy me a bunch of clothes you knew Ramstein was going to bring some back for me."

"I know, but what does he know about women's clothes?"

I huffed out a breath. "I want receipts for all of it."

"I will give them to you but not until you have your money."

"Thank you, Uni. What Ramstein gave me was nice, but

you're right he has no idea about women's clothes."

We spent the rest of the day going through and putting away the clothes she bought me.

Chapter 18

Ilhami

Everything was set up. Ilhami was in place. His great-nephew would be pulling into the warehouse within minutes. All Ilhami needed to do was to get into the warehouse and Takis's office, so he could enslave him without his men finding out. He walked quietly along the far wall of the building until he came to a window about ten feet off the ground. He jumped, easily catching the lip with his hands. He hoisted himself up and looked through the dirt-encrusted window. The warehouse was full of crates and guards. They were scattered around the space looking for anything that did not fit. Getting in was going to be harder than he thought. He could see the office on the first floor in the back of the building.

He continued to climb the wall until he made it to the roof. It was empty, which he thought was interesting. If he was guarding merchandise, he would have stationed someone on the roof. He walked quietly to the skylight near the back, peered in quickly, then retreated. There was a reason no one was on the roof. There was no way to get in or out of the warehouse without power tools. The skylight was covered in expanded metal, welded in place. He could rip it up, but it would make too much noise. He walked to the edge of the roof and looked over. No one was patrolling the back of the warehouse, so he jumped off the roof and landed on the ground almost silently. He was running out of time, he needed to get in before his nephew showed up. He walked along the wall looking for an opening. There had to be another way to get in. He came to an exit only door. There was no door handle, only a flush lock that could only be used from the inside, but there was a flaw: the hinges were on the outside. He made quick work of pulling the pins out, then he waited.

He heard a horn honk and movement inside. He opened the door and went in lightly closing it behind him. He was in the dark office, exactly where he wanted to be. He waited behind the door as he heard a car pull in then shut off. The overhead door closed, and he listened as car doors opened and closed.

"It is nice to meet you," he heard his nephew say with a heavy accent. "I hope this will be the beginning of a long friendship."

"We will see," Takis said. "Did you bring the money?"

"Yes, do you have the product?"

"It is here." Ilhami heard a suitcase being unzipped. Then the clasps of a briefcase being opened. That wasn't the plan, he thought to himself. His stupid nephew was going to ruin everything.

"You understand I need to count this before I let you leave with the product," Takis said, closing the suitcase.

"Of course, can we do it in private? I get jittery with so many guns around," his nephew said, and Ilhami breathed a sigh of relief.

"Yes, the money counter is in my office. Please follow me," Takis said, walking toward the office.

The door opened, Takis came in, followed by Ilhami's nephew who closed it behind him. As soon as the door was closed Ilhami was on Takis. He pulled him around and made eye contact before he could shout in warning. "Quiet, you are going to do everything I say. Do you understand?"

"Yes."

"Good, now here, suck on this." Ilhami cut his finger with a knife and shoved it into Takis's mouth. He sucked as was instructed. When Ilhami thought Takis had enough blood he pulled his finger out of his mouth, took Takis's wrist and bit it. He drank long, enjoying the taste of the man's blood. It was clean, telling Ilhami that Takis did not sample the drugs he sold. He licked the wound closed and cemented the slave bond. "You are mine now. If you disobey me, you will feel pain like you have never felt before. Do you understand?"

"Yes."

"Good now go out there and tell everyone that the deal is done. Nephew, take the drugs and the money and meet me at my house."

Takis turned and left the room with Ilhami's nephew closing the door behind them. Ilhami smiled to himself, his plan was working perfectly. He waited in the office until he heard the garage door open then he exited the way he entered, he put the pins back into the door, and quietly left the warehouse to return home.

"You did well, Nephew," Ilhami said when he entered the house and looked at the bale of marijuana on the table.

"Thank you for setting this up for me. Now I can go out on my own and get out from under my brother." He smiled, looking at the drugs.

"You will need to pay me back plus ten percent of your take." He wanted to help his family, but he needed funds as well.

"Of course, I should have it to you within a week." He zipped up the suitcase and put it on the floor. "I need to go, or I will miss my ride back to the main land."

"Very well, do not get caught and do not smoke it all yourself."

"I won't, thank you uncle." He hugged Ilhami and left.

Ilhami looked at his watch, it was too late to go back out now. He opened his laptop and started to search for Theron's attacker. There had to be a trail, there always was.

Chapter 19

Katie

September quickly turned into October and the season changed from summer to fall. The temperature dropped the leaves changed and fell to the ground. I had to start dressing warmer for my runs, but I no longer needed the backpack for Vinny. He had doubled in size and had no problem keeping up with me anymore.

When Ramstein was in town, he always spent a few hours with me showing me how access security systems and their video feeds. As the days got shorter Uni got bored and started teaching me programing language.

Mordor finally started ignoring me along with everyone else. I did the dishes, helped in the kitchen, and learned how to be a computer nerd. No one else had offered to help me with what I needed, and I was stuck until they did.

Vinny and I were out running one cold, overcast morning, in October. I was jamming out to my music from the phone Ramstein had brought me, pushing hard up the hill overlooking town when I heard a noise I hadn't heard in a long time.

I stopped and pulled my earbuds out to listen. It was the sound of a big truck coming from somewhere on the far side of the mountain. We never had big trucks come in. Deliveries were all made by pickup trucks and this wasn't a pickup based on the volume of the engine. I moved off the road with Vinny and hid behind a large rock. The truck came around the corner and I panicked. It was an armored attack vehicle and I was guessing there was only one reason it was on the road. I pulled out my phone and sent a text message to Uni: *Armored truck headed toward town. Guns mounted on the roof.*

She replied almost immediately: *Stay low, will reply when it is safe to come back. Thanks.*

I looked at Vinny, I didn't want to just sit there while my new home was attacked, but I didn't know what I could do. We stayed hidden behind the rock for what felt like hours, and I kept expecting to hear gunfire or people screaming, but there was nothing. The forest was eerily quiet as if all the birds and animals knew we were under attack and were hiding out just like we were. When I no longer heard the truck, I stood and looked at the hill. If we climbed a little bit higher, I would be able to see town.

"Vinny, we have to be super quiet and climb up this mountain." He looked at me as if he understood everything I said, but I knew better. We slowly started to hike straight up the hill trying to be as quiet as we could but every time a leave crunched under our feet I cringed. The forest was so quiet I thought the men in the trucks would be able to hear me breathing even though I was a mile away as the crow flies.

When I thought we had hiked far enough we cut across the mountain until I could just see the outskirts of town. I looked at Vinny and held my hand up in a stay gesture. He lay down and watched as I belly crawled my way over and looked down on the town. Only there was no town to see. There were ruins of a town, but nothing that looked familiar to me. The truck was stopped in the middle of what should have been Main Street and a bunch of guys dressed in all black with assault rifles were walking around looking at the ruins.

Did they destroy the town with some silent bomb? Kevó had been there not forty-five minutes before and Uni had sent me text message, so she was all right before the truck got there. My heart started to pound in my ears loud enough I was sure Vinny could hear it. I closed my eyes and found my breath. I told myself something was going on, there was no way I had lost another home. I would have heard something. After I found my breath and slowed my heart down. I opened my eyes to watch the men.

There were six of them walking around with assault rifles. They were looking for something. They walked through all the ruins of the city but never opened fire. Finally, one of the men near the truck yelled something and twirled his hand in the air. I couldn't see him or make out his words, but I was guessing he wanted everyone to load up.

I watched as the men ran back to the truck and got in. A horn honked, and the truck started to move down the road through town. I didn't know if they were going to turn around and come back the way they came or if they would keep going; not wanting to get caught by them I waited where I was. After a few minutes of seeing nothing, Vinny and I made our way back to the road then sprinted back to town.

We were five miles from town we I took the road and probably two miles if we went off the track. I took the road, I knew would be quicker and safer. I ran faster than I had ever run, thinking there were going to be people who needed help. Vinny started to lag, but he knew where home was, and he would come as quickly as he could. I had to keep going. When I made it to the outside of town, I stopped and looked around.

It wasn't the town I left. I wanted to fall to my knees and sob, I had killed more people, it was all my fault. If I would have texted Uni as soon as I heard the truck maybe they would have had time to escape. As I looked at what was left, something didn't feel right. I was about to walk through the buildings when a loud grinding noise stopped me. The ground began to shake, and I backed away, not wanting to be hit with falling debris. I looked behind me to see if Vinny was close by, but he wasn't back yet.

The ground twenty feet in front of me started to shift, then rise. I backed up again as dust distorted what was happening and the ruins started to rise and the buildings I knew rose from the earth. "No way," I said, completely mesmerized. Town rising before my eyes. I heard Vinny bark and turned to see him running to meet me. "Come, Vinny," I said and grabbed his collar when he approached me.

Five minutes later, I was standing in front of the town I had been living in for a month. Uni came running out of the alley where her apartment was and barreled toward me.

"Are you OK?" she asked between breaths when she reached me.

"I'm fine," I said, unable to take my eyes off the town. "What the hell was that?"

"Oh, our defensive mechanism. Do you like it? This was the first time we had to use it." She looked around, assuring herself that everything was where it needed to be.

"Yeah, super cool." I was still in shock. It felt like something out of a James Bond movie, not real life.

"Come on, they want to see you over at headquarters." She took my hand and dragged me a few feet before what she said registered, and my feet started to work again.

I followed Uni to the building and walked inside feeling like I would fall through the floor at any moment. We went to the left of the reception desk and down a hallway with cubicles on one side and a wall on the other. She stopped at a door about half way down.

"Why don't I take Vinny while you go in there," she said, bouncing from one foot to the other.

"What is going on Uni?" I asked, as my heart rate picked up again.

"They just want to talk to you about what you know. I can take Vinny to the park while you're gone."

"Am I in trouble?"

"No, at least I don't think so. You saved our asses, why would you be in trouble?" She would not meet my eyes.

"Yeah, why don't you just take him home? We sprinted back and I'm sure he's tired and thirsty. Here 's my key."

"OK, come on Vinny, let's get you some water." Uni and Vinny went home, and I turned to the door. I wasn't sure if I should knock or not, so I erred on the side of caution and knocked.

"Come in," I heard Tad say. I opened the door, and I found myself in a conference room with seven people sitting around a large table.

"You wanted to see me?" I asked, looking around the room. Tad was there, along with Mordor, and a few people I had seen around, but never met.

"Please have a seat," a burly man with a buzz cut, and dressed in tactical gear said, pointing at the seat at the end of the table. I sat down, folded my hands together, and rested them on the table.

I met the eyes of everyone in the room then waited for them to tell me what was going on. I thought I was there because I sent the warning text to Uni, but I squirmed with so many eyes staring at me.

"Do you know who it was?" A man in a button down blue shirt asked.

"I have no idea. I was halfway up the mountain. I moved so I could watch them, but I was too far away to really see anything."

"Who have you told about this place?" Mordor asked, looking smug.

Was I going to be kicked out?

"No one, I have no one to tell." I was starting to get agitated.

"Then how did they find us?" the burly one asked.

"How am I supposed to know? You can look at my phone and my computer I haven't contacted anyone outside of this town since I have been here. I don't even know where here is." I was getting pissed. Why in the world would I tell someone where I was?

"She is telling the truth. Stop badgering her, she is the only reason why we were not found," Tad said, standing, and walking around the room.

"But then who leaked our location?" Mordor asked, turning in his chair to look at Tad. "How can you trust her?"

"I don't know but I will find out. Why wouldn't I trust her? If wasn't for her, we would likely all be dead." Tad met the eyes of everyone in the room. "We all owe her our thanks." He got up and left the room.

They all turned to me. "He's right, thanks for alerting Uni. Our sensor was down in that section," the one in tactical gear said.

"Why are we all trusting what Tad says? Can't you see she's a spy sent here to find out our secrets?" Mordor jumped to his feet.

"Then why did she tell Uni? If she was trying to destroy us she could have just kept going and gotten a ride back with them. You're too paranoid Mordor, get a grip," the man in the button-down shirt said.

"You'll be sorry for letting her go free. Just you wait." Mordor stood and stormed out of the room.

"Are we done here?" I asked, standing.

"Yes," the burly one said. "Thank you for doing what you did."

"No problem, you guys have a hell of a disguise when you want it." I turned and went home. I needed a shower and a nap after everything that had happened.

"How did it go?" Uni asked when I got back to the apartment. I fell onto the couch and let out a sigh.

"They wanted to know if I knew who the guys were. Mordor tried to convince them I had called them in. Everyone blew him off and they thanked me for my help."

"He is such an ass. I knew everything would be fine, why would you warn us if you told them where we were?"

"That was my defense too. I need a shower." I rolled off the couch, my legs already stiff.

"Yeah, I had better get back to work. Do you want to grab a beer at the bar later?"

"Sure, what time?" I asked, walking toward the bedroom.

"I don't know when I'll be done. How about I send you a text?"

"Sounds good to me. Lock the door on your way out please."

"I will, bye, Vinny," she said, closing the door on her way

out.

I took off my clothes and stood in the shower until the water went cold, I would have given just about anything for a hot tub. The run had killed me. I didn't think I was going to be able to walk the next day.

After I was dressed I came out of my room and looked at my watch. It was already three, which meant not only would there be morning dishes, but the lunch dishes would be waiting for me as well.

"Come on Vinny, let's get to work." He looked at me from his dog bed then closed his eyes. "Alright you can stay here, but you had better be a good dog." I patted his head and went to work.

Chapter 20

Theron

Theron put down his phone and looked at the notes he took. Everyone thought he was dead, which meant someone, or someone's, were going to try and fill the gap as head of the Cretan Syndicate. He wondered if any of the other members would throw their hat into the ring.

He looked at the calendar, they would have had their monthly meeting a few days ago and he wondered if they mourned him or celebrated his demise. It didn't matter, when they saw that he was alive he would have his post back. They knew not to mess with him.

He picked up his phone and dialed Serafeim. He was least likely to buy into anyone else's ideas since compulsion did not work on him. As much as he could not trust him, he was an arms dealer after all, he would be straight with him.

"Who is this?" Serafeim asked, after answering on the first ring. "How did you get this number?"

"I am alive," Theron said, trying to make his voice more confident than he felt.

"Theron? Prove that it is you."

"I saved you from the Turkish mob when you were eighteen, they wanted to cut your head off for selling them defective M-16's. You cried for your mom like a baby." Theron smiled, remembering the night many years before.

"How are you alive? Where have you been?" Serafeim asked.

"I have been recuperating in a private hospital. I need to know what is going on with my island, can we meet?" Theron got up and paced while he talked. He had a bad feeling about what Serafeim was about to tell him.

"Yes, but not until later. I have a meeting with the man who is trying to take your place. I'll call you when I am ready."

"Good, I cannot wait to hear all about it." Theron pushed the end button on the phone and kept himself from smashing it in his fist.

Miguel was on his way back from his tailor. He was going to need to be dressed and ready to take the car as soon as he got back. He was about to shower when the doorbell rang. He snuck to the door and looked out the sidelight. There was a man in an EMT uniform holding a cooler. The blood had arrived. He opened the door, signed the paper, and took the cooler without saying anything. He closed the door and went upstairs to the room Vince and Helen were sleeping in. He quickly hooked up the transfusion tubes and left them to heal. He went into the bathroom and showered, since he had woken up he had not been taking very good care of himself. If he was going to win the island back, he was going to have to look the part.

"Theron? Where are you?" Miguel called, coming in the front door with a garment bag over one arm.

"I just got out of the shower. Did you get it?" he called back, coming down the stairs with a towel slung low on his hips.

"Yes, when I told the tailor who it was for, he kissed me." Miguel thrust the bag to Theron.

"Thank you for being my errand boy, I know it isn't something you are used to doing." Theron took the bag into the living room and hung it on the back of a door before unzipping it.

"I would ask you to do the same if our positions were reversed. You can't afford to be seen in anything but your best. Do you have a meeting tonight?" Miguel sat down on the edge of the couch and watched Theron dress.

"Yes, with my arms dealer. He is the most trustworthy member of The Syndicate, have you heard anything about who is trying to take over?" He pulled a white button up shirt from it packaging, and started to put it on.

"No, but no one is going to tell a Spaniard what's going on."

"I guess you're right." Finished buttoning his shirt, he pulled his pants on.

"I did sense another vampire while I was out though."

"What?" Theron dropped his hands from his fly, and put his hands on his hips. "Did you see them? Did you recognize him?"

"No, I only felt him for a moment then he was gone." Miguel looked at his hands. Theron kept a tight leash on vampires on his island. He didn't want to think about another vampire there without his permission.

"I will be on the lookout for him then." He finished dressing and turned to Miguel.

"How do I look?" The suit felt big; he had lost weight while lying unconscious.

"It needs to be taken in, but I don't think anyone will notice. Did the blood come?"

"Yes, I started transfusions for them both. They will probably need another bag pretty soon." Theron picked up his wallet, one of the few things that wasn't destroyed by Alex, put it in his jacket pocket, and his phone in the other.

"I'll go check on them. When are you leaving?" Miguel stood and walked to the base of the stairs.

"As soon as Serafeim calls me back." Theron pulled his phone out of his pocket to make sure the ringer was on. "Can I please have the car keys?"

"Sure, let me know before you leave." Miguel threw him the keys and jogged up the stairs.

Chapter 21

Katie

I stopped outside of the bar that night after receiving a text from Uni. The normal warm atmosphere that I saw most nights when I walked by on my way home wasn't there. The place was dark, and I wondered if it was closed. I also wondered where Uni had gone if it was closed. I pulled on the door, it was unlocked. I walked inside, the lights came on and voices yelled, "Surprise!"

I jumped, then looked around to see almost the entire town smiling in my direction. Uni came to my side and handed me a beer. "We all wanted to thank you for warning us this afternoon. This party is in your honor."

"Thank you everyone, I just did what I thought needed to be done." I took a sip of the beer and smiled. Everyone cheered then started talking to each other.

I actually earned some trust, I thought to myself.

"Karate Kid, this is Hound," Uni said, bringing my attention back to her. A man a few years older than me was standing next to her with a smile on his face. I had no idea where he got the nickname because he looked nothing like a dog. He was tall with blond hair and blue eyes. He had wide shoulders that tapered down to a lean waist. He was wearing a blue T-shirt and jeans.

"Hi, nice to meet you," I said, holding my hand out to him.

"You too," he said, taking my hand, and shaking it once before releasing it. "Ramstein told me you wanted to learn how to access the cameras that are used in public places to help you find people."

"Yes, I would love to learn how to do that. Can you show me how?" I asked, feeling dumb compared to everyone else in the bar.

"Yeah, stop by my office around three tomorrow and I can spend some time with you. Bring your computer and we'll see if it has what it needs to run the programs I have."

"Sure, thank you." I pulled my phone out of my pocket and entered in the appointment. I didn't think I would forget, but if I was out running or doing dishes, I might space out. I hadn't had to be anywhere at a certain time in a long time.

"No problem, here take one," he said, handing me a shot. "We are celebrating after all." He handed one to Uni too. "For giving us the warning we needed."

We clinked our glasses together and threw back the shot. I coughed, I had not drunk strong spirits in months. "What was that?" I asked, wiping tears from my eyes.

"Ouzo, it's made from distilled grapes and anise." He laughed at my reaction to it. "Have fun tonight."

"Yeah you too." I turned to Uni as he walked away. "Please keep me away from any more ouzo."

"I make no promises. This was the first time we had to use our camouflage and it worked. Everyone wants to celebrate." She laughed and took my hand, leading me through the crowd. People smiled at me as we passed, and some of them patted me on the back. I was shocked that I wasn't a pariah any more.

"Karate Kid," a woman about my age called, stopping me in my tracks.

"Yeah?" I asked, looking her over. She was my height, heavyset, with long, copper-colored hair and a friendly smile.

"I'm Copperhead." She extended her hand and I took it. "Uni told me you need to figure out a way to access your money without it being traced back to you."

"Yes, I have almost no cash, and I can't access my bank account without being tagged." I looked around as a few other people listened in.

"I can show you how to move it, set up a new account in a new name, but you need to get a new passport first."

"Really? You would be saving me from living on the streets if you could show me." I could use my own money, not the money Vince let me use, but the money I saved for this trip. I didn't know how far I would get with it, but it would be nice not to owe anyone.

"Yeah, let me know when you get a new identity and I'll show you how to get everything set up."

A waitress with a tray full of shots stopped in front of Copperhead. She took a glass off the tray and gave it to me before taking one for herself. "Opa," she said, clinking her glass with mine, and throwing the shot back.

I cringed, I didn't need another shot, but I didn't want to be disrespectful, and she was going to help me. I chugged it and coughed again as the burning warmth filled my insides. I took a sip of my beer to chase away the anise flavor overpowering my mouth.

"Oh, there's Hound, I need to talk to him about something. I'll catch up with you later," Copperhead said, moving through the crowd to where Hound was talking to another woman.

"She has a huge crush on him," Uni whispered in my ear.

"I can't blame her, he looks like Thor," I giggled as my brain buzzed from the ouzo.

"Are you buzzing? I don't think I have ever heard you giggle before." Uni laughed as I nodded my head and finished my beer.

"Let's go get another beer." I led the way to the bar which was empty except for Tad.

"What can I get you?" The man behind the bar asked, giving me a big smile. He was short, on the rounder side, with olive skin, and kind brown eyes.

"Two beers please." I pulled the twenty-euro bill from my pocket to pay him when he held up his hands.

"Your drinks are on the house tonight. Thanks for sending us the warning."

"Thank you," I said, taking the beers, and giving one to Uni.

Karate Kid, Tad thought to me. *Can I have a word please?*

I looked at Uni. "I'll catch up with you, Tad needs to talk to me for a second."

She raised her eyebrows then winked. "OK, see you in a bit." She turned and was swallowed by the crowd an instant later.

I moved down the bar and took a seat next to Tad, who had a glass of red wine sitting in front of him. "Hi, how are you tonight?"

"I am very well, especially since you sent us the warning about the group who came through." He gave me a tight smile, but it didn't reach his eyes.

"Have you figured out who they were yet?" I asked, praying it wasn't Alex or any of his crew.

"We are working on it. The license plate was stolen, and we are putting the faces we were able to get on camera through a facial recognition software. It will take time for it to finish."

"I was too far away to see if it was the man who's after me." I didn't know why Tad wanted to speak to me, but if it was about Alex, then there wasn't much I could do.

"I do not think it was the man who is after you. I think we have mole in our operation." Tad spun on his chair and looked around the room to make sure no one was nearby.

"You know you can just think at me and I'll hear you." He didn't like my gift, but it was a gift and if he wanted to tell me something in confidence it would be the best way.

"If I need to I will, everyone here is drunk so I do not need to worry about them remembering what I say to you." He turned to face me then leaned in. "Everyone trusts you now. If you hear anything that might tell us who the mole is will you tell me?"

"Of course, I love it here. In some ways it reminds me of home." It was just being in the mountains, nothing else reminded me of home, but I had been on a beach so long it felt like coming home in many ways.

"Good, and thank you for your help today. If it had not been for you, all would be lost, and I would have to go back to living in a cave."

"No problem, I don't know what I would have done if you hadn't taken me in. I want to keep this place a secret too." The bartender put a shot down in front of me when I stopped talking. I looked at it and groaned.

"Opa," he said, clinking his glass with mine before we both threw the shots back.

"Be careful with the ouzo, it has a way of turning on you," Tad said, laughing.

"Karate Kid, where are you?" Uni called from somewhere in the crowd.

"Go and have fun. We will talk more later." Tad turned to the bar and stared blankly at it.

I got up and wound my way through people until I found Uni dancing in place while wildly talking to a tall man with a cocoa complexion. He was gangly with short, curly, black hair, and deep brown eyes.

"Uni, are you OK?" I asked, putting my hand on her shoulder to make her stop swaying. "How much ouzo have you had?"

"I am just perfect," my young friend said, saying each word with perfect enunciation. "This is Barkley, Barkley this is Karate Kid."

"Hi, nice to meet you," I said, shaking his hand when he extended it to me.

"Nice to meet you too. Copperhead told me you need help coming up with a new identity and passport." He took a sip of his beer.

"Yes, I've been made, and I need to be someone else until I take care of a few people." My words were starting to slur. I could not have any more ouzo or things were going to get ugly.

"How many aliases do you have?" He seemed to be stone-cold sober while I was starting to have a hard time standing.

"Um, well there is the real me, the one Vince made for me, and Karate Kid," I said, 'Karate Kid' with my horrible Japanese accent and he laughed. "Sorry, I think I have had too much ouzo."

"It's OK, you're funny when you're drunk." He clinked his beer bottle with mine and we both took a sip. "I can help you come up a new identity. If you want, we can make a few in case you are made again."

"That would be great. When can we start?" I wouldn't feel safe until I was able to travel and access my money.

"I would say tomorrow morning, but I don't think you are going to be up for it, so how about after lunch?"

I pulled my trusty phone out and put it into my calendar. "Sure, I have another meeting at three. Will two hours be enough?"

"No, but we will be able to make a good start."

"I'm so happy everyone is helping you," Uni screamed, and put her hands in the air as a pop song I did not know started playing. "Come on, KK, let's dance."

"KK?" I asked, confused.

"Yeah, Karate Kid takes too long to say." She grabbed my hands and forced me to dance with her. I started to move with the bass and fell into the moment. It had been a long time since I had something to smile about. Who would have thought saving the village from an attack would win me so many friends?

Uni started swing dancing with me, and I followed her lead as she pulled me toward her then pushed me away. We were all smiles and laughs until she spun me out and I ran into the back of Mordor.

"Hey," he yelled, and I let go of Uni to see his shirt covered in beer.

"Oh my gosh. I am so sorry, Uni just spun me too fast and I didn't see you there."

"You need to get yourself under control. Just because you

'saved' us." He held up quotation marks when he said 'saved'. "Doesn't mean that all of us trust you, some of the dumber ones might, but you have no place here. You bring nothing to the table."

The smile fell from my face and my mood darkened. He was right, I did nothing to help them. I was just mooching off them until I could go back on my own. I was about to apologize when Uni spoke up. "When was the last time you had kitchen duty, Mordor?" She pushed him in the chest, and I quickly stepped between them to keep Uni from starting something I would have to finish.

"Uni, stop. He's right, I have not contributed much around here. If there is something I can do to help, then I will be more than happy to do it."

"No, you took over everyone's kitchen duty and he hated it. Besides that, he can't even thank you. He's a dick. Kick his ass."

He took a step toward me as if I was going to do what Uni asked. "Look there is nothing to fight about, Uni has had a lot to drink. Let's just go our separate ways and everything will be fine." I noticed people's conversations had stopped and they were slowly moving away from me and Mordor.

"No, I think we need to settle this now." He handed his beer to the man standing next to him and rolled up the sleeves on his shirt.

"Kick his ass KK," Uni yelled into the now deafening silence of the bar, someone had even turned the music off.

"Listen, Mordor, I really don't want to fight. I was just cutting loose; can't we just forget about this whole thing?" I was a little tipsy, but I had no doubt I could have him on his knees in seconds.

"You need to learn your place," he came at me with his arms out as if he was going to tackle me almost before he stopped talking. I moved out of his way, and he ran into the table behind me. I spun and moved to the other side of the circle as he groaned from hitting the table with his midsection.

"OK, you proved your point, let it go before you get hurt." I finished the beer in my hand and handed it off to someone standing nearby as Mordor started to sidestep around the circle, with his hands palms up, like he was going to lift me over his head and pile-drive me.

"Don't you get it? Nobody wants you here. Why don't you go back where you came from?" He jumped at me and wrapped his arms around my middle.

"Because," I said, trying to get a lungful of air. I wrapped my leg around his calf and pushed him backwards until he fell onto his back. "There is nothing but a pile of rubble there." I was done with the party. I needed to leave. I pushed through the crowd and almost made it to the doors before I heard him running up behind me. I spun around and punched him making contact with his jaw. He stood confused for a second then fell backward to the ground.

Everyone clapped and whistled, but I ignored them. I went out the door and ran back to my apartment with tears rolling down my cheeks.

I slammed the door behind me when I got back to my room, and Vinny ran to me whining. I slid down the door and buried my face in the fur of his neck. Mordor was an asshole, but I was mad at myself for letting him get to me. Goddess, I missed Crete, not just the place but everything the place meant to me. The vampires I had left behind, even if they were dead. It would always be a place where I was happy. The three months I spent there had become my new normal, and now I would never have it again.

"I'm sorry I left you at home tonight, Vinny. There were just too many people in the bar. I was afraid you would have gotten stepped on. Come on, you probably need to go outside." I forced myself to my feet and opened the door.

Vinny and I went out into the cool night and walked toward the park. The fresh air cleared my mind of the alcohol and the homesickness. I never thought I would be homesick for two places at the same time. I wanted to be home with my parents but more than that I would have given anything to be back on Crete with

Theron, Helen, and Vince.

I stiffened when I felt Tad come up behind me. I turned and automatically fell into my fighting stance. "I come in peace," he said, holding his hands up in surrender.

I relaxed, I had no reason not trust Tad, and he had just watched me fight Mordor, so he knew what I was capable of. "What can I do for you?" I asked, as Vinny came back to my side and sat down.

"I wanted to apologize for Mordor, he was out of line." He stepped next to me and turned to look around.

"He was drunk. I understand not trusting people. It is one of my special skills." I put my hands in the pocket of my jacket.

"Thank you for not killing him."

"What do you mean? Why would I kill him?" I asked, pulling my eyebrows together in confusion.

"I have watched you fight, I have watched you train. You were very gentle with him. From what I have seen you could have ended it before it started if you wanted to." I felt him smile.

"Well, I just got everybody on my side, most of them want to help me. They might change their minds if I kill him."

"You say that like you know from experience."

"No, just a feeling. You have a family here and as much as they say they don't like him, it probably would change if I killed him."

"You said before that you killed Theron's third in command. Did he hold it against you?"

"No, it was a life or death situation. He was pissed that his man tried to kill me." I turned so I could watch Tad's face.

"And what happened in the bar wasn't life or death?" he asked, pulling his eyebrows up high on his head.

"Mordor? No, unless he had a weapon. He wasn't going to kill me." I let out a half-laugh. "But I guess I put him in his place. Do you think he will leave me alone now?"

"I doubt it. Once he is focused on something he rarely lets it go until he gets what he wants. The good news is that you probably won over any of the others who were not sure about you. We all know how difficult Mordor can be. But why did you run off?"

"He brought up Crete, and I'm drunk. I lost everything on Crete. I spent my first week here trying to figure out if I was going to survive the loss."

"You must have decided that you are going to survive." Tad began to walk, and I walked with him.

"For now, I won't give up until the ones responsible for the massacre on Crete are dead, even if I die in the process."

"What will the Goddess think?" He sounded serious, but he felt skeptical.

"I don't care what she thinks. I lost the love of my life on Crete and two of the best friends I have ever had. Lolita is the key to this, it's because of her I had to leave the real me in San Sebastian. My parents, the ones who raised me, think I am in a witness protection program."

"You have lost everything."

"Yes, even a way to fund what I need to do," I gasped, trying not to cry. Damn ouzo, I hadn't cried about how shitty my life was in weeks. A few shots and I was a sobbing idiot.

"But you made contacts tonight who are going to help you start over." We stopped walking as we came to the alley where my apartment was.

"Yes, and thank you for letting me stay. I don't think I would have survived long without your help."

"You are welcome. Sleep well you are going to have a long day tomorrow."

Vinny and I went back to our apartment and settled in for the night. The fight had sobered me up and I fell into a dreamless sleep.

Chapter 22

Ilhami

Ilhami pulled his phone out and dialed Serafeim's number. He had no plans of going after the man who had killed Theron, but he wanted the members of The Syndicate to think that he was. He would feel safer with a gun anyway, he didn't trust them not to start a gun fight.

"Ilhami, how did you get this number?" Serafeim asked, answering the phone.

"I wanted to speak with you about making a purchase." He walked to the window in the living room of his house, ignoring the question. He could just see the bay from his position. The moon light shone on the gently moving water causing the light over the ripples to seem to glow from under the surface.

"What kind of purchase?" Serafeim knew what he needed to buy, he just wanted him to say it out loud.

"When I find the one who killed Theron I will need something to take care of him with. I wasn't able to bring my weapons with me when I came to Greece." Ilhami rolled his eyes and walked into the kitchen to get a bag of blood from the fridge.

"What do you need?"

"What do you have?" Ilhami didn't think the man was taking his request seriously.

"I'm sure I have everything you need to take care of the group who did this to our comrade."

"What do you mean group? At the meeting you said the man who planned it, not all of them." Ilhami grabbed the bag out of the fridge and popped it into the microwave for twenty seconds.

"After you left we talked about it. If you kill one, it's likely the others will want revenge. We do not want to start a war that might effect civilians, you need to take care of them all," Serafeim said over the noise of a bar.

"Very well," he seethed. He needed to enslave this man as soon as possible. "When can I see what you have?"

He looked at his watch. "I have time now."

"Perfect. The sooner I have the weapons, the sooner I can take care of the problem. Where do you want to meet?" Ilhami took the bag out of the microwave and tore the lid off.

"I will pick you up. Where are you?" Ilhami heard him start to move through the crowded room.

"I can meet you." He didn't want Serafeim to know where he was staying.

"Nonsense, I will pick you up, tell me where."

Ilhami reluctantly gave him the address of his house and hung up the phone. He went into the front hall and waited for Serafeim to arrive. He told himself it would not matter if Serafeim learned where he lived. He was going to start the bonding process before the night was over, but it still made him nervous.

Headlights bounced off the wall in the entryway and he got to his feet as a horn blew. He left the house walking tall, Serafeim's men were nothing to him. They would be his men before long. He got into the backseat of the Land Rover and nodded his head at Serafeim.

"Thank you for the ride." He closed the door and the SUV turned around in his driveway.

"Do not mention it." Serafeim looked out the window as they drove down the street.

"Where are we going?" Ilhami asked.

"To my showroom, I hope you brought cash."

"Of course," he said through clenched teeth. These men were not being very helpful, given the fact that he was pretending to avenge the loss of their leader.

"Good, you understand I am a businessman. If I give you something for free, then everyone will be asking for a discount. I'm not a charity; I have to watch my bottom line." Serafeim relaxed against his seat and looked out the window.

"Of course, how else would you be able to survive?" Ilhami asked, wishing he could just reach over and sink his teeth into the man, but the driver and guard in the front seat were keeping a close eye on them through the mirrors.

The car came to a stop outside a white, concrete building no windows, the only door was set in the middle. The edge of the roof was covered in coiled razor wire, and he wondered if there was another door in the back. The security of this building made Ilhami think it must have been filled with gold, but then again guns and munitions were gold to many people. The SUV stopped by the front door and they got out. Serafeim went to the door, pulled out a keychain, and unlocked the door. He went inside and Ilhami moved to follow him only to be stopped by a guard.

"Wait here until he disarms the alarm." The man ordered, holding his arm in front of the door.

Ilhami took a step back and put his hands in his pockets, trying to play it cool and calm when all he wanted to do was throw the human against the wall. He turned and looked around. The building was in a light industrial area surrounded by small mechanic shops and warehouses. There were no homes nearby, the location was no doubt strategic. If there was a war, Serafeim would not want to endanger the lives of civilians.

Stupid man, Ilhami thought, it would make it that much easier to get into. Serafeim came to the door and waved him in. He walked into a long, narrow room filled with glass display cases. The lights were on and as he walked through the room he noticed all sorts of weapons. From small .22

caliber handguns to .50 caliber sniper rifles. There were cases filled with different grenades and launchers, there were plastic explosives, knives, and even some swords.

"What do you need?" Serafeim asked, from the other side of the glass case filled with hand guns.

"I am going to need a long-range sniper rifle with a silencer, a high caliber handgun, and the ammo to go with them." He was making it up as he went. He looked up and locked eyes with Serafeim. "Tell your guards to leave," he said, forcing his compulsion onto the man.

Serafeim blinked and looked around. "Why would I do that? I do not know you, or trust you. I think I will leave them where they are."

Fuck, Ilhami thought to himself, he was one of the few humans that compulsion did not work on. "Very well, how much for what I need?" He backtracked quickly, pretending he hadn't said a thing.

"Depends on which rifle you want. Come over here and I will show you what I have." He moved to another case and pulled out a small briefcase. "This is your standard .7mm Winchester, it breaks down into two pieces, plus the bolt and the snap-in scope. The serial number has been sanded off making it untraceable."

It was a gun Ilhami would not mind owning. He picked it up and pulled the bolt back, it was unloaded, as was expected, he closed the bolt and brought it to his shoulder. It fit him perfectly and the trigger was just how he liked it. He put the gun back on the felt cloth on top of the table. "How much?" He kept his face passive, trying to not reveal how much he wanted it.

"This one is four thousand euros, cash," Serafeim said, watching Ilhami closely for a reaction.

"For that price it includes the silencer, case, and a case of ammo correct?" He looked down at the rifle then at the other ones arranged in the case.

"The silencer is extra, but I will include a case of ammo since we are friends." Serafeim folded his arms across his chest.

"You drive a hard bargain. I could pick up the same thing with a silencer for half the price in Moscow."

"But we are not in Russia, are we? It is very difficult and therefore expensive to bring guns to Crete. I am forced to pass the costs along to my customers." If The Turk bought the gun at the price he gave him, he would make over a hundred percent profit on it.

"What kind of deal will you make me if I buy the Colt in the case over there as well?" He nodded his head to the case with only one gun sitting on the shelf. It was a 1911 Colt, with ivory grips, night sights, a grip safety and an attachment for a flash light.

"That gun is the most expensive handgun in my collection. It's ten thousand, it is an original with elephant ivory grips. It has been completely restored and reworked. It is said that Hitler carried it."

Ilhami restrained from rolling his eyes. "How much for both?"

"Fifteen thousand and I will throw in the silencer and a case of ammo for each," Serafeim said, wondering how much longer this was going to take. He wanted to meet with Theron, he would not believe he was alive until he saw him for himself.

"Very well, I will need to arrange for the funds. I brought some cash with me, but not enough. Can we complete the purchase tomorrow night?" Ilhami looked around, pretending to admire the other items for sale, when he was really trying to figure out where he was going to get the money.

"Of course. Call me when you are ready, and I will make arrangements to meet. Now, if you will excuse me I have another meeting I must get to." Serafeim extended his arm toward the door.

"Of course." Ilhami exited the store and waited while Serafeim locked everything back up.

"Can I drop you somewhere?" Serafeim asked, putting the keys back in his pocket.

"No, if it is all the same to you I think I will walk for a while. I will have one of my men meet me when I am done."

"Very well, we will be in touch."

"Yes, we will."

Ilhami walked around the neighborhood, taking in all the details of the buildings and businesses around it until he was a half mile away. He wanted to get the lay of the land in case he needed to break in. He pulled his phone out and called Takis. "I need a pick up." He gave the man his location and turned to look up at the sky. There was no way he was going to be able to get his hands on the cash he needed for the guns. Well, he could, but he would be left with nothing and he needed some walking around money.

A car stopped in front of him flashing its lights. He walked to the passenger rear door and got in. "What took you so long?" he asked, sitting directly behind the driver who wasn't Takis.

"I am sorry, I was asleep when Takis called me to give you a ride. I got here a quick as I could."

"Take me to him, now." Ilhami's voice dropped to a dangerously calm level. When Ilhami told Takis to pick him up, he meant for Takis to come himself not delegate it to some underling, but it gave him an idea.

"He told me he did not want to be disturbed for the rest of the night." The man's voice shook with every word.

"If you want to live long enough to see the sunrise I suggest you take me to him." Ilhami sat back in his seat and relaxed. If this one did not do what he asked, he would compel him. He still did not know where Takis lived and it was annoying him.

The man drove him to the outskirts of the city and pulled off the road at a gate. He rolled down his window and entered a code. When the gate opened he pull the car through and stopped when he reached the front door.

"Now wait for me. I am going to need a ride home." Ilhami

got out of the car and rang the doorbell then stepped back. The house was dark, but he heard a noise after a minute and a light came on. He waited impatiently while Takis unlocked the door and opened it.

"What is the meaning of this? You can't just come to my home in the middle of the night. My family is sleeping." His robe was tied tightly around his middle, his brown hair was pushed to one side of his head, and his shoeless feet danced back and forth.

"When I tell you I need a ride, I expect you, to give me that ride." Ilhami flicked the invisible rope that bonded Takis to him causing the pain he used to control his slaves. It wasn't as much as he could inflict if the slave bond had been complete, but it was enough to bring him to his knees. "Do you understand?"

"Yes," Takis said between clenched teeth, holding his head with his hands.

"Good now invite me in." Ilhami let go of the man's mind and waited while he got to his feet and opened the door wider.

Ilhami walked through the door then waited while Takis closed it. "Where can we talk privately?"

"This way," Takis led him through the foyer and down a hallway. He went through a door on the right, leaving it open for Ilhami to follow. He clicked on a lamp on his desk. "What can I do for you?"

"I need fifteen thousand euros by sundown tomorrow." Ilhami took a seat and waved his hand for Takis to sit down across from him.

"Why would I loan you fifteen thousand euros?" He folded his hands together and rested them on his stomach.

"I did not say I wanted to borrow fifteen thousand. You are going to give me fifteen thousand." Ilhami did not bother to compel him. He was going to bring the slave bond one step closer to being complete in a few moments.

"Again, why would I do this for you? You come onto my island and expect us all to bow down to your rule without any reason. What have you done for Cretans? What have you done for The Syndicate?"

"Nothing yet." Ilhami used his compulsion then. "Come and drink from me."

Takis got up from his chair and fell to his knees before Ilhami. Takis took a knife from the pocket of his robe and cut Ilhami's wrist. "Drink deep slave." Ilhami shoved his bleeding wrist into the man's face. Takis took the wrist in his hand and started to drink. When he had enough Ilhami took his wrist back and pulled Takis between his legs shoving his neck to the side. His fangs slid into his neck and he drank the crimson nectar, feeling the bond grow as he took his fill.

"Now about the money," Ilhami said, pushing Takis back before regaining his feet.

Takis turned and went to the painting behind the desk, he pulled on the lower right corner and one side opened like it was a door, revealing a safe. He dialed the combination and opened it revealing stacks of cash. He started pulling out neat piles of money and setting them on the desk.

"Do you have a bag?" Ilhami asked, looking around the room.

"I will get one in just a second." He pulled out a few more bundles, sat down at the desk, and opened a drawer. He brought out a gym bag and put the money in the bag. "Here you go."

"Thank you, now go back to bed." Ilhami turned, walked himself out of the house, and back to the car.

"Drive to a secluded beach." He told the driver and relaxed back in his seat with the money he needed to buy the guns next to him. All wasn't lost, but he was still pissed he wasn't able to compel Serafeim. He was going to be a problem, but easily enough dispatched. He would enslave the rest of The Syndicate then take care of Serafeim.

"This is a private beach, and the owner is out of town. Is it secluded enough for you?" The driver asked.

"Yes, this will do nicely. Get out of the car we are going to go for a walk on the beach."

Chapter 23

Theron

An hour later Theron's phone buzzed in his pocket. "Yes?" he asked, after pulling it out and pushing the answer button.

"I am done with my meeting where would you like to meet?" Serafeim asked, over the sound of a car engine.

"Somewhere private where no one will recognize me." Theron said, going out the front door to his BMW.

"Let's meet in the cave then, I will leave my bodyguards at home."

"I'll be there in fifteen minutes." Theron hung up the phone and started the car driving quickly to the parking area near the cave.

The cave was where he had first met Serafeim eighteen years before. Serafeim was just starting to break out as a known arms dealer, and Theron needed a cut if Serafeim was going to put his island at risk by allowing scumbags from all over the world on Crete. They struck a partnership, and Theron loaned him the money to buy a warehouse near the port, making it easier for him to move his product on and off the island while keeping most of the civilians out of the crossfire if something went wrong.

Before then, clients had to go all the way to the cave. This meant they had to go through town, then park on a public road where the police often patrolled, or they could take a boat. There were too many civilians between the town and the cave. Theron wanted Serafeim's clients to come onto the island, buy their guns, and leave. It was the deal he made with Serafeim. His clients were allowed on the island for no more than four hours before they had to leave. If they were coming for vacation with their family it was one thing, when they were coming to buy munitions it was another.

He found the rarely used trail and followed it down to the cave's entrance without issue. He had not ventured to the cave in many years, and he found he missed the solitude. Miguel would probably disagree with him after the months he spent hiding in the cave on the island across from his compound, but in small doses it made him appreciate where he was in the world. When he reached the mouth of the cave he found the torch they had used many times while dealing with Serafeim's clients. He pulled a lighter from his pocket and lit it. Serafeim would need the light to find his way.

Theron sat down on the rock and looked at the blanket of stars above him falling toward the earth and swallowed by the water. He wasn't at full strength and he was tired, almost winded. He could not remember the last time he had been so weak. He closed his eyes and rested, he could not let anyone know that he wasn't at one hundred percent yet. He trusted Serafeim, but showing any weakness would only get him into trouble later. He heard steps on the trail and he got up quickly moving into the shadows. He was positive it was Serafeim, but he could not be too sure, with how quickly things changed on the island it could have been anyone. He stood silently as a middle-aged man stepped into the light and looked around. He was short with the beginnings of a pot-belly, his brown hair curled around his ears, and even in the light of the torch he could make out the watery brown eyes looking for him.

"Theron, are you here?" Serafeim asked, as Theron heard his heart rate pick up.

Theron stepped from the shadows and opened his arms. "Serafeim, it is good to see you."

Serafeim whirled around, startled, pointing a gun at Theron. "Theron? Is it really you?" His voice was tight, but he lowered the gun.

"Yes, I am alive and well. Look, good as new." Theron turned in a circle, letting the man get a good look.

"Thank the gods." Serafeim took him in a hug that lasted a few seconds too long.

"Did you miss me, Serafeim?" Theron pulled away from him and held him at arm's length.

"You have no idea, the man, if you could call him that, who is trying to take your place is a pain in the ass." He lowered his arms and started to pace.

"What is his name?" Theron sat down on the rock and gave him his full attention.

"The Turk, but he said his first name is Ilhami." He continued to pace back and forth in front of Theron.

"How old would you say he is?" Theron asked. The only person he had ever known by the name had been expelled from the island over fifty years ago. He would be an old man now.

"He looks to be in his late twenties or early thirties, but accent is different than any Turk's I have ever heard. Do you know him?"

"I'm not sure. Do you have a picture of him?" If it was the man Theron thought, he would have to be a son of the man he exiled or a vampire.

"Yes, he came to my store tonight to buy a few guns." Serafeim pulled his phone out and thumbed through a few screens before he handed it over. Theron took the phone and almost let a gasp pass his lips before he caught it.

"Yes, I know him. He is a very dangerous man. Has anyone seen him in the daytime?"

"No, he is staying in a rental. He goes home early in the morning, before the sun comes up. We have yet to see him during the day. Do you think he's like you?" Serafeim asked; he did not know what Theron was, but he knew his habits.

"I am afraid so. Tell me how he made himself known to you and the rest of The Syndicate." Theron got up and started to pace as Serafeim told him about how The Turk had crashed their monthly meeting and the outrageous demands they gave him to join.

"Really? You are making him find the man who attacked my compound?" Theron let out the first laugh he had since the attack, it felt good. "You have no idea how badly he wanted to be the one to kill me."

"Why does he hate you?"

"I was forced to kill his whole family to gain control of the island many years ago. He always threatened that he would come back and kill me for what I did. He thinks he was too late and now you have demanded he kill the man who supposedly put me in the ground. Thank you for paying me respect when you thought I was dead." He laughed again.

"You didn't think we respected you enough to find out who did this and kill them? You are the one who made every single one of us who we are. We are not good men, but we all respect you and what you have done for us." Serafeim put his hands on his hips and brought his eyebrows together in anger.

"No, but I hoped you would, and you would not let our island fall into the wrong hands. Tell me who else has he met with since the meeting?" Theron sat back down on the rock.

"None that I know of, but when I saw Takis, earlier this evening he was acting strange."

"Call everyone and tell them not to meet with him alone, and not to make eye contact with him." Theron wanted to save the members of The Syndicate, but it looked like it was too late for Takis. If Ilhami had already started the slave process Katie was the only one who could fix it and who knew where she was or even if she was alive.

"I met his eyes tonight, is it too late for me?" He ran his hands through his hair and stared wide-eyed at Theron.

"No, you're special, he cannot control you like he can the others." Theron hated telling him the secrets he had kept from them for so many years, but they were on the brink of war and if the other members became slaves to Ilhami then it would be harder to win.

"I am?" He made it a question and smiled broadly.

"Yes, now go and spread the word."

"What are you going to do?"

Theron thought on it for a time. "I am going to send a friend of mine to Agapios. I want him to watch over him and protect him from Ilhami. Don't tell the others that I am alive yet, if he gains control over them I don't want him to know until I rip his head from his body."

"What do I tell Agapios about the new guard?"

"You will think of something, tell him it is just to be on the safe side, you know what a pansy he is."

"Yes, I will think of something."

Theron went back to the house a little while later to find Miguel sitting in the living room, reading a book. "You look very at home here in this shack," Theron almost laughed as Miguel looked up from his book.

"How did your meeting go?" Miguel asked, ignoring the insult Theron threw at him.

"It was good, there's good news and bad news. I am hoping you will be willing to help me." Theron sat down in the chair across from Miguel.

"What do you need?" He closed the book and put it on the end table.

"I need you to play bodyguard to Agapios. He is weak-minded. We think Ilhami has already enslaved Takis, our drug lord. I have no doubt he will try to enslave everyone in The Syndicate. If that happens I will not be able to hold the island." Theron ran his hands through his hair and looked at the ceiling.

"So, I will have to hang out in bars, and whore houses?" Miguel asked, his tone dry, like he would rather do anything else.

"Yes, Agapios is easy to watch, but he is an important member. I would hate to lose him."

"How did he end up as the leader of the entertainment industry, if

149

he is so weak?" Miguel did not understand. To oversee such an industry, one had to be clear-headed and not be afraid of getting his hands bloody.

"He's very smart, and vicious. Many people died during the battle for this position, he wasn't merciful. Believe me, we want him on our side."

"Why haven't you made him your slave?" Miguel asked, confused, it's what he would have done.

"Because I made a promise when I won the island, I would give all of my leader's free will. I am starting to regret it now. If they were my slaves it would be harder for them to succumb to Ilhami's advances."

"I admire that you keep your promises, I have never been very good at it."

"So, I've heard." Theron thought of Katie and wondered where she could be. Vince would kill him if he didn't have some information on her when he woke up.

"I know. I ruined everything with Katie, and now she's out there on her own." Miguel hung his head, wishing he would have killed the mercenaries on his island when he had the chance.

"She isn't stupid, and Vince gave her the tools she needs to survive almost anything. I am sure she's fine, but I must start looking for her. If I'm empty-handed when Vince wakes up, he will probably kill me."

"How are you going to track her?" Miguel asked, looking up with his eyebrows high.

"I have my ways and I think it will best for everyone if you stay out of it. I need you here right now, not running off to find her. You'll do nothing but scare her if you find her, and she'll kill you."

"I am almost expecting it from her. I treated her so badly, thanks to my ego and Lolita. I doubt she will ever forgive me." Miguel looked back down as his feet. "When do you want me to start guarding Agapios?"

"Tomorrow night. Serafeim is going to call me at sundown and tell me where Agapios is going to be." Theron got up from his chair and walked to the stairs.

"I will be ready," Miguel said, picking his book back up. "Would you mind checking on Vince and Helen? They're probably ready for new bags."

"Yes, I will, enjoy the rest of your evening."

"You as well."

Theron went into his room and booted up his laptop. He didn't have very many ways he could track Katie, but he had to try. He pulled the security footage from the port on the day of the attack. He watched his BMW pull into the parking lot and a woman who must have been Katie get out of the car, but it did not look like her. The woman had blonde hair, a clear complexion, and none of the bruises she had after her fight with Ben. She carried a suitcase and a plastic bag from a big box store. She must have stopped and given herself a makeover. She wasn't dumb. She knew Alex would be looking for her.

He watched her board the ship and was about to turn the camera off when he saw a Land Rover pull into the parking lot and Alex jump out. Theron smiled, at least she made it off the island safely. He looked up the route the ferry she took. It stopped at three different islands before it made it back to Athens. He sighed, it was going to be a long night. He didn't have access to cameras anywhere but on Crete. If he was going to track her down, he was going to need help. He picked up his phone and called a number.

"Who is this?" Zoi's curt voice flowed through the phone at Theron's ear.

"Hello to you too, Zoi," Theron smiled into the phone; she was one of the few female vampires Lolita had not taken down. He wasn't sure what side she would fall on, but he needed her help.

"Theron, you are dead. Are you calling me from the grave?" she asked, still not sounding like she believed it was him.

"Not dead just unconscious for a while."

"I'm glad to hear it. You're not just calling to tell me you are alive." It was almost hard to understand her with the thumping bass in the background.

"You know I'm not. I need a favor."

"What is it?" she asked, as the music abruptly cut off.

"Will you please grant me access to the security cameras at the port?"

"Who are you looking for? The one who attacked you?"

"Him and others."

"Very well, it is a small thing to ask. You will have access within the hour. Is your email still the same?"

"Yes, and can you please not tell anyone I am alive? I am dealing with a hostile takeover attempt. I do not want him to know I am alive yet."

"Of course, but you must promise to come for a visit, once things have calmed down." Theron could hear the coy smile in her voice. Zoi had exotic tastes in the bedroom and Theron had to be in just the right mood to play with her.

"Yes, I will come for a visit once everything is under control."

"Good, look for an email with a user name and password within an hour." The call ended, and Theron went into the room where Vince and Helen were. Their bags of blood were empty. He went to the cooler and got out another bag for each of them. Once the blood was entering their system he sat down in the chair and looked at Vince.

"Katie made it off the island on her own. She is smart, Vince, she dyed her hair and put on a bunch of makeup." He smiled at the thought of Katie dying her hair in a bathroom sink. "She is somewhere, and I'm trying to find her, but it would be easier if you would wake up. You know her better than I ever will. I need your help too. The Turk, the one whom I banished when I took over The

Syndicate, is back. Someone changed him, and he is trying to take over the island. Miguel is helping. I know you want to kill him, but I will not be able to keep the island without him. I think he is truly sorry for everything he did to Katie. Hurry up and get better, I miss talking to you."

He moved his chair over to Helen. "That goes for you too. How am I supposed to do my job when you are lying around all the time? You are my second in command and I need you at my side. It is going to take all of us to get rid of The Turk." Theron leaned back in the chair and rested his head against the wall. He didn't know how much longer he would be able to stand this house, with only Miguel for company. He needed to be out recruiting more vampires since his were all lost. When Vince and Helen woke up they would have a memorial for all who had died during the attack, then he would start to rebuild. His new home would be bombproof. He did not care how much it cost.

After a short nap he went back to his computer and found the email Zoi promised to send with the login information he needed to access the security footage from the port. He cued it to the date and time Katie arrived and watched as groups of people disembarked. She was one of the last ones off and she looked nervous. She was looking around left and right until her eyes found what she was looking for. She moved quickly and joined a group of people laughing and talking. He had to switch cameras as she left the view of the first one and it took time to get the timing of the footage where he needed it on the second, but once he did he found her and a man holding a photo. It must have been who she saw before she joined the group. When she walked past him she dug into her bag keeping her head down. The man completely missed her. Theron could not help the smile on his face as he watched her leave the group and get into a taxi.

"Opa," he yelled, doing a fist pump. He ran back into the room where his friends slept. He went to Vince's head and whispered in his ear. "She made it past the man waiting in Athens. You have to wake up now. I need you to help find her." He waited for any reaction from Vince but got none.

Theron got up, turned the light out, and went into his own room to sleep. He didn't know where Katie was, but she had gotten past Alex and his men three times. The woman was so much smarter than anyone gave her credit for.

Chapter 24

Katie

I woke up the next morning feeling better than I thought I would after all the ouzo I drank the night before. It snowed during the night and Vinny was terrified of it at first. After I showed him there was nothing to be afraid of we went on our morning run. When we got back I ate breakfast then went back to the kitchen to start on the dishes.

"Hi Lucy," I said as Vinny and I walked into the kitchen.

"Hi Karate Kid, what are you doing here?" she asked, turning from the pot on the stove she was stirring.

"The dishes." I gave her a confused look, then heard someone banging pots and pans back by the sink.

"No one told you?" She laughed and went back to her pot. "You are officially off kitchen duty."

"Why?" I asked, leaning around the corner to see who was doing the dishes.

"Mordor started the fight, Tad said it was his punishment for being an asshole last night. You kicked his ass." She chuckled to herself.

"Great now he is really going to love me." I looked at Vinny, how was I going to fill my time if I didn't have dishes to do? "Well, I guess I'll see you later then."

"Enjoy your day dear," she called, not looking up from her pot.

"Well, what should we do?" I asked Vinny, as we walked back toward our apartment. "Train of course." We went back to the apartment, I picked up my katana and we went to the park. It was empty for a change and I worked through my forms undisturbed. I set my katana on the picnic table when I was done and pulled a ball out of my pocket.

I had just thrown the ball for Vinny when I heard someone behind me. I turned to find Mordor holding my sword staring at it. "Please put my katana down," I said, moving to the far end of the table.

"Have you ever used this in battle?" he asked, holding it like a baseball player holding a bat. Only he was letting the sword rest on his shoulder instead of just above it. I was pretty sure he thought he looked like a badass, but he actually looked like a drunk American in Japan.

"Yes, unfortunately I have. Please put my katana down." My voice was even and calm. If he didn't put it down I would be anything but calm.

"Why? Is it a bad thing?" He brought the sword around his body in a chopping motion.

"Because I didn't want to kill the man, but I had no choice. Please put the katana down."

"There is always a choice. I like it, I think you are going to have to make me put it down."

"You're right, I chose not to die. Don't make me hurt you, just put the sword down and you won't get hurt." I closed my eyes and found my breath. It was going to take all my control not to kill him.

"I would like to see you try while I am holding this." He spun it around erratically, trying to put on a show.

I let out a breath and moved, with my hand flat and fingers together I stabbed him in the throat. He dropped my katana and grabbed his neck fighting for air. I caught it before it hit the ground and leveled it on his throat.

"You bitch. I was going to say I was sorry about last night, but I'm really not. You shouldn't be here. You are doing nothing but

156

wasting our resources," he croaked as his eyes went from the tip of sword to my eyes then back, and all the color drained out of his face.

"I'm sorry you feel that way, but I have nowhere else to go and if you ever touch my katana again, I will send you to the hospital, if not the morgue." I backed up and went to the table to get my scabbard. Vinny let a low growl out. "Come on, Vinny, let's go home."

"This isn't your home, Karate Kid, you won't last long. I'll make sure of it," he called after me, trying to sound tough, but his voice cracked, and he coughed like a lifetime smoker.

We walked home, then I sat on my couch thinking about Mordor. I didn't know what I had done to him to make him dislike me so much, but I needed to keep an eye on him and my katana. I had a lock on my door, but it would not take much for someone to break in. I needed some rope, then I could make a sling and I could keep my katana with me all the time. My katana and my quail necklace were the most important things I owned. I fingered my necklace and kept myself from shedding a tear.

We went to the general store to buy parachute cord, I pulled up instructions for weaving a sling on my computer and got to work. I was about half way done when my phone pinged. I picked it up to see I only had five minutes to get to Barkley's office. Leaving my sling, I picked up my computer bag and called to Vinny.

When we arrived outside Barkley's office I knocked lightly on the door. "Come on in," a voice called from the other side of the door.

I opened the door and we went inside. "Hi, how are you?"

"Good, have a seat. How are you feeling after all the ouzo last night?"

"I'm good, I think the fight helped sober me up." I looked around the room taking everything in. There were six different printers, three computers, a camera on a tripod in front of a green screen, and a few other machines I had never seen before. Barkley's desk was clear other than a laptop, a notepad, and a pen.

"Mordor has always been an ass. He wants to keep the town small and thinks everyone needs to pull their weight for the greater good. He doesn't understand that we are here to help people and you need help." He shook his head and turned his computer around to show me what he had. "I have a few different programs I use to create new identities. I would give you the software for your computer, but you need a lot of printers to get it done."

"Yeah, I see what you mean. I never really thought about how to make them." I was disappointed. I wanted to be able to create my own documents but traveling with all those printers would be impossible.

"Don't worry I'll help you set up as many as you want. It should keep you safe for a while." He laughed and pulled his computer back in front of him.

"So, we aren't stealing people identities, right?"

"No, we're just creating new ones. You won't have a lot of background if someone really digs, but it will be enough to get you through customs and set up bank accounts if you need to."

"OK, good. Where do we start?" I was finally taking a step toward being self-sufficient. I still had no idea how I was going to get around the cameras, but I wasn't willing to undergo plastic surgery to stay off Alex's radar.

"I need a mug shot. Will you stand with your toes on the line in front of the camera please?" He pushed back from his chair and stood.

"Vinny stay," I said, getting up, and standing in front of the camera.

"Good, I'm going to take a few different pictures then I will show you how we are going to make them look like they were not taken on the same day."

"I never thought of that. It would look strange if you had the same photo on everything." I stood straight and pulled my shoulders back.

"That is why I'm the professional. Now smile for the

camera."

After Barkley took ten different pictures of me, some smiling some with a neutral expression, some with me slouching, and one with me frowning he moved the chair I had been sitting next to his. "Now watch and learn."

He opened a program and imported the photos. "With this I can change your shirt, change the background and even the highlights in your hair." He brought up a photo and started to manipulate it.

"Do I get to pick my new name, or do you have a list somewhere? Where will I be from? I want make sure I know a little bit about the area, in case someone questions me." I was thinking about my old alias. I had been to San Diego, so I was prepared if someone asked.

"I have a list, and don't worry I will give you a short background on who each one is. I am going to show you how to make the first one and you are going to make the rest of them."

"I don't know how I will ever be able to thank you for this." I wasn't only going to have one new identity but as many as I could make.

We went back to manipulating the photos. When we were done I had forty different photos I could use for my new identities. "When can we do the next step?" I was excited; part of me wanted to blow off Hound and finish making my new cover, but I needed to find a way to find and track Lolita too.

"I have time tomorrow around ten." He leaned back in his chair and put his hands behind his head.

"OK, I have been relieved from kitchen duty, so I can be here whenever." I leaned against the door and scratched Vinny behind the ears.

"I heard Tad gave it to Mordor for a month. I would watch my back if I were you. He holds one hell of a grudge."

"I ran into him this morning, and it didn't go very well. I'm going to try and stay away from him as much as possible."

"Good plan, have fun with Hound."

"Thanks, see you later." Vinny and I went back to the first floor to find Hound.

My meeting with Hound didn't take as long as I thought it would. I ended up leaving my computer with him, so he could load the software I would need to find people. He was going to show me how to use it after he had everything loaded.

As Vinny and I walked back to the apartment I felt like I was moving forward for the first time since I left Crete. I had already done my training, started on my fake ID's and my computer was being loaded with programs I could use to find Lolita and Alex. It was cold outside when we exited headquarters, so we went back to the apartment and I worked on the sling for my katana.

At six o'clock there was a knock at my door. I got up and looked through the peep hole to see Uni standing outside. I opened the door and waved for her to come in. "Hurry its cold out there."

"No kidding, and its only October, you would think it was January. What are you doing?" she asked, as I went back to my almost completed sling.

"Making a sling for my katana. That asshole Mordor was looking at it a little too closely this morning and I don't trust the lock on the door." I made the next knot as I talked.

"You have to watch him. Once he finds someone he doesn't like he puts all his energy into destroying them. I've seen him do it, you are going to need to be careful with everything important to you." She sat down on the couch and folded her arms over her chest.

"That is what Barkley said earlier. How was your day?" I asked as I worked.

"Brutal, I drank way too much last night. It feels like someone hit me on the head with a hammer. I've been drinking sports drinks like I was an Olympic athlete. How are you feeling?"

"I'm good, I think the fight burned most of it out of my system before I went to bed."

"Must be nice, I have gotten almost nothing accomplished today. All I wanted to do was curl into a ball in a dark room and wait for the pain to end."

"I've been there. I'm sorry, that ouzo is brutal. What are we doing tonight?"

"Dinner, then I have to get back to work. I'm hoping food will help me find some energy. Are you almost done?"

"Yeah I just need a few more minutes." I came to the end of my sling and tied it off. I took the sheath of my katana and fitted the sling to it. I pushed my arms through the loops and adjusted it, so it would sit against my spine.

"That looks good. Will you show me how to make those?"

"Yeah, I just looked it up on the internet." I reached behind my head and pulled the sword from the sheath to get the feel of it. It took too long. "This is going to take a while to get used to." I got it back in the sheath on the third try.

"It doesn't look like you are having any problems to me," Uni joked. "Let's go eat, then you can practice with it."

"OK, let me get my coat." I put the leather coat Uni had given me on over my sword. It was snug, but I liked the idea of having it under my coat, and it would not draw as much attention as it did when I held it.

The three of us left the apartment and hurried to the cafeteria. Everyone must have been hungry at the same time because we had to wait in line for the buffet. I waved to Hound who was standing with Copperhead a few people in front of us.

"Hi Hound, how's it going?" I asked.

"Good, I have almost everything loaded on your computer. I'll have it ready tomorrow to show you how it works."

"Great, I can't wait."

"Do you guys want to sit with us?" he asked, looking nervous standing next to Copperhead.

"Sure, if you guys don't mind a dog under the table." I looked down at Vinny.

"No problem," Copperhead said, looking relieved to have company.

I made eye contact with Uni and raised my eyebrows and she winked at me.

When we finally made it to the buffet there were no plates. I could hear Lucy yelling at Mordor to hurry up or all her food would be ruined. He came out of the back with a pile of plates in his hands. He threw them onto the table and tried to run back before everyone saw him, but there must have been some water on the floor because he slipped and fell on his ass. Everyone laughed except for me, I felt bad for the guy. Not only was he stuck on kitchen duty, but falling on his ass in front of everyone was only rubbing salt in the wound. He slowly got to his feet and walked to the back with his head held high. At least he wasn't letting everyone get to him.

We got our food and went into the dining room. Copperhead and Hound were sitting across from each other at a table by the window, so I took the seat next to Hound while Uni sat down next to Copperhead.

"You so missed it," Uni said, putting her napkin in her lap, and picking up her fork.

"What happened? I heard everyone laughing." He took a bite of his salad.

"Mordor brought out a pile of plates, after he put them down he tried to run out of the room, but he slipped and fell." Uni cut a piece of chicken and brought it up to her mouth.

"I wish I could have been there." Copperhead laughed, and took another bite of her food.

"I feel bad for the guy," I said, digging into my own food.

"Why? He hates you and keeps trying to get you kicked out." Copperhead gave me a pointed look.

"He's already in trouble for the shit he started last night, now he's being punished and falling just added insult to injury."

"Well, he is a big boy, I'm sure he will get over it," Hound said. "I meant to ask you if you had a picture of who you want to find?" he asked, changing the subject.

"No, I'm going to have to find her, get a picture from a camera, then keep track of her." I frowned, wishing there was a way to make it easier, but vampires didn't have their photos taken very often for fear of being discovered.

"Do you know where to start?" he asked, bringing his eyebrows together in concern.

"She is in Europe, other than that I have no idea. I have a few places to start though."

"Good, you can start tomorrow, and I have another program that might help you."

"Great," I still couldn't believe how much help these people were giving me after they all but ignored me a few days ago.

"What is everyone doing after dinner?" he asked the table.

"I should get some work done, but what are you thinking?" Uni asked.

"I don't have any plans," Copperhead said while I kept quiet.

"Do you guys want to come over and watch the new Avengers movie?" he asked.

"Isn't it only in theaters?" Copperhead asked, sounding skeptical.

"Yeah, but I have my ways." He looked at her wiggling his eyebrows.

"Yeah, it sounds like fun. What about you two?" Copperhead asked, looking from me to Uni.

Uni was about to say yes from the smile on her face when I stomped on her foot.

"I would, but wow I'm tired. It's been a long day. I think I am going to turn in early, so I can catch up on some sleep. Last night kind of kicked my ass. Don't you have work to catch up on Uni?" I glared at her; Hound wanted Copperhead to himself.

"Yeah, I have gotten nothing done since yesterday." She looked down at her food, trying to hide a frown.

"Are you sure, I have plenty of room." Hound was being nice; but I didn't think he really wanted us to join them.

"No, I'd probably fall asleep in the first five minutes. You guys have fun."

"Yeah, have fun," Uni said, staring at her plate.

We finished eating, took our trays to the trash, and stacked them on top of the can. "So, I'll see you tomorrow morning?" I asked Hound.

"Yeah, do you know when you will be coming by?"

"I have to meet with Barkley at ten. Do you want to work before or after?"

"Let's meet at eight, then you will have the software to mess with for the rest of the day. I'm sure it is going to take a while for Barkley to do his thing."

"OK, I'll see you tomorrow then. Have fun with the movie." Uni and I waited outside the cafeteria, while Hound and Copperhead walked toward his apartment.

"What's the big deal KK? I really wanted to see that movie." She pouted, kicking an imaginary rock with her foot.

"You said she had a crush on Hound. I thought we would be nice and let him go on a date with her."

She looked up at me with a smile on her face. "You're right. They will have more fun without us and maybe Hound will let us borrow his copy."

"There you go. I'm going home and going to bed. Have a good night."

"You too, see you tomorrow sometime."

Vinny and I went back to our apartment and I pulled my book out to keep myself entertained until sleep claimed me.

I woke up the next morning with tears running down my face. I'd dreamed of Vince. He was taking me on a date. We had dinner on a beach, then went to the house on Crete, and he made passionate love to me. I had not had many dreams since I moved to the Kevó, but when I did it was always about Vince and I always woke up crying.

I wiped the tears away and looked at the clock. It was early, but if I got up, I could get my run in before I had to meet with Hound. I got ready quickly and ran out the door with Vinny at my side and my katana on my back. It took me a while to get used to running with it, I had to stop to adjust it until it fit snug and would not hit me in the back of the head every time I took a step.

When I got back I had just enough time to take a shower and grab a bagel before I went to Hound's office. I knocked on the closed door when I arrived. There was a loud 'thunk' and voices on the other side. I took a step back and leaned against the wall next to the door. I wasn't sure what was going on, but I didn't think anyone was being hurt, it was probably the complete opposite.

The door opened a minute later, and Copperhead came out with her hair looking frizzy and her shirt inside out. "Morning," I said, unable to stop smiling.

She saw me, and her face went from pale to fire engine red in a heartbeat. "Morning, I was just, ah . . ." She fumbled for words. "I'll see you later." She sped past me down the hall.

Hound appeared in the doorway a second later. "Hi KK, I didn't realize what time it was. Please come on in."

"Looks like you must have had fun watching the movie last night," I said, following him into his office, and sitting on the chair I sat in the day before.

"Yeah, I'm glad I finally found the guts to ask her out. Thanks for not going last night. If you want I can still hook you up with the movie." He moved around his desk and sat down in front of my computer.

"I would love to watch it, but I don't have a television." I watched as he turned my computer on and entered the password.

"Your apartment didn't come with one?" He looked up surprised.

"No, but I don't watch a lot of TV anyway so it's not a big deal."

"You can watch it on this though," he pointed to the computer. "Remind me when we are done, and I will give you the copy I have."

"OK, so what did you do to my computer?" I asked, ready to get to work and not think about what he and Copperhead were doing to before I arrived.

"I installed three different applications. The first one is the latest and great facial recognition software." He clicked on the icon on my desktop and a basic looking program opened. "All you have to do is upload a photo," he opened the photos folder and clicked on a picture of the President of the United States and dropped it in the program. "Then you click the button that says search, and it will comb over every video feed in the world looking for him. You can narrow your search by country, region or even state." He clicked on an icon that looked like a map and a window popped up with empty fields. "If you want to search in specific places you enter them, with your broadest area first." He entered United States of America in the first field, then dropped down to the next one and entered District of Columbia, then entered Washington DC.

"Can you narrow it even more? Like if you know they are in certain part of the city?" I asked, looking at all the empty search boxes.

"Yeah, but you have to be very specific. You put in the boundaries in a square." He started typing addresses into the fields. "If you miss one, the whole search will error, and you'll get nothing." When he was finished he hit the start button and the program started clocking. "It will take a while, depending on the area you are searching, this one should only a take a few hours and it will run in the background."

"Can I use it anywhere in the world, or do I have to be connected to your server?" I asked, watching as nothing popped up on the screen.

"That is the beauty of the program, as long as you have internet you can use this program. It's the first one of this kind. It can't be traced either. Part of the code makes the IP address bounce all over the world."

"Wow, did you write it?" I asked impressed.

"It was a joint effort by almost everyone here. It is our baby, I'm glad we can give it to you." He minimized the window and opened a different program. "This one will allow you to view live feed from almost any surveillance camera in the world." A window popped up and asked for an address. "The only thing you need is the location of the camera."

"I'm guessing you don't have a list of cameras around the world?" I asked, wondering how I would find the cameras. Would I have to walk around the area and write down the addresses?

"No, but all it takes is a few internet searches to find them. Nobody likes Big Brother spying on them, so people post their own lists. If you have an idea of where you want to search you can find the cameras."

"What about inside places? Like a train station or an airport?"

"Most public places will show up." He typed in Grand Central Station, New York and hit the enter button. A few seconds later the screen filled up with a grid of all the cameras in the train station.

"Wow that's so cool." I looked from one video to another. "Can you record them?"

"Yes, you just hit the record button. If you hit this button, you can say when to record, so if you want to get some sleep you can have it record for eight hours then review it later. Just remember to delete it when you are done unless you really need to save it. Otherwise you will fill up your hard drive within days."

"Thank you so much for putting this on my computer. Now I just need a place to start looking." I had no idea where Lolita was.

"How are you going to find her?" he asked, pulling his eyebrows together.

"Well I was going to start looking for clues in newspapers, and stuff." I didn't tell him that I wanted to follow missing person's reports or random dead bodies.

"If you need help I'm here. Let me show a few more things." He pushed the computer over to me, and he had me run a few searches on people who would be easily found. An hour later the original search found the president walking outside the White House.

I would have given up a lot to have a picture of Lolita I could plug into the program.

When we were done, I thanked Hound and went up to the second floor where Barkley would likely be waiting for me. His door was open, and he was talking to someone when I got there. I knocked on the side of the door. "Hi Barkley, sorry I'm late."

The man he was talking to turned and I was careful to keep my expression blank. The man could have been Vince's brother. He was tall with the same wide shoulders and deep brown eyes. His chin was a little more pointed and his hair was shorter, but I almost ran to him thinking he was Vince. He stood and gave me a warm smile.

"Karate Kid, this is Vangel. Vangel this is Karate Kid, or as we call her, KK. Vangel works in the field most of the time. I was just telling him about what you did for us when the commandos came through." He leaned back in his chair and laced his fingers behind his head.

"It's nice to meet you," I forced myself to say as I offered him my hand.

"Nice to meet you too. Thanks for saving the town. The world would be a sadder place without these knuckleheads." He shook my hand and let go. "Barkley, are we still on for lunch?" he asked, looking down at Vinny and offering him the back side of his hand to sniff. Vinny sniffed it then gave it a quick lick. Vangel gave him a scratch behind the ears.

"Yes, is one all right? We're going to be busy here for a while." Barkley looked at me.

"Sounds good. See you around, KK." He left the room, and I turned to watch him leave.

"All the girls love him." Barkley said, then gestured toward the chair sitting next to his.

I shook my head and took the chair. "It's not that, he reminds me of someone." I kept my voice even, but my chest was tight, and if I relaxed my hand, it would shake too hard for me to type.

"I see. Well, he's a really nice guy. If you want someone to spar with he would be the one." He clicked open his computer and opened a program.

"How long is he going to be here?" I asked, hoping it would not be long. I didn't know how many times I could see him and hold myself together.

"You never know with him. It could be a day or a month. It depends on what's happening and where we need him to be. So, yesterday, we prepped a few of your photos. Today we are going to turn them into the best fakes money can buy."

"Let's do it," I said, ready to roll up my sleeves, and get to work.

We spent the next two hours printing, cutting, laminating, and putting together my first alias. It was a long and for the most part boring process. I only paid attention because I wanted to make six more of them.

When we were finally done I looked up from my new passport. "I don't know how to thank you Barkley. This is a huge step in the right direction for me." I hugged him quickly then took a step back.

"You did us a solid when you saved us from those guys." He blushed and went back to his chair.

"When can I start another one?" I asked. I wasn't used to everyone thanking for sending a text message. I looked at my watch as my stomach growled.

"Tomorrow afternoon will be good for me." He pulled up his email program.

"OK, I'll come by after lunch tomorrow then."

"See you later."

Vinny and I went to the cafeteria and grabbed a sandwich to eat. All the tables were full when I came out of the buffet line and I stood there for a second before I saw Hound, Copperhead and Vangel sitting at a table. I wanted to sit with Uni, but I didn't see her. She must have been catching up on her work. I was about to find a quiet corner in the kitchen when Copperhead saw me and waved me over.

"Here we go," I said, to Vinny as we walked over to their table. "Hi." I sat my tray down and took a seat. "Sit, Vinny," I said, and he sat down next to me.

"How was fake ID class?" Copperhead asked, taking a bite of her salad. "Are you ready for me to show you how you can access your bank account?"

"Good, we have one done, and tomorrow I make my own. I am ready whenever you are." Getting access to money would solve one of my biggest problems. Once I had it, all I had to do was find Lolita, come up with a plan, and kill her. Then I would do the same to Alex. I took a bite of my sandwich.

"Why don't you stop by my office after lunch, and we will get your money," Copperhead said around a mouthful of food.

"Sure, I need to pay Uni and Ramstein back for all the stuff they bought me since I've been here." I could not wait to have my money back, I felt crippled without it and no way to make anymore.

"OK, it won't take very long, and you will be ready to go."

"Do you go everywhere with your sword?" Vangel asked, eyeing it behind my back.

"Yes." I didn't look up. Every time I looked into his eyes I saw Vince, and my heart could not handle it.

"Why?" he asked, eating a chip.

"Oh, Mordor is being a complete asshole to her. She doesn't trust that he won't try to steal it," Uni said, coming up behind me with a tray in her hands. "Thanks for waiting for me."

"Sorry I didn't know we were meeting." I moved closer to Hound, and Uni sat down next to me.

"Mordor isn't someone you want on your bad side," Vangel said, before taking a bite of his sandwich. "How did you get on his bad side?"

"Well you know how I told you how KK warned us about the commandos who came through? Well we had a big party to celebrate and he got all pissed that we all trust her now. He got in a fight with her and she kicked his ass." Uni was laughing obnoxiously when she finished telling the story.

I shook my head at Uni. "I wasn't trying to create an enemy, but I guess I can add him to my list especially since Tad gave him kitchen duty for a month." I took the last bite of my sandwich and chugged the rest of the water in my bottle.

"Are you ready to go?" Copperhead asked, seeing that I was about to leave.

I really needed to put some time in with my katana, but I needed access to money more. "Yeah, that would be great."

"We'll see you guys later." She stood with her tray.

"OK, see you guys." I got up, took my dishes to the return counter with Copperhead, then went to her office.

A few hours later I was walking back to my apartment with a smile on my face and cash in my pocket. The Kevó had a bank, so after I set up my new account, I transferred money to the bank and got enough to pay back Ramstein and Uni. It eased my mind knowing I didn't owe anyone money and I wouldn't have to worry about it anymore.

When I got back to my apartment I changed into my warmest leggings and top. I put on the snow boots I bought from the general store then put on my hat and gloves. I went to the park and started with my katas. When I was done with them I took my gloves off and put them in the pocket of my coat and pulled my katana out.

I moved through the forms Theron had taught me. I tried to keep my mind on the moves, but I kept thinking back to Vangel and how much he reminded me of Vince. I knew vampires could not have children, but he looked so much like Vince I could not help but wonder. If Vince had not been thousands of years old I would think he might have fathered Vangel before he was turned.

Halfway through my forms I noticed someone watching me. They were on the other side of the park and were not coming any closer, so I ignored them and continued. When I was finished I put my sword in my scabbard only struggling for a minute before I had it. It was going to take a while to get used to pulling it off my back and putting it back in its scabbard.

My hands were frozen, so I put my gloves back on and decided to practice pulling the sword out from my back and putting it back a few more times. The gloves were not making it any easier. The man who had been watching me started to come over. I cursed under my breath then I recognized him, it was Vangel. I ignored him and continued practicing.

"What are you doing?" he asked, stopping a few feet away from me.

"I'm practicing pulling my sword out of my scabbard from my back." *What did it look like I was doing?* I thought to myself.

"You are very good with the sword, why is pulling it out from your back so hard?" He cocked his head to the side as if he was trying to figure me out.

"Thanks, I just started carrying it on my back, and it is taking me a while to get used to it." I pulled it out again, each time was a little smoother.

"Where did you learn to use it?" He moved to stand at my side with his hands behind his back.

"A friend," I said, trying not to dwell on memories of Theron. "I lost him recently."

"I'm sorry." He brought his eyebrows together in concern. "Is that why you're here?"

"One of the reasons." I really wanted him to go away, I didn't want to talk to him.

"What happened?"

I put my katana back in its sheath and let out a breath. "Did you hear about what happened in Crete?"

"You mean the attack on the head of The Syndicate's compound? Yeah, I heard about it." He took a step closer to me.

"It was because of me. It was all my fault and I lost everyone I cared about." I blinked and for the first time, talking about it didn't bring tears to my eyes.

"Wow, were you there?"

"Yeah, I got out, barely." I was done talking about. I turned to walk back to my apartment.

"Alex is after you?" he asked, falling into step next to me.

"How do you know about Alex?" I asked, stopping in my tracks. Was this guy going to tell him where I was? I put my hand on my sword without thinking.

"I worked with him a long time ago." He stopped and looked at my hand on my sword.

"Are you going to tell him I'm here?" I tightened my grip.

"There is a reason why it was a long time ago. The guy is a nut job. I saw him do things that made it hard to sleep. I would love to see him taken down."

I wished he was a vampire, so I could tell if he was lying or not. I was safe for the moment, but if he was going to run to tell Alex where I was, I needed to take him out and move on. I let my hand fall back down to my side. Trust went both ways and I would have to trust that he would not tell Alex where I was, if only because he would not want Alex to find Kevȯ.

"He is on my shortlist," I said continuing to walk toward home.

"You have a list?" he asked, still walking next to me.

"Yeah, there are three people on it."

"Do I know any of them besides Alex?"

173

"I doubt it, none of them are here."

"That's good to know. These people are my family, I would rather not have to fight you to save one of them. Even if it was Mordor." He laughed at the thought.

"Mordor is an asshole, but he's not on my list. He hasn't tried to kill me yet," I said, as we reached the alley where my apartment was.

"Well, if you want someone to train with, I'm no slouch at martial arts."

"OK, thanks." I didn't know if I could handle sparring with him. It might trigger the black hole. "See you around."

"Hey, I know you told Uni you were going to play with the software Hound gave you for the night, but he gave me a copy of the new Avenger's movie. Do you want to come over later and watch it?"

I wasn't sure if he was asking me on a date or if he was just trying to be friendly, but I needed to be alone for a while. "Thanks, but I need to figure this software out. Maybe another time."

"OK, see you around."

"See you." I went back to my apartment, wondering what his story was, and why he looked so much like Vince.

Chapter 25

Vince

Vince blinked, not recognizing the room he was in. He was weak, and hungry. Something was wrong. His head was killing him. He brought his hand up and rubbed his face and found an IV in his arm. He looked up to see an empty bag of blood hanging from a pole with a tube running into his arm. What happened?

He remembered watching Katie sleep after she killed Ben, remembered her being a smartass about her test and the fight. The thought of her lips on his and how much he wanted her. They were moving to the mansion. Lolita had put a bounty on Katie's head. He was with Theron in his office when Katie's panicked voice found him. They were under attack. They ran for the tunnels after the first bomb went off. The house he shared with Katie was gone. She wasn't there though. *Get a car, run, I'll find you.*

Theron, Helen, and he were in the tunnel, they were running to the garage to try to reach Katie before she left. A huge explosion went off rocking the ground all around them. They stopped as the sounds on explosions continued. There was nothing they could do but hope the tunnel did not collapse and that Katie got away. They heard someone running down the tunnel and they stopped. It was dark, and if it was human they would not be able to see them waiting there. Vince hoped it was Katie, he did not want her to leave his sight. Three men came around the corner, and in the lead, was Alex.

Theron and Helen faced off with two of the men while Vince set his sights on Alex. "Alex, why are you doing this? Katie was your friend," Vince said, as they faced off against each other.

"She was never my friend, she used me, just like you're using her. You two were fucking the whole time and she never told me."

"I wish that were the case, I have never slept with her. She was telling you the truth," Vince said, as Alex lunged at him with a knife. Vince batted his hand away, and Alex's knife went flying.

"Please, why else would she turn me down?" Alex kicked at Vince, but missed as Vince spun out of the way.

"Because she only wanted you as a friend. I am sure she told you that multiple times." Vince rolled across the ground and came up with the knife in his hand.

"Women never know what they want. If it hadn't been for you, she would've left with me. I would have been able to keep her safe." Alex dodged Vince's first attempt at stabbing him.

"It still doesn't explain why you would want to collect the bounty." He kicked Alex in the knee, and Alex fell forward. Vince jumped forward trying to stab Alex with the knife, but Alex turned, and Vince was only able to cut his side.

"She was never going to be mine. Why would I let you have her? Plus, it's a lot of money." Alex touched his side, brought up his hand, and saw his fingers covered in blood. Anger got the better of him and he pulled a handgun from his ankle and aimed it at Vince's head when dirt began to fall between them. They both looked up as the tunnel collapsed between them. Vince took a step back to get out of the way when something hit him on the side of the head and everything went black.

He yelled at the top of his lungs. Where was Katie? How long had he been out? How did he get to this house? He looked around and saw Helen in a bed on the other side of the room. He went to her on shaky legs and knelt. He shook her shoulder, but she did not wake. She must still be healing. Where was Theron? They had been all together when the tunnel collapsed.

A knock at the door had him crouching ready to attack whoever was on the other side. He was weak, it was taking everything he had just to stay on his feet, but he would not go down without a fight.

"Who is it?" he asked; even his voice sounded weak.

"Theron. Can I come in?"

"Thank the Goddess. Yes, come in." Vince staggered back over to the bed and sat, hunched over.

Theron opened the door and stepped inside with a human behind him. "Let me take the IV out then you can eat, and we can talk." He took the needle out of Vince's arm and put a cotton ball over it.

The man behind Theron sat down next to Vince in a daze. Vince took the man's wrist and bit into it. The hot blood on his tongue was the best thing he had ever tasted. It was metallic, and clean almost as if he were a virgin. This man did not drink or smoke, and there was no hint of even over-the-counter medication. He did not want to stop, he tasted so good.

"Vince, that's enough. You don't want to kill him, do you?" Theron asked, shaking his shoulder. Vince let go, licking the wound to coagulate the blood and stop the bleeding.

"Thank you, I don't think I would have stopped without you." He let go of the man, feeling stronger and more himself already.

"Go downstairs and wait with the others," Theron told the man, who got up and left the room at Theron's command.

"Where's Katie?" Vince asked as soon as the door was shut.

"I don't know." Theron sat down on the bed next to Helen. He took her hand in his and squeezed it. "One of my cars was found at the ferry port with the keys locked inside it. I followed her using security cameras until she got into a taxi in Athens."

Vince let out a breath. "Did you find my cell phone?" He wanted to call her.

"No, but here is a new one." Theron pulled it out of his pocket and gave it to him.

He dialed his old phone number and hit the button that would take him to voicemail. He entered his password and the robotic voice said, "You have one new message."

"I hope you're OK. I'm alive. I'm running. I don't know where I'm going, but it will be far away from here. I'm ditching this phone. You'll be able to find me when you can. Take care Vince . . . I . . . I love you." The message ended, and Vince hit the save button, then ended the call.

"She is hiding somewhere safe. I know you will be able to find her." Theron said, trying to be gentle.

"How long have I been out?" Vince asked, trying to calculate how quickly he would be able to find Katie.

"I was out for a week; you have been out for six." Theron looked at Helen, hoping she would wake up soon as well.

"Six weeks? Wait you were out for a week, how do you know?"

"How do you think I am sitting here talking to you? We were rescued." Theron was avoiding the question, but he had to tell him.

"By who? Katie did not come back did she?" He sounded hopeful.

"No, Miguel saved us." Theron moved his chair back as the words left his mouth, fearing Vince might lash out at him.

"Miguel is here? Wait, where is here?"

"We are in a house near what is left of the compound. Miguel tried to warn us about the attack, but he called during Katie's final test and you know what happened after that. I didn't check my voicemail until I woke up to verify Miguel's story. He came over the night after the attack and started looking for survivors. We were the only ones he found." Theron started past Vince, remembering all that he had lost.

Vince forced himself to find his breath. As much as he hated Miguel, he made the right decision by not killing him when he found out he was so close to Crete. He would tolerate him, but he could not guarantee what would happen when Katie found out he was with them. "I'm sorry you lost so many of your people." Vince was tired. He put his feet up on the bed and lay down.

"They will be hard to replace but it's my own fault for letting Alex stay here in the first place. If I had not given him sanctuary, this would have never happened."

"There was no way to know that. Looking backwards will never show you the way forward. Do not let it bring you down."

"Miguel wants to see you. What do you want me to tell him?" Theron asked, letting go of Helen's hand and standing.

"I am not ready to talk to him yet. Tell me what has happened since I have been asleep."

"The Turk is back." Theron let the words hang between them.

"The Turk? He should not be a problem, he has to be in his seventies by now." Vince did not understand.

"He is in his seventies, but someone changed him in his early thirties. He is trying to take the island from me." Theron's voice was just above a growl.

"Does anyone know you are alive?"

"Serafeim, is the only one I have trusted to contact since he cannot be compelled. I need your help. I can't let The Turk take over."

"I will help you, but we have to find Katie first." Vince would not be able to think of anything else until he knew Katie was safe. She had been on her own for six weeks. Anything could have happened to her in that time.

"Vince, if we do not take him down now, I do not know if we will be able to later. He has already turned Takis into a slave."

Vince closed his eyes and found his breath. As much as he wanted to run out the door, take the first plane to Athens and find Katie, his only child needed his help. Theron had helped Vince by allowing Katie to take refuge on his island. Theron would still have his compound if he had not brought her there. He owed it to him. "OK, but let's get it done as quickly as possible.

How many vampires does he have?"

"None, that I have found. There are only four vampires on the island at this point."

"What do you have in mind?" Vince asked, formulating a plan.

"The Syndicate's next monthly meeting is in a week. I plan to attend and show them that I am alive. They will help us get rid of the Turk. From what Serafeim has told me they do not like him. He is making impossible demands and is undermining them wherever he can. Miguel has been playing body guard to Agapios since he is the most susceptible to be compelled."

"How do we keep Ilhami from attending the meeting and what are we going to do about Takis? He will tell Ilhami everything he wants to know about the meeting."

"We are going to meet without him. Serafeim will tell him the meeting is in a warehouse near the port while we are actually going to meet in the cave."

Vince thought about it. It might work, but only if The Turk wasn't having them watched. "How do we make sure they are not followed?"

"Everyone is going to arrive at the dock, where the meeting is set to happen. When they enter the building, they will be led to the basement which has a tunnel only I know about. They will take the tunnel to the marina where they will get on boats and will be taken to the cave."

"Who is going to be piloting the boats?" Vince was impressed. Theron had thought this through, but they needed to make sure no one was involved with Ilhami.

"I hired them from Athens. They think it is for some tycoon's weird party, they have no idea what's really going on."

"Very well, I need to eat more and not from a bag." Vince touched the IV bag, hanging from the pole near his bed.

"I will have someone brought to you tomorrow. It is too late to go out now and you need to rest."

"Yes, I am weak, but I am pissed as well." Vince lay back and stared at the ceiling thinking of Theron's problems and wondering what kind of mess Katie had gotten herself into.

"Thank you for agreeing to help me. I cannot do this on my own." Theron looked over to Helen.

"She will wake up soon Theron. We need time to heal, and she is still so young."

"Yes, I think it will take all of us to win my island back. Then we will find Katie and put an end to Alex and Lolita." Theron left the room, and Vince closed his eyes to let sleep take him.

"Where is my daughter, Gladiator?" Asteria asked, shaking Vince.

"I do not know, Goddess. I have been unconscious for six weeks. All I know is that she made it off the island. She could be anywhere in the world right now."

"She was in Athens the last time I felt her, but it is like she dropped off the face of the earth. You are her protector, you must find her." She let go of Vince and began to pace.

"When did you lose her?" He wanted to find her just as much or even more than Asteria.

"The night after the attack."

"Do you think Lolita has her?"

"No, I can feel Lolita, if Katie was with her I would have felt her."

"What about Alex? Could he have her?"

"The human who attacked Crete? I cannot feel humans unless they have ingested vampire blood. She could be with him, but I don't think she is. Do your job, Vince." The Goddess disappeared before his eyes, and he jerked awake to see one of the people he would like to kill, if only he was strong enough.

"What do you want Miguel?"

Chapter 26

Katie

After I showered and fed Vinny I sat at the table with my computer. I brought up the surveillance program. I put in the address for my dad's work. I knew I was asking for trouble, but it had been so long since I had talked to, let alone seen my parents, I wanted to make sure they were all right.

The screen popped up and everything was dark. With the time difference it was the middle of the night back home. I set it up to record the next morning, and I found a few other places to record while I slept. I just wanted to make sure my parents were safe.

I had just finished setting up the last camera when someone knocked on my door. I locked the screen on my computer and shut the lid. I went to the door and looked through the peephole. I groaned, it was Vangel and he had a box in his hand.

"I know you are standing at the door, just open up," he said, looking at me through the peephole.

I shook my head and opened the door. "What can I do for you?" I asked, catching a whiff of cheese and pepperoni.

"It was pizza night and I didn't see you, so I thought I would bring the pizza to you. We only have pizza night a few times a year, you don't want to miss it."

"Thanks, I forgot about dinner," I said, wondering if it would be rude to take the box, and shut the door in his face. "Please, come in," I said instead, and pushed the door open for him.

I sat down on the couch and moved my book off the coffee table. Vangel came in and kicked the door closed behind him. Vinny sniffed his legs then the box. "Sorry, Vinny, pizza is for humans only."

He set the pizza box on the table then took his coat off and hung it on the hook beside the door. "Do you want me to take my shoes off? They are kind of wet from the snow."

"No, its fine." I didn't want him to get too comfortable.

He went back to his coat and brought out two bottles of beer from his pockets then sat down on the far side of the couch. "I forgot to get napkins and plates do you have any?" he asked, opening the box.

"Yeah, I think I do." I got up and went to one of the built-in drawers in the wall between my bedroom and the living room. I pulled out a stack of paper plates that had been there when I moved in. "Here we go."

"Great, I hope I didn't ruin your plans for the night," he said when I came back over and offered him a plate.

"No, I was just finishing messing around with the programs Hound gave me." I sat down on the other side of the couch, my mouth watering at the sight of the pizza. I could not remember the last time I had it.

"You don't have a TV?" he asked, looking around the room.

"No, this apartment didn't come with one. I never watched a lot of TV anyway. I can turn some music on if you want."

"No, that's ok. What do you do to unwind?" he asked, putting a slice of pizza on my plate before serving himself.

"Unwind? I don't know, read?" I had not thought of unwinding in months. "I never seem to have much time to unwind."

"You stay pretty busy then?" He took a bite of his pizza and opened his beer using the edge of the coffee table as an opener.

"Yeah, I train a lot." I didn't understand what this guy was doing. "Then I sleep." I looked down at my pizza, picked up the slice, and took a bite.

"You're in great shape, why do you train so hard?" He took a long sip of his beer.

"I need to stay in shape, the people who are after me are better than me. If I stay in shape I might have a chance of winning when the time comes." I tried to open my beer the way he had but could not figure it out. Every time I hit the lid the bottle just slipped.

He extended his hand for the bottle. "Are you sure it will be a hand-to-hand fight?" He angled the beer on the coffee table, so the cap was wedged into the edge, hit the bottle cap, and the top popped off.

"Thanks, and no, but hand-to-hand is all I know." I brought the beer to my lips and took a swallow.

"What do you want to learn to do?" he asked, finishing his first piece, and grabbing another slice.

"I want to learn everything. I have never shot a gun before, and it would be nice if I knew how to use one. And maybe a sniper rifle." I finished my first piece of pizza and took another piece. "This pizza is so good."

"I could teach you, if you teach me how to use the katana. It is the sexiest weapon I have ever seen," he said around a mouthful of food.

"Do you have any martial arts training? My sensei didn't let me start training with the katana until I had karate down." I was really hoping he wasn't coming on to me. The last thing I needed was another man who wanted me when I didn't want him back.

"Yes, what they taught me in the military."

"Well, we will see. You will need your own sword though. I'm sorry, I can't share mine." It was my sword, if I let him use it I felt I would be insulting the blade. "I don't mean to be rude, but I have bonded to my katana and I feel like I would be insulting my sensei's memory if I let you train with it. Besides it's better if you learn with your own. No two are alike. If you train with mine, you might make a mistake when you have your own because you have not used it enough."

"I will get one then. We can start with guns tomorrow." He drained the rest of his beer. "I don't mind sharing those." He winked at me.

"You will? Thank you."

"No problem." He ran his hand through his hair, and I saw glint on his finger.

"Where's your wife?" I asked, recognizing his wedding ring.

"She was killed during a mission." He rested his head in his hands and leaned forward.

"Wow, I'm so sorry. I had no idea. I just saw your ring and . . ." I trailed off.

"It's OK. I show up at your door with pizza and beer. I figured you might think I was coming on to you. I'm not, I just couldn't stand to watch Hound and Copperhead flirt with each other anymore." He got to his feet.

"Yeah, all I had to do was back out of watching a movie with them." I laughed and felt better knowing he wasn't interested in sex. I was still mourning; I didn't know if I would ever find someone I could love after Vince. Even though Vangel looked just like Vince, there would be no replacing Vince.

"So, when do you want to start?" he asked, bending down, and giving Vinny a scratch behind the ears.

"Whenever you have time. I am meeting Barkley tomorrow afternoon. I usually go for a run around eight, then work with my sword."

"OK, I'll meet you and run with you, then after you're done with your martial arts training I will take you to the shooting range." He walked to the door.

"OK, but I am warning you. I do eight-miles a day." I followed him to the door.

"Good, I won't get soft while I'm here. See you on Main Street at eight?" he asked, putting on his coat and opening the door.

"See you then."

He left shutting the door behind him. I locked the door and leaned against it. I was starting to feel like I wasn't on my own anymore, and it felt good.

Chapter 27

Ilhami

Ilhami walked into the nightclub at the edge of the bay in Heraklion and smiled. It was a nice place. He would probably end up spending most of his time there once he was established. He walked around to get the lay of the land. It was located in an old warehouse that had been refurbished into a nightclub. The bottom floor had a bar running down each of the walls, with a DJ booth elevated at the back. The dance floor was huge and full as the DJ played a song laced with bass. The front of the club had a coat check and a few tables and sofas. A bouncer guarded the stairs to the second floor, Ilhami thought it must be the VIP section. After he had the layout of the main floor down, he moved to the base of the stairs and the bouncer moved to block his path.

"Name?" the bouncer asked, looking at the list on his clipboard.

"The Turk. I should be on there," Ilhami said, expecting there not to be a problem. Agapios knew who he was, and he would be placed on the list.

"Sorry, you're not on the list." The bouncer looked up and made eye contact with Ilhami.

"Yes, I am. Don't you see it, right there?" Ilhami asked, pointing to a random name, and capturing the bouncers mind.

"Go ahead, sir." The bouncer moved away from the stairs and Ilhami climbed them.

It was lavish, no wonder Agapios spent most of his time there. The floor had blood red, low pile carpet. There was a bar at the top of the stairs. Booths lined the walls and couches arranged for conversations took up most of the floor. Along the back wall there was a stage with a woman dancing indecently to the music from below. The other side was open to the dance floor on the first floor with a cat walk allowing customers to walk around and watch everything happening below.

He found Agapios where he expected him, sitting in a booth near the stage. He was watching the woman on the stage dancing. Ilhami went to the bar and ordered a glass of wine. When the bartender wasn't looking he poured a little bit of blood into the glass from a flask he always kept on him. He took the glass and approached Agapios but was forced to stop when a short man stepped into his path. "Agapios is not accepting visitors right now," the man said in Greek but with a Spanish accent.

"Tell him The Turk is here. He will see me." Ilhami took a step back and waited.

The man went over and whispered in Agapios's ear. He shook his head and the man returned to Ilhami. "He asked me to tell you, you can wait if you would like, but he is watching his wife dance. When she is done he might be ready to see you."

Ilhami tensed, he wasn't to be ignored, no matter who was dancing on the stage. "Look at me," he commanded the guard.

The man looked up into his eyes. "Your mind tricks will not work on me."

Ilhami took another step back and looked at the man. "I know you."

Miguel raised his eyebrows. "I know you too. When did Lolita release you from service?"

"On my fiftieth anniversary. What are you doing here?"

"I have never visited Crete before, Theron never liked me. Now that he's gone I decided I would spend some time here." Miguel folded his arms over his chest.

"Why are you playing bodyguard? Don't you have your own city to look after? How is the rebuilding going?"

"It is going well. Believe me, I left my most capable vampires in charge. As for why I am playing bodyguard," Miguel paused, trying to come up with a reasonable excuse. "This is a profitable island. I wanted to get to know the people who are running it, see if there was anything I could do to help the transition since Theron is gone."

"There is no need to worry, I am taking his place." Ilhami folded his arms in front of his chest.

"You have already gained the support of The Syndicate? I have heard that is not easily done." Miguel kept his hands at his side.

"I am working on it. You're right, they are not easily won over. Maybe you can help me." He let his arms fall to his waist.

"I will do what I can. Come sit down at my booth," Miguel said, using his hand to direct Ilhami to the seat.

When they were both seated he lowered his head and looked around. "They want me to pay them fifteen million euros to join."

"That is a sizable amount of money. Did my sister pay you enough to have it?" Miguel knew she paid her men half of what they were worth.

"No, I have nowhere near that kind of cash."

"Are you asking me for a loan? I am sorry but most of my money is tied up in rebuilding my city." Miguel was surprised he had the balls to bring it up. He barely knew the vampire.

"No, they gave me another option. If I avenge Theron's murderer I would be in. The problem is I have no idea who did it." He ran his hand through his hair and looked at the ceiling. He knew he should not give the game away, but he was running out of options. If he wasn't able to enslave all the members of The Syndicate, he was going to have to kill the man to earn their trust.

"Oh, you mean Alex? He's a mercenary, I had a chance at him before the attack, but I let him go to see what he was up to.

"Alex, Alex what? How am I going to find him with only a first name?" He slammed his fists down on the table, causing people in the nearby booths to stop to stare.

"I'm sorry, you know how mercs are, they usually have twenty different aliases and never go by the same name twice." Miguel wished he could help him. Alex was a liability they did not need right now. "I will make some inquires and if I find out anything I will let you know."

"Thank you, I know you, above most realize how important it is to stake a claim in this world." Ilhami looked past Miguel, Agapios was still watching his wife dance. "I will leave you to your duties, and try to catch up with him another night."

"Be well." Miguel said, standing when Ilhami stood to leave.

"You as well." He turned and left the bar swiftly. He could not shake the feeling that Miguel wasn't slumming it for the fun. His excuse that he'd never been allowed on the island made Ilhami wonder how many other vampires would be planning trips to Crete now that Theron was gone. He needed to take control before anyone else got the same idea.

His plans for the evening blown, he walked the tourist zone and watched as people from around the world enjoyed the pleasures of Crete. He wondered how often Agapios checked on his other clubs. An idea crossed Ilhami's mind. He went into the next bar he came to and started to compel people to answer his questions.

Chapter 28

Miguel

He did not know how Theodore did it. Miguel had been following Agapios around for a week. For overseeing the entertainment industry, he was the most boring guy Miguel had ever met. Each night Miguel would pick him up from his house take him to the same club and watch as Agapios sat watching women dance. He had lied to Ilhami, he wasn't watching his wife. His wife was at home with his children while Agapios would go and just watch. Miguel appreciated that he was true to his wife but doing the same thing night after night had him wanting to kill the man on principle.

He was ready to give up and let Ilhami turn him into a slave, maybe then he would do something fun. It was Sunday night, the club was dead, and Miguel had to try to get him to do something fun. Instead of taking the booth in front of Agapios's he sat down across from him. "Can I ask you something?" Miguel asked, trying to look as harmless as possible.

"Of course, Miguel. What is on your mind?" He did not look at Miguel while he talked, he kept his eyes on the dancer and her gyrating.

"What do you do for fun?" If the man thought this was fun, he needed to go to Amsterdam and see a real dancer.

"I like doing this and spending time with my family. When I was younger I would dance all night, drink too much, get into a fight, and carouse like most young people. I am too old for all that now." His eyes dropped to his lap for a second before returning to the girl on the stage.

"If you do not mind me asking, how old are you?" Miguel thought the man could not be in his fifties yet.

"I am thirty-nine."

"What are you talking about? You are not too old to do the things you did when you were in your twenties." Miguel could not understand why someone so young, who had so much power, could be so boring.

"I want to, believe me, but I made a promise to my wife when we were married. I promised that I would not get into any more trouble. It was fine for a while, we had fun together and had sex like rabbits, but then the children came, and all of her attention went to them." He looked down again and scratched the side of his nose with his finger. "I am the head of the entertainment industry; I have to be seen. I cannot stay home every night and play with the young ones. So, I come here and remember how much fun my wife and I had before they were born."

"What about your business? Don't you have to bust some skulls occasionally?" Miguel oversaw everything in San Sebastian, and it seemed there was always someone pushing him. He had to assert his authority at least once a week.

"I run a tight ship. Everyone falls in line. I have not had to beat anyone in, let me see," he started to count on his fingers. "Five years, I think."

"When was the last time you checked on your other clubs?" Miguel had a bad feeling about this.

"I stop in once every few months. Everything is running smoothly, they show me their books. They add up to what they are paying me, so I leave them alone."

"I think you should make an unannounced visit to a few of them." Miguel said, only imagining how many sets of books each club could have.

"Do you think they're screwing me?" His face was starting to turn red and Miguel didn't know if his anger was at him or at the owners of the clubs.

"I doubt it, but I have found that if you drop in on them unannounced you will get to the truth of the matter." Miguel drummed his fingers on the table.

"Very well, beginning tomorrow night we will start to drop in on my clubs and see what they are up to.

Chapter 29

Katie

I woke up thinking about my parents. I had not had a chance to look at the recordings of their offices yet. I jumped out of bed and went to my computer. I opened the one at my mom's company first and watched as the parking lot slowly began to fill with cars, but I never saw hers enter. Maybe she was just taking the day off, I thought, and clicked over to my dad's office. I watched as his forest green Subaru entered the parking lot and he got out of the car. He was moving slow, and I couldn't tell if he was limping or not. I watched him make his way across the lot and paused the feed when he was close to the camera.

I had to do a double take, it was my dad, but he looked ten years older. His hair looked thinner, there were more wrinkles around his eyes and he looked too skinny. Tears sprung into my eyes, this was all my fault. Losing me had taken years off his life. What other choice did I have though? If I contacted them someone would find them and hurt them to get to me. I had to leave them alone, at least until I killed Lolita and took care of the bounty on my head. I wiped the tears from my eyes and looked at the time. I needed to go if I was going to meet Vangel.

Five minutes later Vinny and I stepped onto Main Street looking for Vangel. I was dressed in my waterproof trail running shoes, warm leggings, a lightweight long sleeve shirt and a windbreaker. I had a stocking hat on my head and gloves on my hands. I adjusted my katana on my back, so I wouldn't hit my head on it as I ran.

It was cold, but the sun was out, and the wind was calm. It was going to be a nice day for a run. I looked up and down the street again, still not seeing Vangel. I wasn't going to wait for him all day. "Come on Vinny." I walked up the street toward the trail I normally ran. When I got to the end of the street I turned to see if Vangel was anywhere. With no sign of him I did a few stretches and took off down the trail.

I was about a half-mile into my run when he caught up to me. "Hey, sorry I forgot to set my alarm." He slowed down to my pace, breathing heavily.

"How did you know which way I went?" I looked at him out of the corner of my eye. He must have sprinted to catch up with me.

"Hound told me you normally went this way, so I guessed." He huffed out.

"Do you want to stop for a second to catch your breath?"

"If we could just slow down for a minute, I almost have it back."

We slowed down for about a quarter of a mile, when his breathing regained its normal rhythm I picked it up a notch.

"Why didn't you ask me how my wife died last night?" he asked, as we descended a hill marking the halfway point.

"What? Oh, well I didn't think it was any of my business." If he wanted to tell me he would tell me.

"It's normally the first question people ask."

"I didn't, say I didn't want to know, of course I do, but everyone has their secrets. If you want to tell me, I'll listen and keep it to myself, but I'm not going to beg you to find out what happen."

"We were on a job, taking out an ISIS cell in the outskirts of Paris. Everything was going as planned. I was set up in the building across the street from the apartment they were staying in. The plan was for me to take out the targets with my rifle while she took out anyone trying to exit. The problem was, they got to her. I told her I was in position and she could go in, except she didn't go in. She started firing on me. I escaped, barely, and called it in. Before I could even try and find her to talk some sense into her, the local government stepped in. They blew up the top three floors. After what happened at the football match in Paris, they were not going to risk any more lives."

"That must have been horrible. Are you sure she died?" I asked, trying not to lose my breath as we pushed up another hill.

"Her body was found, and I had to identify it." He sucked in a hard breath but didn't miss a step.

"Why are you telling me this?"

"My wife changed teams and I will never know why, but at the time I didn't care. I had just lost my best friend and the woman I loved. I know how it feels if you need to talk." We started up the next hill, and I dug in a little harder.

"Thanks, I'm doing better now. I still have some dark days, but I am working on moving past them. I'm sorry you had to go through it. I can't even imagine how horrible it would be."

"I live by, 'what does not kill us only makes us stronger and if we are lucky, smarter'. I don't see myself ever getting serious with a woman again. That's why I still wear the ring." He held up his hand between pumping his arms. Finally, at the top of the hill we increased our speed on the decline. "What about you. What do you do?"

I had no answer, I couldn't tell him I was the prophesized queen of the vampires, he would never believe me. "Survive, is all I have been doing for a while now. I graduated college in May, I was going to be a teacher, but now I have no idea where I am going end up."

"Sounds like life threw you a curveball."

"You have no idea." I hadn't thought about a future where all my enemies were dead, and I could be normal. I didn't know where to start.

"Well, I'm sure you'll figure it out." We reached the bottom of the hill and ran on. He was starting to tire, and all talk stopped for the rest of the run.

When we got back to the park we stretched then he followed me through my katas. He had some skill, and while I could tell he had never done the katas I was showing him, he knew the moves.

"How can you still be up and moving?" he asked, sitting on top of the nearby picnic table.

"This is nothing compared to my old training program." I pulled my katana out, found my breathing, and started moving through my forms. Once I began I blocked everything out and concentrated. I don't know when it happened, but at some point, my katana had become an extension of my hand. When I was done I bowed and turned around to see Mordor and Vangel glaring at each other. Vinny was on his feet with his head lowered, standing between me and Mordor.

"What is going on?" I asked, keeping my hands wrapped around the grip of the katana.

"Are you so afraid of me that you hired a bodyguard?" Mordor asked, using his head to indicate Vangel.

"I don't need protection from you. Didn't you learn your lesson yesterday?" I asked, making a show of putting my katana back in its scabbard, I didn't want him to think I was scared. "Why are you here?"

"I just wanted to watch you play with your sword."

"Well I'm done playing with it, please leave."

"The park is open to anyone." He sat down on the picnic bench.

"Vangel, are we still going to the range?" I asked, ignoring Mordor.

"Yeah, do you want to shower first? You might want some warmer clothes too. It's usually pretty windy up there."

"OK, I need to eat too. Do you want to meet in an hour?" I looked at my watch.

"Yeah in front of the cafeteria?"

"See you later, come on Vinny let's go eat." I walked to the cafeteria, wondering what I was going to do about Mordor. He was escalating the situation while I was trying to ignore it. I knew if it came down to a fight, I would hurt him badly, and I didn't want everyone to take his side when I wiped the floor with him.

I would not throw the first punch, I vowed as I took a tray and plate from the buffet line and filled it up with food. It was getting late and the seating area was almost empty.

After I ate I went home, showered, and changed into jeans, a long sleeve shirt with a flannel shirt over the top, my thick socks, and snow boots. I pulled a clean knit hat out and mittens that could be pulled back, so I could use my fingers. I was about to leave when I thought of Vinny. I never left him at home, but this was one place I didn't want him to go with me.

I squatted down and looked at him in the eye. "Listen buddy, I am going to need you stay here and guard the house OK? Make sure no one comes in. You're not going to like where I am going. It's going to be really loud and it will scare you." He whined in response, and I gave him a hug. "Be a good boy OK?"

He went into my room and I heard him jump up on the bed. I left feeling guilty that I wasn't bringing him with me. Vangel was walking down the alley as I locked the door. "Looks like you're ready," he said, when he was a few feet away.

"Yeah, let's do this." I put my hands in my pockets, and we made our way to the parking garage. "Where is the range at?"

"About ten minutes from here. We'll take my car." He pulled his keys out of his pocket and went to the driver's door of a Volkswagen Golf.

I laughed, going to the passenger side, and getting in.

"What's so funny?" he asked, putting his seatbelt on and starting the car.

"I figured you would drive a Land Rover, or a Hummer. Do I need to cover my eyes?" I asked, looking out the window as we crept through town.

"No, I got permission from Tad to show you where the range is." He turned left at the end of the street and shifted, picking up speed as we drove down the snow-packed road.

"That's a nice surprise."

"We are an extremely paranoid group of people. Mordor being the worst."

"No kidding, I don't know how I am going to get him to back off without sending him to the hospital." I looked out the window, admiring the jagged mountains that reminded me of home.

"Avoiding him would be the best thing to do." He turned off the main road onto a snowy two-lane track. "It's just up here." We traveled about a mile down the road until it ended at a small low building with no windows. "Here we are."

"This is the range?" I had never been to a gun range, my only reference was movies, and they always seemed to be in a basement or a cement building. I was surprised it was outside where the shots would echo forever.

"Yeah, we are far enough away from towns that no one will hear us." He got out of the car and went to the back to open the hatch.

I got out and followed him around and watched as he pulled out two long gun cases and a suitcase. "Can you grab that ammo box please?" he asked, walking toward the building.

I grabbed the big green box out of the back and almost fell over. It was a lot heavier than I thought it would be. I closed the hatch and followed him toward the building, shivering as the wind blew across my face. I went through the door, hoping the building would be heated, but there was no sign of a heat source. It would have been pointless anyway since the room was missing an entire wall. It was open to the hillside in front of us. The only protection from the wind was a long bench and table that ran along the missing wall. Vangel put the suitcase and the gun cases on the bench and was opening the suitcase when I closed the door.

I put the ammo box on the table next to the suitcase and stepped back to watch him pick up a gun, drop the clip and pull the slide back.

"What do you know about guns?" he asked, placing the gun on the table and putting the clip next to it.

"Not very much. I know they kill people and you need bullets unless you are in a movie." I was trying to make him laugh, but he ignored my remark, and pulled a spotting scope out of the suitcase.

We spent the next thirty minutes going over basic handgun etiquette. Being from the States, I probably should have known most of it already, but my parents were not into guns. I learned not to point it at anything I didn't want to kill, which was harder than it sounded, then I learned to how to load it, hold it, aim, and use the safety.

Once Vangel thought I could be trusted, he put a target out for me to shoot at. "Go head and take aim." He stood behind me, as I picked up the gun, and lined the bead up. "You never pull the trigger, you squeeze it. When you are ready, squeeze it on your exhale. Handguns do not typically have a hair trigger, so you will have to squeeze it all the way back for it fire." He took a step back. "Fire when ready."

I took aim and squeezed the trigger. The gun bucked in my hand and I closed my eyes afraid something was going to hit me. I opened my eyes and looked at the target expecting there to be nothing left of it based on the sound of the explosion.

"You hit low," Vangel said, trying to hide a smile. "Do it again, don't jerk, the gun isn't going to hurt you. Keep your eyes open."

I lined up again, knowing what to expect this time, and squeezed the trigger, forcing myself to stay still. I saw snow fly behind and to the right of the target.

"That was better, keep going. Shoot whenever you are ready until the clip is empty."

"OK." I did the best I could, trying to find a way to hit the target. I finally hit the target with the last bullet in the clip. The hole was as far away from the bullseye as it could be while still being on the paper.

Vangel took his ear protection off and gave me a smile. "You can take the ear protector off now. Go ahead and reload the clip and you can go again."

I pulled my ear muffs down, so it rested around my neck while I pulled the box of ammo out and started to load the clip. "Why is this so hard?"

"Because you are using different muscles and you have to learn to judge distance. You are improving, you hit the paper on your last shot. We will have you in the circle in the next round."

After I finished loading I got ready to shoot again. I closed my eyes and found my breath before I brought the gun up and stared at the center of the ring, I lined up and squeezed the trigger. It went off and I hit the outer circle. I continued to shoot making sure I kept my breathing even and supported my shooting hand to keep it from shaking. The last bullet hit the inner circle, and I jumped up and down with the gun pointed at the ceiling.

"Good job. Now we can move on to the rifle." He took the handgun from me, reloaded the clip quicker than I ever could and put it in the suitcase.

"Can I go get the target?" I asked, squinting at it.

"Yeah go ahead." He went to the other gun case and unzipped it as I ran out the door to the target. I picked up the box and walked back to the building. There were holes all over the target, but I could see my progress from barely hitting the paper to my last shot hitting the inside ring.

I looked up to see Vangel holding a rifle. "Are you ready for the big guns?"

"Let's do it." I put the box down and moved closer to him.

"This is a Remington .223 semiautomatic rifle, with a ten-power scope. It is also known as an AR-15, most NATO countries use it. It is also used by hunters for medium-sized game, like coyotes and wolves." He held the gun with both hands. The muzzle was pointed toward the hill side. One hand was on the underside of the barrel while the other was around the back, near the trigger. "It has a range of about four hundred yards. This is set up a little differently than the Smith & Wesson you were using before. This is the slide that ejects spent casings and reloads the chamber." He pulled a piece of metal back, opening a door in the side of the gun. "You can lock it in place by pulling it until it clicks." A bullet flew at me, and I caught it. "To release the clip, you hit this button." He pushed a button near the clip and it fell into his waiting hands.

He handed me the rifle and I mimicked the way he held it. "So, you load it the same way, there is a safety here." He pointed to the safety on the side. "Load it and turn the safety on."

I took the clip from him and pushed it into the slot until it clicked, then I pushed the metal piece attached to the door and it snapped shut. I engaged the safety catch and waited for the next step.

"Have a seat." He waved me toward the bench in front of the table. He grabbed the spotting scope on the tripod, brought it over and sat down next to me. "There are a lot of differences between a handgun and rifle, but there are a few things that will never change. The first one is that you never point the gun at anything you do not want to kill. It's a little easier to make sure you aren't pointing it at someone with the rifle because of the longer barrel. Another similarity is when you pull the trigger, bullets will fly. Don't put your finger on the trigger until you are ready to shoot. This rifle has a scope on it to help you get a closer look at your target. I want you to bring the gun up and hold the butt of it tight against your shoulder and look through the scope."

I pulled the gun up holding the back half of it with my right hand near the trigger and used my left hand to hold up the barrel. I looked through the scope and saw nothing but black. "I can't see anything."

"Lean your head forward a touch," he said, with laughter in his voice. I tilted my head forward, and I felt the scope touch my eyebrow. "If you shot the gun now you would end up with a black eye or worse. Move your head back so the rise of the stock rests against your cheek."

I moved back and blinked, the hillside was magnified so much that

I could make out the needles on the pine trees. "OK, I can see the hillside now."

"Now put the gun down for a minute."

I put the gun down and looked over to him. "What now?"

"Can you see the orange target about two hundred yards out?" he asked, pointing.

I looked and squinted my eyes. "I see it. How big is it? It looks like it is the size of a quarter."

"Good now find it in your scope." He looked down at the spotting scope and started moving it around. I picked up the rifle and started looking for the small target. I scanned the area where I thought it would be, but found nothing. I took my eye off the scope and found the target, then I brought the rifle up to my eye and looked for it. Finally, I found it in the scope, it was a human cut-out painted orange. "I found it."

"Put the gun down for a minute. Are your arms tired?"

"Yeah, I was holding the gun for a long time." I shook the cramps out of them.

"We are sitting at a table for a reason. Pick the gun up and rest your elbows on the table. You will be more stable that way and put your ear protection back on." I did as he suggested, and it was much more comfortable. "Good now find your target." I looked through the scope and found the target.

"I have it."

"Good, now take the safety off using your trigger finger." I felt around for the safety and turned it off. "Good now when you are ready, squeeze the trigger just like you did with the S&W, only this one will pull much easier."

I found my breath, put the crosshairs on the target, slowly exhaled, and squeezed the trigger. The gun went off, jumped, slammed into my shoulder and the scope hit me in the face.

"Hit," Vangel called, looking through the spotting scope.

"Great, can we go back now so I can get some ice?" I asked, holding my hand to my eye.

He looked up and cringed. "What happened? It was a great shot."

"I'm not sure but I think the gun just kicked my ass." I brought my hand down from my face and looked at the blood. "Do you have a first aid kit?" My eye was killing me, and my shoulder hurt. It wasn't the first time I had bleed from my face, and I was sure it would not be my last.

"Yeah come on, it's in the car." He took me by my good shoulder and walked me to the passenger seat. He started the car to get the heat going then knelt between my legs with a sterile cotton pad. He dabbed at my face cleaning the blood off. "The good news is I don't think you need stitches."

"What's the bad news?" I asked, hissing as he cleaned the wound with an alcohol swab.

"You are going to have one hell of a black eye." He took a tube of something out of the bag. "I'm going to superglue the cut together, hold still." I sat, trying not to move as he glued my face back together, wondering why I had wanted to learn to use a gun in the first place. "OK, wait here and I'll go get all the stuff, I think we are done for the day."

I didn't want to quit, but my head was killing me and the vision in my right eye was blurry. I needed to get warm and find some aspirin for my splitting head. "OK." I put my feet in the car and closed the door. I leaned my seat back, moved the vents allowing the warm air to hit me, then closed my eyes and wait for him to come back.

I heard the hatch open, and turned to watch as he put the suitcase, gun case, and ammo box in, then shut the hatch. He came around to the driver's door and got in. "I'm sorry, I could have helped you put everything way. I am just being whiney."

"It's all right, I know how bad it hurts to take a scope in the eye. Just be glad it wasn't a bigger caliber gun," he said, as he pulled back onto the road and took me back to town.

By the time we got back, my head hurt even worse than it had when the scope hit me. Every bump in the road made it pound even harder.

"Thanks for showing me how to use a gun," I said, getting out of the car.

"We are not done yet. We are going to go out again tomorrow," Vangel said, leaning forward in the seat.

"We are?" I asked. I could barely think around the pounding in my head.

"Yep, you still have a lot to learn. Go get some rest and I will check on you later." I shut the door and he drove down the street to the underground parking garage.

I walked back to my apartment wanting to do nothing more than lay down and sleep off my headache. I unlocked the door and Vinny came spilling out whining. He smelled the blood on the leg of my jeans where it had dripped from my face and whined some more. I bent down and wrapped my arms around him. "I'm all right, don't worry. Come on, I'll take you to the park." I shut and locked the door, and we walked to the park. There were a few people on the street, and as we walked by, I said hi to them while they looked at me slack-jawed.

I frowned, had I done something to make them all mad at me again? We got to the park and Vinny ran around sniffing things. The ground was covered with snow and he dug around in it for a while before doing his business. When he was done we went back home and I took off my clothes with the intention of taking a shower, until I looked in the mirror.

No wonder everyone was staring, my eye was completely black, I was surprised I could open it with the swelling. Changing my mind about the shower I pulled on a pair of yoga pants and a zip-up hoodie. I went to my mini-fridge and pulled out an ice pack. I lay on the couch and put the ice pack on my face. I was just starting to relax when someone knocked on my door.

"Who's there?" I called, not wanting to get up.

"Uni, Vangel said you got hurt. Can I come in?"

"Yeah, it's unlocked." I closed my eyes, wishing the pain in my head would go away.

"Oh my gosh. What happened?" she asked, sitting on the coffee table next to my head while Vinny begged her for attention.

"I got scoped while shooting a rifle." I moved the ice pack, so she could see.

"Oh man, you look rough. You still have blood all over your face. Why don't you go take a shower?"

"My head hurts too much to move. After I am done icing my eye I'll take a shower."

"Is there anything I can do to help you?"

"No, I just need this headache to go away."

"Well shoot me a text if you want me to bring you some soup or something."

"I will, thanks for stopping by."

"Anytime. Later." Uni left, and I drifted to sleep before I even thought about a shower.

I woke up later to someone pounding on my door and Vinny barking. I rolled off the couch grabbing the now warm ice pack before it fell to the floor. I looked through the peephole and saw Tad. "Vinny sit," I commanded, and he sat down, and stopped barking.

I opened the door. "Tad, what a surprise. Would you like to come in?"

"Yes, I am sorry to intrude." He walked into my small apartment and looked around as if he never seen it before.

"Sorry, I was just taking a nap that lasted most of the day, it looks like." I looked at my watch. It was six in the evening. "Please have a seat."

"No thank you, this will only take a minute. I heard you were injured today I wanted to make sure you were all right." He looked at my eye and frowned.

"I'll be fine, my headache's gone and it's not my first black eye."

"Did Vangel do this to you?" He brought his eyebrows together, and I wondered where his sudden concern for my safety was coming from.

"No, the scope on the rifle did it to me. He warned me it would happen. I was too close to the scope the first time I pulled the trigger. Why the sudden concern?" I sat down on the couch, still half asleep.

"The last thing I want to do is make you mad. You could tell your mother where I am." He paced back and forth across the living room. "Why are you still in this apartment? I told Mordor to move you to one of the newer units last week."

"Tad, please calm down. I'm not going to tell her where you are. Unless you give me to my enemies I would have no reason to tell her your secret."

"Really?"

"Yes, you have done nothing but help me. If Vangel had done this to me on purpose I would have taken it up with him. I would never take it out on you."

He stopped pacing, and sat down on the chair across from me. "Have you been able to find out who our spy is yet?" he asked, changing the subject quickly, and folding his hands together before resting them in his lap.

"No, I haven't seen anything out of the ordinary from anyone, but no one would even talk to me before the soldiers came through, so I may not be your best place for information."

"I know, but sometimes fresh eyes are the best eyes. I will leave you to recover. If you find anything else, please let me know." Tad rose from his chair. "I will arrange a new place for you to stay as well."

"No, this is fine. It has everything I need. Please, I don't want to be a bother."

"Very well, if you are sure."

Chapter 30

Vince

"What do you want?" Vince sat up, forcing Miguel to back away from him.

"Seeing if you were all right. Vince, can I please talk to you without you trying to kill me?"

"What do you have to say?" Vince asked, pushing against the bed, and resting his back against the headboard.

"I messed everything up with Katie. I did some things I don't deserve to be forgiven for. All I want to do is tell her I'm sorry, I regret everything that happened in San Sebastian. I want to make it up to her and to you." He sat back down on the chair, leaned over, and buried his head in his hands.

"Just because you are sorry does not mean you will be forgiven. You fucking raped her Miguel. How could you?" Vince had dreamed of confronting Miguel about what he did to Katie for months. It was too bad Vince was too weak to fight, he really wanted to kick the shit out him.

"She was driving me crazy. She wanted to leave, and I couldn't let her. Lolita said I needed to show her who was boss. It was wrong, I was so wrong. I know she will never take me back. All I want is for her to forgive me."

"Good luck." There was no way Katie would ever forgive him for what he did to her.

"Please, you have to help me gain her forgiveness." He stared at his hands as he spoke, gripping them so hard they turned white.

"Why would I? I appreciate you saving me, but what else have you done other than terrify her and hurt her? You are going to have to do more than this to gain her forgiveness." Vince needed to be out there looking for her, not sitting in this bed listening to a brokenhearted shell of a vampire beg him for something he could not give.

"I'm trying to sleep over here. Would you two please shut up," Helen said, from the bed on the other side of the room.

They both turned their heads to look over at her. "You're awake," Miguel said, getting up and going to her.

"Yes, how long have I been out?"

"Over seven weeks. I need to go and tell Theron, he is going to be so pleased." Miguel got up and ran out of the room.

"What happened and who was that?" Helen asked, looking over at Vince.

"We were buried in the tunnels and that was our savior, Miguel," Vince said dryly.

"That bastard saved us?" She rolled her eyes and looked at the IV tube running to her arm.

"Yes, I do not know how I feel about it yet."

"Is Katie safe?"

"I do not know. Theron knows she got off the island and made it to Athens without being caught but he has been unable to track her any further. I need a computer, then I can see where she has been spending money."

"If she was captured and taken to Lolita what do you think will happen?"

"I think we will be doomed. Lolita is going to try and take over Europe. Knowing her, she will not do it quietly. Before you know it, the humans are going to start vampire hunting again and we will be forced to live in caves and who knows what else."

"Well, she's a smart girl, I bet she's fine. How long were you out?" she asked, rolling on her side to see him easier.

"Six weeks, but we have more important things to talk about. There is trouble on Crete. Do you remember The Turk?" Vince asked, resting his head against the wall and staring at the ceiling.

She drew her eyebrows together in thought. "Maybe. Wasn't he trouble around the time Theron made me?"

"Yes, you were in the middle of fighting your blood lust and he asked me to help him secure the island. We killed all The Turk's family and sent him away, forbidding him to come back. When he heard Theron was dead he came back as a vampire. Lolita changed him when he was in his thirties."

"Is he trying to take over?"

"Yes, and Theron needs our help to stop him."

"Helen, you're awake." Theron ran into the room with the first real smile he had since before the attack.

"Yes, and I am hungry for more than bagged blood."

"I will have a donor come by this morning. How are you otherwise?" he asked, sitting down on the bed next to her.

"I'm pissed off, Theron. Our home is gone because of a human we all trusted. I want to find him and slowly bleed the life out of him. I haven't skinned anyone in a long time, I would love to practice on him."

"You will get your chance, but first we need to win our island back before The Turk takes it over. Then we will find Katie and Alex." Theron pushed the hair back from Helen's face. "You need to rest. I will wake you up when the donor gets here."

"What time is it?" Vince asked, trying to see out the blackened window.

"It's four in the morning the sun will be up soon."

"I need access to a computer and the internet, now." Vince pushed to his feet. His head swam for a second before he steadied himself. He looked down, all he had on was boxers. "And some clothes."

"Check the closet, I think Miguel bought some clothes for you and Helen weeks ago. You should be able to get by with them for now. I will go get you a computer."

Vince staggered to the closet. He was going to need to eat a few more times before he would be of use to anyone. At least he would be able to see if Katie was all right or not. It had been six weeks, she probably thought he was dead, and she was out there all alone with Alex and Lolita after her. He found a pair of shorts and a T-shirt in the closet with Yoda on it. He flashed back to the T-shirt Katie had given him when they first arrived on the island. He was going to wear it when he was done with her training, but he had never had the chance.

"Miguel," he bellowed, putting the shorts on but grasping the T-shirt in his hands.

"What?" Miguel asked from the doorway.

"Where did you get this shirt?"

"I bought it at the store. I can get you a different one tomorrow if you don't like it."

Vince let out a breath, the one Katie gave him was probably incinerated when the house blew up. This one still had the tag on it. He had taken the tag off the one Katie gave him. He took a breath. "It's fine, thank you." He shoved his arms through the holes and pulled it on. She might not have given it to him, but it made him feel close to her. He went back over to the bed and sat down. His whole body hurt, his muscles had atrophied from being unconscious for so long and it felt like part of him was missing without Katie nearby.

Theron came back into the room with a laptop and handed it to him. "I just got it yesterday, but it's all set up. You need to rest."

"I will rest when I know Katie is safe." Vince spat. He needed to know where she was more than he needed rest, he could rest when she was safe and in bed next to him. He opened the screen and started working. She would have to use the credit card he had given her. She had no other money.

He pulled up his credit card's website, logged in and scrolled down the list of transactions. She bought a plane ticket to the

Bahamas, stayed at least two nights at a hotel in Athens and went shopping. The day after the attack was the last time she used her credit card. Where was she? He brought up the tracking program for the flash drive he had given her at the airport in San Sebastian. He did not think she had it in her go bag but there was always a chance. The program loaded, and he clicked on the device, it could not be found. Probably buried in the rubble somewhere on the property. He logged into the fitness program that synchronized with her activity monitor, the GPS would show him where she had been running. There was no data, even from when she was Crete. Someone had wiped it clean. She was trying to fly under the radar, and he had no idea how he was going to find her.

"Well?" Theron asked, when Vince frowned at the computer.

"She made it to Athens, but beyond that there is no trace of her. She bought a plane ticket, I will have to see if she used it. But either way she has not used her card for anything since the day after the attack." Vince closed the computer screen.

"Well, that could mean a couple of things." Theron sat in the chair beside the bed and glanced over at Helen. "She most likely went off-grid. Maybe Alex figured out her alias and she had to stop using it. "Or he found her and took her to Lolita."

Vince wanted to throw the computer against the wall in frustration. "The Goddess does not think she is with Lolita. She cannot sense Katie, wherever she is."

"The Goddess talks to you?" Theron pulled his eyebrows together in disbelief.

"I'm her daughter's protector. When she cannot find Katie, she comes to me and she is super pissed right now. Just like me. I need to get to Athens." Vince's new phone vibrated from the nightstand.

Vince closed his laptop screen and picked up his phone. It was an alert from his bank. Someone had just withdrew money from his account. Excitement replaced his melancholy, had Katie accessed his account? He opened his laptop up again and logged into his bank account.

"What is it?" Theron asked, looking eager.

"Someone pulled a hundred thousand euros out of my bank account." He clicked on the transfer but did not recognize the account number. He picked up his phone and called his bank.

"Was it Katie? Where is she?" Theron moved to sit next to him on the bed, to look over his shoulder.

"I don't know but I am going to find out."

Forty-five minutes later he hit the end button and thought about throwing the phone across the room. Katie had moved the money, but that wasn't why he was irritated. He was mad because no one could tell him where the money went, or even what bank it went to. It was like she plucked it out of the internet and disappeared with it.

"You need to heal Vince; you can barely stay on your feet for more than five minutes as it is. We will help you, but you have to let yourself heal, or you won't be any use to her," Theron said, knowing he had his work cut out for him, Vince could be a pain in the ass when he wanted to be.

"Theron, you don't understand. I must find her. I must tell her I'm alive. She is going to think I'm dead, that we are all dead."

"We will find her, it's just going to take some time. Calm down, sleep. We will talk more about it tonight."

"How can I sleep when I have no idea if she is safe or not?"

"Vince, you trained her. She is not the timid little girl she was when you brought her here. You need to have faith in the training she received. She is fine." Theron wanted to tie him to the bed and make him relax, but there was nothing he could do to calm him except talk to him.

"I just wish I knew where she was."

"We will find her. I have resources we will use, but not until you are recovered, and The Turk has been taken care of. I need to go check on Miguel. Rest." Theron left the room, closing the door behind him.

Vince lay back on the bed; what strength he had was gone. Theron was right, he needed to recover. Even if he found Katie, he would be more of a liability than a benefit as he was. He closed his eyes and tried to relax. Katie could take care of herself.

Chapter 31

Miguel

Miguel picked Agapios up from his house as he always did, but before pulling away Miguel turned in his seat. "Where do you want to go first?" Miguel asked.

"Let's go to the bar at the end of the tourist zone. The man who owns it is known to be shadier than the others."

"Very well, let's go have some fun," Miguel pulled out of Agapios's driveway and drove to the first bar on the list.

Miguel parked the car in front and got out. He made a show of opening Agapios door then followed him inside. It was early, and the place was half-empty. They walked to the bar then each took a stool. The bartender came over smiling until he saw who was in the bar. "Agapios, what can we do for you? We weren't expecting you tonight."

"Surprise visit, please tell Spyridon I'm here, and would like to meet with him to go over his books." Agapios spun around on his stool and looked over the bar. "They have redecorated since I was here last. It looks good."

The bar was designed as a sports bar, with dark woods and heavily plastered walls. There were photographs of Greek sports teams hanging on the walls around the twenty televisions taking the rest of the wall space.

"I like it," Miguel said, watching the football match on one of the TVs.

"Yes, it would be fun to watch world cup games here."

"Agapios, how good to see you," a short frumpy man with a mostly bald head said, coming out from the back room. "What can I do for you?"

"I want to see your books." Agapios stood.

"Why? They are the same as they were last week when your man came in to look at them" Agapios was starting to turn red in the face, and Miguel put a calming hand on his shoulder.

Agapios head shot up. "What man?"

"The Turk, he said he was working for you." The man's eyes glazed over for a second. "Please Agapios, I had no idea that he didn't work for you. He made me pull out my real ledger and made me pay him for the money I owed, plus interest. I don't know how I am going to stay in business after I paid him."

Miguel pulled out his phone and sent a text message to Theron.

We need to take care of The Turk, he is pretending to work for Agapios and stealing from him.

"He does not work for me." Agapios's face turned a brighter shade of red. "I will let you go for now. If you ever lie to me about how much money you are making I will kill your family and make you watch before I castrate you."

"Thank you Agapios. What should I do if he comes back?"

"Call me immediately. Start a telephone tree, call everyone, and tell them to call me if he comes in asking to see the books. Tell them he is trying to take over my territory. Damn Turks."

"I think it is too late. I have spoken to a bunch of owners. Some have already closed their doors, while others have no idea how they are going to recover from the money they paid him. Are you saying that you have not seen the money?" The color drained from the man's face.

"No, I have not and as of right now I have no plan to collect it from you. I will get it back from The Turk. Call me if you see him again."

"I will, thank you Agapios."

They left the bar and did not speak until they were safely in the car. "What do you want to do?" Miguel asked, turning in the front seat, so he could see Agapios.

"I don't know, I have not been challenged in so long. What would you do?" he asked, pulling a handkerchief from his pocket, and mopping the sweat from his face.

"I would kidnap his family, and torture them until he came to me, then I would make him watch as I killed them. After that I would spend at least a week torturing him before I let him die. I would let some of my less than trustworthy men watch so they would spread the word about what happened if they went against me."

"Let's do that." Agapios said, almost jumping with excitement. "I have not tortured anyone in years."

"Unfortunately, it will not work with him. He has no family; we will need to find another way." Miguel drove to another bar. "Let's get a drink, and we will think of something."

Chapter 32
Ilhami

A week later Ilhami was in the black. Not only had he paid for the guns he wanted from Serafeim thanks to Takis, he was now taking a cut of the gross sales from half the bars on the island. All Ilhami had to do was say that he was checking up on things for Agapios when he went into a bar or whorehouse. The owner would show Ilhami the books he would have shown Agapios. Ilhami would review them, then compelled them to show them their real books and he collected on the back taxes and interest. A few of the bars had close down, but really, they were cheating The Syndicate and they deserved it.

Word had gotten around, and owners had been busy fixing their books making sure everything matched but they still kept the real books and he could compel anyone to give them up. He walked inside the first bar on his list for the night, Thekla, and looked around. It was a Monday night and the crowd was thin.

"What can I get you?" the bartender asked, without looking up from the glass he was polishing.

"I would like to speak with the owner on behalf of Agapios." The man looked up at his words and all the blood left his face.

"Of course, we have been expecting you. Please follow me and I will get him for you." He came out from behind the bar and led the way to the backroom. "Let me get the light," the bartender called, moving to the back of the room. "It is back here."

Ilhami wanted to laugh, they thought they were setting him up. He could hear the heartbeats of the five men in the dark room from half way across the bar. The first one tried to grab him from behind and hold him down. Ilhami broke the hold and jerked his head back to meet the nose of the man. Who then flew backwards and hit the wall. The others came at him together. Punching, and kicking at him in the dark. Ilhami easily ducked and countered the attacks.

The lights came on suddenly and he pulled the Colt from his waistband firing four rounds quickly, hitting each man once in the center of their foreheads. The bartender held his hands up in surrender. "They made me do it. They said The Syndicate was asking for too much."

The man was telling the truth, but it did not stop Ilhami from making an example of the bar. He tied the bartender to a chair then exited the room. The patrons did not notice as he emptied liquor bottles on to the wood bar and lit a match. He went out the front door, slammed it closed then barred it before casually walking across the street to watch the concrete building turn into an oven filled with human pot-roast. When the sirens from the fire department were blocks away he got into his car and drove off. Word would spread about how The Syndicate was handling anyone who did not want to pay.

He went home after his adventure in the bar. It would be pointless to go anywhere else. Everyone would be on guard after what he had done. He almost regretted it, but when he thought about the thugs waiting in the back room for him, and his guilt slid away.

Chapter 33

Katie

After Tad left, I took a shower then I sat down at my computer and thought about who might have outed the town. Mordor was the first person who came to mind, but only because he hated me and tried to pin it on me in the first place. I wanted it to be him, but he loved this town more than any of the other residents save Tad. No, someone else must have done it.

I made a list of everyone I knew, which wasn't very long, but they all seemed capable. It could not be Vangel, he wasn't there when it happened, but it could have been one of the others. I had no idea how to sneak around and find out stuff about these people. Plus, by nature of what we did, everyone kept their secrets even closer to their chest than people normally would. I had no idea how Tad wanted me to find all this out. There was a knock at my door and Vinny sat down in front of it. It must be one of the good guys since he was sitting and not barking.

I opened the door to find Uni standing outside, hopping from one leg to the next. "Uni what's wrong? Come in out of the cold." She came inside, and I shut the door behind her.

"I just saw Tad leave. What did he want?"

"Oh, he wanted to find me a new place to stay." I didn't know why, but I didn't want to tell Uni that he wanted me to find the mole.

"Oh, cool, are you going to move? This place is pretty basic." Uni moved to the couch and sat down.

"No, I'm fine here. There is no point in moving. I have everything I need. Plus, Vinny likes it here." I sat down next to her, and rubbed Vinny behind the ears.

"How long do you think you are going to stay?" Uni asked, kicking her shoes off, and crossing her legs under her.

"I don't know. Probably until I can find Lolita and come up with a plan to kill her."

"What about Alex?"

"He is on the list, but first I need to take care of Lolita. After she's dead I'll find a way to get Alex off my back." I leaned back on the couch and stared at the ceiling. I had made some progress. The trail of disappearing people had lead me to Paris, where they had been disappearing weekly for months, but it suddenly stopped a few weeks ago. Maybe she moved, but I had no idea where she moved to.

"Why her and not Alex?"

"Because she's the reason Alex came after me in the first place. She put a bounty on my head and Alex wants to collect. If I don't kill her, there will always be someone gunning for me." It was nice to talk to someone about my problems for a change.

"Can I help?" She turned to face me. "I'm almost done with my project, so I have the time."

I looked at her for a minute and studied her. I didn't want to get any more humans involved with what I was doing, but if she helped find Lolita she would not be in any danger. If Lolita never found out I had help, she would be safe. "OK, I would love some help."

"Where do we start?" Uni sprang to her feet and put her hands on her hips.

"Let me show you what I have so far." I got up and led her to the table where my computer was sitting. I sat down in front of it. "Pull up a chair." I pointed to the only other straight back chair in my apartment.

She pulled the chair over and sat down next to me. "Lolita

is a killer." It was the best explanation I could come up with. I wasn't going to tell Uni she was a Vampire. "And she is building an army to try and take over Europe. So, I have been tracking missing persons. When she takes someone, they are normally never seen again."

"She really is a bad person," Uni said in a small voice as I pulled up a map of Europe with red and blue dots covering it.

"Yes, she is. The red dots are where people have been reported missing. The blue dots are where people have been found dead with no leads." I pointed to an example of each of them

"So, it looks like there have been a lot of disappearances around Paris. Do you think she's there?" Uni asked, staring at the screen

"I think she was there, but there has been no activity around there for weeks. Based on how many people went missing she probably was forced to move." I let out a breath and switched screens. "Since the last missing person in Paris, it's like she dropped off the face of the earth. Here is a map of the missing persons for the last two months." There was no pattern, and no concentration of missing people. I was at a dead end.

"Do you think she gave up?"

"I doubt it, I think she must be getting close to unleashing her army, and believe me when I say if she unleashes them, it will be a blood bath."

"Yeah, I see what you're saying. It doesn't look good." Uni pulled the screen over to her.

"Where did you get the information about the missing persons?" she asked, zooming in on the big cities for a closer look.

"Newspapers, social media and the like." I got up, went to the fridge, and pulled out a bottle of water. "Do you want some water?"

"No, I'm good. Let me see what I can come up with. Can you email me your research? Maybe a fresh set of eyes is what you need."

"Yeah, here." I went back over to the computer and emailed her all the documents I had on the missing and murdered people.

"I'm too tired to look at it tonight but I can tomorrow. What are you going to do when you find her?" she asked, getting up, and putting her shoes on.

"I am going to cut her fucking head off or die trying. She can't be allowed to live. She is the most sadistic person I have ever known." My voice was calm and even. I didn't know what Uni would think of it, but it was the truth.

"Really? Is she worse than Hitler?" She went to the door looking surprised.

"If she is allowed to live and if her war takes place, she will be worse than Hitler. She won't kill people in gas chambers she will turn them into mindless slaves."

"OK, I'll see what I can do tomorrow. We will find her KK."

"Thanks Uni, see you tomorrow," I said as Uni left, closing the door behind her.

For the rest of the week I split my time between Barkley, Hound, Vangel, Copperhead and Uni. I practiced shooting guns with Vangel, made a dozen new alias with Barkley, moved money from Vince's account to a new account for each of my new aliases and had Hound teach me how to find security cameras.

"I think I found something," Uni said, almost breaking my door down one day. Her laptop was in one hand with her power cord dangling behind her.

"Come in, you're crazy." I opened the door, and she ran to the table and plugged her computer in. "I need a new battery. I have one on order but it's not here yet. She opened her computer and started to click on images.

"What did you find?" I asked, standing behind her.

"I found a pattern. If you look at all the missing people after August, they fall off, right?" She pulled up the map I had sent her the week before.

"Yeah, go on."

"So, I started to look for other stuff. You said she was

building an army, so she would have to house them somewhere. I looked for recent real estate transactions for places big enough to house and train soldiers. There weren't that many in the last few years. I narrowed it down to three." She clicked over to her internet browser and showed me the first one. "This is a huge ranch in Germany. It is five hundred acres of farmland. It has four barns, and twenty cabins. The prior owners were running a resort where people could hunt, fish, horseback ride, you know? What do you think?" she asked, clicking through the pictures. There was a big house surrounded by smaller ones. There was a long wide barn that was probably an indoor arena with stables. The other barns looked like they were used to store hay and feed for the animals.

"Go back to the picture of the main house," I said. There were a lot of windows facing south and west. They weren't the heavily tinted ones Theron and Miguel had on their homes. She would have to spend a lot of money fixing them. "Let's look at the next spot."

"OK this one is a chalet in the Swiss Alps. It is in the middle of nowhere. The land was sold with one hundred acres. There is a main house and some outbuildings." Uni clicked over to it.

"That's not it. It's too far from a big city. She is going to want to be close to or in town." I shook my head.

"Then this one might be it." She clicked to the next property. There was a bunch of rundown buildings surrounded by trees and ivy.

"Where is this?" I asked, looking closer at the photos as she clicked through them.

"An island in Venice, it's called Poveglia. It is known as the most haunted place in the world. There's a lot of history there, but the most important thing is that it was sold a few years back and major renovations have been going on there since."

"Tell me the history," I said, sitting down at my computer, and running a search on the name of the island. I went straight to the images as she talked.

"First the Venetians built forts on it to help protect the lagoon that leads to Venice proper. In the seventeen-hundreds they turned it into Venice's version of Ellis Island. Anyone entering Venice had to stop there to make sure they were not bringing disease with them into the city. Then it became a hospital for plague victims. In the nineteen-hundreds it was turned into an insane asylum. Thousands of people are buried there."

Most of the images I looked at made the place look creepy. It would be perfect for Lolita. It would give her the privacy she needed to keep her army and it was just a boat ride away from an iconic city. "I bet that is where she is," I whispered, more to myself than to Uni.

"Really? She has that kind of money?" She looked up from her computer.

"Yes, I'm sure she does. I need to record all the cameras nearby, see if I can get her on tape. Then I can track her movements."

Uni and I spent the next few hours setting up timers to record traffic cameras around the city. She didn't understand why I only wanted to record them at night, but she went with it. "What do we do now?" Uni asked, standing, and stretching.

I looked at the clock, I hadn't gone on my run yet and it was almost noon. I was supposed to meet Vangel for target practice in an hour. "I need to go for my run or my day is going to be crap. Would you mind telling Vangel that I am running to the shooting range and I'll meet him there?" I asked, looking down at Vinny. "Would you mind if Vinny hung out with you while I am gone?"

"No problem. I will keep working on finding a photo of Lolita in the meantime."

"Thanks Uni." I went into my room and got ready for my run. When I came out Vinny and Uni were gone.

It was a longer run than I normally did, but running on the road was easier than the trail I normally ran on. It was a warm day with no wind. I could still see my breath, but I didn't mind. I was close to finding Lolita, so close I could feel it. I had spent the past two and half months getting ready to find her, and thanks to Uni I almost had her. How was I going to kill her though? I was good with the long rifle. I could shoot her through the head from a distance, but a bullet to the head was not the same as decapitating her, I didn't know if it would kill her. I wanted to make sure when I took her down that there was no doubt she would die. I was going to have to get close to her and take her head. It was a huge risk, no matter how much I trained, she had centuries on me. She would always be faster and have more experience. I was going to have to be smart and lucky when it was time. I would take the skills that Vince, Theron, Helen, and everyone in Kevó had taught me and kill her.

I was lost in my thought when I heard a vehicle behind me. I turned thinking it was Vangel, but it wasn't him and whoever it was, was coming straight for me. I jumped out of the road and into a snow drift. The SUV slammed on its brakes and started to reverse. I thought they were coming to check on me since they ran me off the road. I swam through the snow, away from the road until it was shallow enough for me to stand up. The SUV backed past me then stopped. I looked at the windshield and tried to figure out if I knew the person driving but the glare from the sun was too much and all I saw was a reflection of me. The SUV shot forward, aiming right for me, I turned and started to run for the trees. They were about a hundred yards away and the SUV wouldn't be able to follow me in there. I zigzagged through the brush as fast as I could, listening to the roar of the engine getting closer and closer. The trees were less than fifty feet away, but I was slowing down, the snow was getting too deep for me to run. The SUV continued to gain on me, and I thought I was done for until I reached the shade of the trees and the snow lessened. I ran into the trees about twenty feet, then stopped and pulled my katana out from its sheath on my back.

I edged around the tree. I wanted to know who was trying to kill me, but I could not see anyone. I heard tires spinning and gears grinding. Whoever it was had high centered in the snow. I slowly made my way to the tree line, staying in the shadows, and looked around a tree trunk, trying to get a look at the driver. It was Mordor. The bastard was trying to kill me. I heard another car coming down the road and backed deeper into the trees. Mordor didn't have a lot of friends, but he could have called for help. When I saw Vangel's Golf come into view I let out a sigh of relief, but wondered if he would see the SUV since we were so far off the road. The car sped by us then stopped and backed up. The engine cut off and I heard his door open and close. The SUV engine shut off and I watched Mordor get out of the car with his back to me.

"Are you, all right?" I heard Vangel call. I wanted to run out and tell him to bring a gun, but I had no idea if Mordor was armed or not. Plus, I was supposed to be finding out who the mole was. This might give me a chance to overhear an important conversation. Vangel walked over the crusted snow quicker than I had run through it. He stopped at the SUV. "Mordor? What are you doing?"

"Oh, I was just out here messing around. I think I'm stuck."

"It looks that way. What were you doing? Your tire tracks are all over the place."

"New tires. I wanted to see how good they were off-road." I heard him say. "Do you want to give me a push?"

"A push isn't going to do it, man. You're high centered. Do you have a shovel?" Vangel took a step back to get a better look.

"No, I forgot it." Mordor's voice cracked as he spoke.

"You came out here to see how your new tires were and you didn't bring a shovel?" Vangel was starting to sound skeptical.

"No, I didn't really think about it too much. It looked like fun. What are you doing out here? Shouldn't you be pumping iron, getting ready for your next big mission?" I watched Mordor shift from foot to foot.

"I was on my way to the shooting range. Who were you chasing?" Vangel's voice dropped and dripped with distain.

"OK, there was a deer in the field. I thought it would be fun to chase it around a little bit." Mordor let out a nervous laugh

I wasn't going to find out anything to lead me to the mole. It was time to make my presence known to Vangel. "Why don't you tell him what you were really doing Mordor?" I asked, stepping out from behind the tree with my katana raised.

"KK? What are you doing out here? Uni said you were going to meet me at the range." Vangel reached behind his back and pulled out a gun.

"Mordor ran me off the road then chased me through the field. I don't know if he was trying to kill me or scare me, but I'm done putting up with his crap." I took a step toward him, holding my katana at my waist, with both of my hands on the grip.

"I wasn't going to kill you," Mordor said, taking a step back toward his SUV.

"Then what were you going to do?" Vangel asked, raising his gun.

"Do you know who she really is? Do you know how big of a price is on her head?" Mordor asked, pulling a gun out of his waistband.

"What are you talking about?" Vangel asked.

"How did you find out who I was?" I asked, fear was beginning to override my anger.

"Facial recognition, baby, I knew there was something about you. Tad said to leave you alone, but I knew there had to be more. Did you know she got all her friends killed when someone tried to collect the bounty? What do you think will happen if we don't collect it ourselves? It is only a matter of time before someone finds out she's is here. Do you think we'll survive?"

"KK is he telling the truth? Is there a bounty on your head?" Vangel was pointing the gun at Mordor, but he lowered it a fraction and looked at me.

"We all have our secrets." I looked between the two of them.

"How much is she worth?" Vangel asked.

"Enough to fund our company for the next three generations, if we bring her in alive. If she's dead, it's a little less." The greed in Mordor's eyes was all I needed to see. I was about to take a step toward him when Vangel spoke stopping me mid-step.

"Why don't we take her back to town. Tad will want to know what we're planning."

I looked at Vangel shocked. How could he do this to me? I thought he was my friend, all everyone in Kevȯ talked about was doing things for the greater good. Was he just as greedy as Alex?

"Why don't you and I just take her, then we could retire to a beach somewhere and never worry about the horrible things that go on in this world ever again?" Mordor asked, taking a step toward me.

"That won't work, and you know it. We need to follow the rules, and taking her to Tad is part of the deal. Plus, you know what they will do if we leave with her." Vangel aimed the gun at me. "Drop the katana KK. Don't make me shoot you." His voice was gruff, but his eyes shifted between me and Mordor.

I thought through my options. Vangel was an excellent shot, if I turned and ran for the woods I wouldn't make it. I didn't think he would kill me, but my chances of getting away with a bullet wound were not as good as trying to get away later without any wounds. I wasn't going to put my katana on the ground though. I lifted it and put it back in its sheath. "You bastard. I thought I could trust you." I put my hands up in surrender.

"Let's walk back to the Golf. We will get your car unstuck later." Vangel pointed with his gun. "KK, you go first. Keep your hands at your sides."

I did as he asked, walking slowly toward his Golf. I looked from side to side trying to figure a way out of the situation, but my mind was so full of panic I couldn't think straight. I didn't know what Tad would do, but I knew Mordor would never stop and if he had truly recruited Vangel there was nothing to stop them from kidnapping me.

"Vangel what are we going to do if Tad tells us we can't turn her in?" Mordor asked, walking behind him.

"Then we will have to make a tough decision. Do we leave and never come back, or do we let her be?"

"Let's just go now. I would rather not have anyone else involved with this. We turn her in and split the payoff."

"We could do that, but then we would be looking over our shoulders for the rest of our lives. You know Tad won't let it go."

"True, maybe it's time for the whole place to go up in flames."

"It was you, wasn't it?" I asked, still a few hundred feet from the car. I found my breath and started to think.

"Was what me?" Mordor asked.

"You were the one who leaked our location to those mercenaries."

"No, I would have been captured as well. I wish I knew who did it though," he said, sounding angry.

"Why did you try and blame me then? Don't you want to know who tried to ruin you?"

"Because I never wanted you here. You have done nothing but distract people from their jobs and I knew whatever trouble you were in would follow you here."

"It only followed me here because you started looking for it." I had to do something, if I got into the car my life would be over. I didn't want to kill anyone, but this was quickly becoming a situation where I needed to decide if my life was more important than theirs.

"Well, we all make our choices. You chose to go running in the middle of the day and I decided it was time to retire."

"You're such a pussy. You couldn't even do it by yourself. You had to rope someone else in to help you." I needed to make him come after me. If I could disable him I might have a chance of fighting off Vangel.

"Don't call me a pussy. I am just as brave as anyone here."

"That's a load of shit. Not only did you have to get someone to help you bring me down, but you ran me off the road using your SUV. Are you afraid of a little girl? You're a big strong man and can't take care of me without a car or help. The only reason you have me is because of that asshole." I motioned with my head toward Vangel.

"Hey, don't bring me into this," he called.

"Why not? You are selling me out, just like Alex did. I hope you are proud of yourself. I will probably never trust anyone ever again."

A fist came flying toward the side of my face. I ducked, and I kicked my leg behind me at the same time. My leg connected with Mordor's shin. I didn't break it, but he lost his footing in the snow and fell onto his back. I spun around and kicked him hard in the ribs. There was a loud cracking sound and he curled into a ball. I pulled my leg back to kick him again when I heard a gun cock. I looked up from Mordor and found the barrel of a gun an inch from my nose.

"KK, stop I think you broke half of his ribs. Unless you want to kill him, you need to stop," Vangel said, as I held my hands up. "You shouldn't believe everything you hear." He clicked the safety on the gun, and offered it to me, butt first, and I took it.

"Why did you go along with him then?" I asked, pointing the gun at the ground, but ready to pull it up if I needed to.

"I wanted to know how much he knew, and how far he was willing to go. You know what happened with my wife, we cannot afford to have someone who would trade one of us for money, no matter how much it is." Vangel kicked Mordor in the gut for good measure.

"What are we going to do with him now?" I asked, looking at the still conscious, but barely moving man on the ground.

"We take him to Tad. He will know what to do." He bent down, grabbed Mordor by the ankles, and dragged him toward the golf.

"What about his car?" I asked, looking over my shoulder at the stuck SUV.

"I'll come back later with a truck and pull it out." He stopped at the rear hatch of the car and stood to stretch out his back.

"Do you want some help?" I asked.

"Please." I unloaded the gun and stuck it in the waistband of my pants as I walked over to him.

"You are getting pretty good with that," he said, with a knowing smile.

"I had a good teacher," I said, thankful I had gotten over how much he looked like Vince in the past few weeks. They looked like twins, but he was very different from the vampire I loved.

We loaded Mordor into the car and took off back to town. Vangel parked in front of headquarters and we pulled Mordor out of the back. He tried to run when we set him on his feet, but we each took him by the arm, and forced him down the steps to Tads office. When we reached the reinforced door at the bottom of the stairs I knocked. A few seconds later the lock disengaged, and we went inside.

"KK, it is good to see you," Tad said, walking back to his desk. "It looks like you brought company." He turned, sat down in his chair, and waved his hand around inviting us to sit.

Vangel pushed Mordor down into a chair and we stood behind him. "Thank you for seeing us," Vangel said, keeping a hand on Mordor's shoulder.

"Don't listen to them Tad, they tried to kill me." Tears started to trickle down his cheeks.

"KK please explain what is going on." Tad leaned back in his chair, folded his fingers together, and rested them on his stomach.

"Mordor found out about the bounty on my head, he tried to run me down with his car. He was going to take the money, leave Kevó and never tell you." I tried to make it as matter-of-fact as I could.

"Vangel is there anything you would like to add?"

"He was going to split it fifty-fifty with me, but I am loyal to Kevó and everyone protected by the town." Vangel let go of Mordor's shoulder, and stood at parade-rest with his hands behind his back.

"Mordor, what do you have to say for yourself?" Tad asked as I felt the magic pour out of him. He was compelling him to tell the truth. I had never seen it done before and my jaw dropped open.

"Tad, it's a lot of money. We would be set up for the rest of our lives, she is just a stupid girl. I wanted the money, I wanted her out of my town. It's the best of both worlds," he said while the tears continued to fall.

"Mordor, you signed a contract to protect everyone and everything in this valley." Tad stood from his chair.

"I know, I'm sorry. Will you give me another chance?" he asked, still making eye contact with Tad.

"There are no second chances, especially since you tried to kill someone who needs our protection. You have forfeited your life." Tad looked away from him and looked at us. "Vangel, thank you for assisting Katie with this matter. I need to speak with the two of them alone now."

"She didn't need me; she would have had him on her own if I hadn't come along. See you later," Vangel said, before turning, and leaving the room.

Once the door was closed Tad began to speak. "The contract that everyone signs states that, if you endanger the life of anyone here you forfeit your life." Tad got up and moved around the desk.

"Are you going to kill him?" I asked, not knowing if Mordor deserved to die or not.

"Oh no, there is a reason, the contract says, forfeit your life, and not death. How do you think I survive up here? I can't very well live off the blood of my town's people. It would be a mess."

"You are going to use him as a donor?" I hated the thought of anyone becoming a blood donor to a vampire.

"Yes, and I am going to make him my slave. I will be able to keep a better handle on him this way." Tad walked around Mordor. "Why are you upset? What punishment do think would fit his crime?"

"I have no idea; it is not for me to judge." Did Mordor deserve to die because of what he wanted to do with me? I had killed Ben for the same reason, but Ben was a vampire.

"But you are judging. Did you not tell me that you killed the last person who tried to collect your bounty?"

"Yes, but he was trying to kill me." It was the only excuse I could come up with.

"Wasn't Mordor trying to kill you as well?" He stopped and looked into Mordor's eyes.

"Yes, I guess I have a double standard." I felt horrible, but the more Tad spoke the more my prejudice surfaced in my mind. How had I missed it? I was always trying to keep humans from getting involved with my situation because I was scared for them. I thought vampires were superior creatures, that I needed to protect humans from them. They needed blood to survive, but that didn't mean I wanted to watch them drink it or allow them to make slaves. I loved Vince, even though he was a vampire, but I still resented them.

"What would you have me do with him?" He caressed Mordor's cheek and cocked his head to one side.

"If I am to be queen I need to treat everyone the same. I leave it to you. Do what you will to keep him from betraying my location." I hated saying it, but I had to do it. If it had been Tad who was trying to turn me over to Lolita I would have killed him without a thought. I needed to figure out why a vampire's life was less important to me than a human one.

"Very well, I am going to use him as a donor and enslave him. He will not bother you again." Tad took Mordor's hand and led him out of the room.

I exited headquarters a little while later numbly walking back to my apartment questioning every belief I had. How was I supposed to be the leader of the vampires when I thought human life was more important than theirs? Every life was important, at least that is what I thought I believed.

Now that Tad had pointed it out to me, I realized how one-sided I had become.

I blamed Lolita and Miguel, and the way they treated me in San Sabastian. They had scared me more than I realized. Now I would fix it, judge people by their actions and not by their species. If I judged Mordor by his actions, then he got what was coming to him.

Chapter 34

Theron

Theron was sitting at his computer looking for Alex when his phone rang. He looked at the caller ID. "Yes, Serafeim?"

"Theron, things are getting out of hand when are you going to make your existence known?" he asked, and Theron listened to the sound of sirens and people talking on the other end of the line.

"What has happened?" Theron surged to his feet ready to take off to help save people.

"Someone burned down Thekla."

"Are you sure it was on purpose? Maybe someone left a lit cigarette in the bathroom."

"It was a hit. Whoever it was, shot the owner's sons in the head then broke all the liquor bottles, lit a match, and barred the door, trapping everyone inside. It was like an oven in there. Twenty people are dead, most of them were civilians."

"Did you call Agapios?" Theron started to pace, he was going to have to make a move soon, but wasn't sure Vince and Helen were up to full strength yet.

"Yes, he is on his way here. It wasn't him or his men."

"I have a good idea who it was. Give me a week and this will all be over." Theron hit the end button on his phone, wishing for his punching bag more than he had in years. He paced around the room, looking at his watch. Miguel would not be back for some time if he and Agapios were going to visit the bar. It was time to come up with a plan.

"Did you see what was left of Thekla?" Theron asked Miguel as he walked in the door.

"Yes, it was gruesome. Do you normally involve civilians in your wars?" Miguel asked, wanting to shed the suit he had on. He could still smell the residue of burnt flesh all around.

"No, it is against all of our laws. The Syndicate is not going to take this kindly, the only problem is proving that Ilhami did it. There are no cameras on that side of town." Theron was ready to march over to The Turk's house and set it on fire.

"Is it time for you to make an appearance?" Miguel asked. Agapios was distraught when he dropped him off at his house. They were criminals, but they had a code, civilians were not to be harmed and The Turk completely disregarded it.

Theron was about to answer when he heard movement from the stairs and watched as Vince slowly descend them. "How are you doing?" Theron asked, when Vince reached the bottom.

"I am slowly getting better, but a five-year-old human could kick my ass right now."

"I was the same when I woke. You will be back to yourself before you know it." Theron clasped him on the shoulder.

"Has there been any change with The Turk?" Vince asked. He wanted to get Theron his island back, so he could search for Katie.

"He turned Thekla into an oven earlier tonight." Theron put his head in his hands. "The owner tried to lure him in and kill him. Ilhami ended up killing the owner and his son's instead, then he set the inside on fire and barred the doors. Twenty civilians baked in the flames."

"We will get him; do you know where he is staying?" Vince asked.

"Yes, he rented a house in the tourist zone. I know we could

242

burn him alive during the day, but I need to make an example of him. To keep away any others who might want to take over." Theron looked up with dull eyes.

"We will get him, and you will not only rebuild your compound, but your family." Vince felt the pain of loss right along with Theron. He only had one child while Theron had so many, but it not matter, losing Theron would be like losing everything he was.

"I will. I'm determined, but I will not start until we have dealt with our enemies. I don't want them to be cannon fodder." He rubbed his hand across the top of his head.

"Good plan. Theron. He is one vampire, with few or no friends. We will get him, just give me some time to recover, Helen too."

"I just want this over already. We need to find Katie. She is more important than anything, but it will be easier to take The Turk down now then it will be later." Theron leaned back on the couch and stared at the ceiling.

"I agree with you. As far as we know, Katie is fine, she is probably drinking a cocktail on a beach somewhere." Vince took the seat next to him.

"Do you really believe that?" Theron asked, stroking his goatee.

"No, but I must believe she is safe. Otherwise I will go insane." Vince laced his hands behind his head and blew out a breath.

"Then think what you must. Thank you for staying and helping me. We will find Katie as soon as we get rid of The Turk." Theron punched him on the shoulder.

"Thank you for your optimism, but let's talk about the meeting with your leaders."

Chapter 35

Katie

The next morning, I got up and went straight to my computer. I had hours of video to review but I had to download it first. I started the download then took Vinny for a run. After breakfast I went back to my apartment and started combing through the video feeds of Venice. It was daunting work. I recorded video from every camera that would cover a way into the city from the island where we thought Lolita was living. There were over thirty different routes for someone to access the island and I had to watch ten hours on each of them. After the first four hours I was ready to start crying. As soon as a boat would come into view, I would pause the video, and zoom in trying to make out the faces of the passengers. I fast-forwarded through the times when there was no traffic, but Venice was a busy city.

Someone knocked on my door and Vinny sat down in front of it. "Come on in, its unlocked," I called, blinking again before looking back at the screen.

"Did you find her yet?" Uni asked, coming in, taking off her coat and shoes. She went to the couch and pulled her computer out.

"No, and it's taking forever," I said, leaning back, and rubbing my eyes.

"I'll help. What does she look like?" Uni asked, opening her computer, and plugging it in to the wall outlet next to the couch.

"She is about five-foot-two with platinum blond hair, she's super pale, almost albino," I said, remembering the last time I saw her in person. It had been right after she took a chunk out of my neck.

"So, she looks like a vampire?" Uni asked, with a laugh.

I gaped at her, and almost asked how she knew about vampires, but realized she was joking. "Yeah, she looks just like a vampire." I turned back to my computer.

"Which camera are you looking at?"

I told her, and we got to work. I watched video after video hoping to find her, but coming up with nothing. "Maybe we have the wrong location," I said, getting up from my chair to walk around.

"Maybe she didn't go out last night," Uni said, not looking up from her screen.

"I have a feeling she always go out; she loves to club. I'm going to go get a sandwich. Do you want me to bring one back for you?" I asked, sliding my feet into my boots.

"No, Hound is going to bring us food. Get back to your station. You might miss something." She pointed her finger back at the computer. "We still have fifteen more feeds to watch."

"Yes, sir," I stood at attention and saluted her before going back to my computer and staring at the screen.

Hound brought us food an hour later and Uni made me eat while I watched. "Who knew you were such a slave driver?" I asked around a mouth full of food.

"I know, but we can't afford to miss anything. Wait, come here, is this her?"

I jumped out of my seat and ran to the couch. I looked at the frozen image of a woman. She fit my description of Lolita perfectly, but it wasn't her. "Too old. Lolita looks like she is eighteen, maybe even younger."

I went back to my computer and stared at the screen. There was a beautiful teak boat coming into view. There were five people in it. Four of them were spread out looking out at the water while the fifth sat in the seat looking straight ahead. I slowed the video down until the boat was as close as it could be to the camera and paused it. "Bingo."

"You found her?" Uni asked, putting her computer on the coffee table, and coming over to stand behind me.

"I am about ninety percent sure it is her. Do you think this will be good enough for the facial recognition software?"

"There is only one way to find out." Uni watched while I saved the frozen image and uploaded it into the facial recognition software. I set up alerts for Venice and sat back in my chair.

"What do we do now?" I asked. Part of me wanted to run to Italy and get it over with.

"We wait and see where she pops up." Uni went to the mini fridge and pulled out two beers. "What are you going to do now?"

"I am going track her, figure out her routine; figure out a way to get her alone, the figure out a way to kill her." I took the open beer from Uni and took a sip.

"There isn't any way you could talk her out of killing you?" Uni asked, cocking her head to the side.

"No, she either wants me dead or as her slave and I refuse to be either."

"Are you sure you're just not after revenge?"

"No, it's more than simple revenge. She is planning on taking over Europe, and believe me you don't want her in charge." I took another sip of my beer. "A lot of it is revenge though. When I ran from her the first time I had to leave my real identity behind, my parents thought I was dead for a month. I was finally able to tell them I was in a witness protection program. If I go home she will follow me there, and I can't risk my parents. Then she killed everyone I loved when she took out the hit on me. She has done everything in her power to make my life hell and I want to make her life hell for a change."

"Mortal enemies, such a pain in the ass." Uni shook her head before drinking more of her beer.

"Yeah, I just want my life to go back to normal."

"Do you think it ever will?"

"No, but I can pretend." I smiled at her. It was hours before the sun would go down in Venice, and I was anxious to see where Lolita went so I could start formulating a plan.

I spent the next week tracking Lolita's every movement. She went to the same club every night at the same time. I tried to find out who owned the club, but it was owned by a corporation that kept everything quiet. Her four bodyguards never left her side. I hacked the security system in the club, but she was always in the VIP section and there weren't any cameras in that part of the club. It made me think that it was vampire owned. She could have her dinner without anyone finding out what she was.

A plan was starting to form in my mind, but for it to work I would need to be in the best shape of my life. I stepped up my training, and started to practice with knives. As much as I wanted to take her head off with my katana, I didn't think they would let me through the front door of the bar with it on my back. My life revolved around watching Lolita, and training to kill her. One of us was not going to walk away from the fight, and I was going to do everything in my power to make sure it wasn't me.

Chapter 36

Vince

Vince opened his eyes to look at the ceiling of the room he was still sharing with Helen. He was getting stronger. He wasn't one hundred percent yet, but he was close. He had enough strength to take down Ilhami, that much, he knew. They would be meeting everyone in the cave in a little while and he was excited to see what kind of plan they could come up with to make an example of The Turk. He got out of bed and went into the small bathroom to shower and get ready for the night.

He had not slummed it in such an ill-equipped house in years. He was looking forward to staying someplace with a real shower and not a half bathtub with a shower wand. After he was clean, he went back to his bedroom and removed the garment bag from the closet. Theron's tailor had made Vince a suit and it was beautiful, there were no other words for it. Charcoal grey, single breasted and slim fitted, which wasn't very slim for him. He dressed in silk boxer briefs and an Egyptian linen, ivory, button down shirt with French cuffs. He rarely dressed so well, especially for a meeting in a cave, but they would be meeting The Syndicate and dressing well would demonstrate Theron's strength. He sat down on the bed and put on his socks and leather shoes. He pulled the blood red tie out of the bag and tied it around his neck before putting on the jacket and buttoning it. He left the bedroom and went down stairs to see if Miguel, Theron, and Helen were ready yet.

"Do you always have to make an entrance?" Miguel asked from the couch, as Vince entered the room.

"No, but tonight I am feeling pretty good, so I thought I would." Vince adjusted his tie and looked around at his friends who were all impeccably dressed. "I hope none of us fall on the hike down to the cave."

"My tailor would cry," Theron tried to laugh, but it never reached his eyes. "Shall we go?"

They piled into the BMW and drove to the overlook where the trailhead to the cave was. They made it down the steep incline without any falls. When they reached the cave, they lit torches then waited for the members of The Syndicate to arrive.

Leonidas arrived first and gasped when Theron stepped out. "Theron, you are alive? How?" He embraced Theron as Miguel offered him a glass of wine from Leonidas's own vineyard.

"I will tell you when everyone is here, I only want to go over it once." Theron patted his back then pulled back. "Let's wait to talk about business until everyone is here. How is your family?"

Vince stayed back in the shadows. This was Theron's island and it was his job to have relationships with these people. Vince was there for muscle, nothing more. He caught himself leaning on the wall, then thought about how much the suit cost and stood straight. He wondered what Katie was doing as he watched the other members arrive. Was she trying to find Lolita? Was she a prisoner? Was she safe? He hated not knowing the answers to his questions.

"Vince, Helen, Miguel, everyone is here. Please come and join us so that we can get back to our families," Theron called.

"Where is Takis?" Evangelos asked, as Vince came out from behind the wall.

"He is not himself and cannot be trusted," Theron said, leveling a stare at Evangelos.

"How are we going to stop The Turk? He killed twenty innocent people in that bar." Agapios asked.

"I think we should bomb his house, then we could blame it

on the same people who bombed Theron's compound," Serafeim said, crossing his arms over his chest.

"We need to make an example of him," Theron started to walk around the inside of the circle they were standing in. "We need the world to know that Crete is not ready for a takeover, and anyone who tries can expect a fate worse than death."

Leonidas's phone started to buzz, and he pulled it out to see who was calling. "It's Takis, should I answer it?"

"Yes, tell him the meeting was canceled due to extenuating circumstances," Vince said, watching the other members of the group, looking for any sign that they had been enslaved.

"Takis, how are you?" Leonidas asked into the phone.

"Where is everyone? The Turk and I are waiting in the arranged spot, but no one is here," Vince heard Takis say.

"Did you get the message from Serafeim? We canceled it, we all had too much going on this week to meet."

"No, I did not get the message. We have a lot to talk about. I like this Ilhami guy. I think he will help us accomplish great things if we let him join us."

"We will talk about it at the next meeting. In the meantime, go out and enjoy yourself," Leonidas said, into the phone.

"Where is everyone?" A new voice asked, and Vince thought it must be The Turk.

"Who is this?" Leonidas asked.

"The Turk, tell me why I wasn't notified that the meeting was canceled?"

"Have you fulfilled the obligations we required of you to join?" Leonidas asked.

Vince loved working with people who knew how to deal with assholes, it was going to make this whole ordeal so much more entertaining.

"No, but I was still going to join you." His voice was less harsh now, as if he had been talking to his mother, and she had chided him for having bad manners.

"Well, maybe next time." Leonidas hit the end button on his phone. "Serafeim is right, Takis is in league with The Turk."

"The only question now is, how are we going to get rid of him?" Agapios asked.

Chapter 37
Ilhami

Ilhami drove into the center of the island and Leonidas's estate. It was huge and beautiful, full of grape vines, date, and olive trees. He thought about taking it as his own, but it was too far from town to be useful. He parked the car at the front entrance and compelled the guards and valets to ignore him. He was at the front door when he felt movement from his left. He turned and looked across the trees and short brown grass beneath them. There was no one there. He heard no heartbeat, no breathing, but he was sure he felt something move that wasn't a tree.

He shook his head and went inside the house. He heard laughter to his right, so he went in that direction. The servants gave him stares as he walked through the villa as if he owned it. When he entered the dining room he smiled wide and held his arms out. "Good evening everyone."

All the members of The Syndicate were there with their wives. They looked up at him, their mouths dropping open, and their eyes widening. Leonidas stood letting his napkin fall to the floor. "What are you doing here? This is a private party."

"Yes, well, I decided to crash your party. Have your server set another setting, we need to speak." Ilhami took a chair from the wall and pulled it up next to Takis and his wife. "Takis, how are you this evening?" He had finished the slave bond the week before and Takis was paying him a good wage to keep things quiet on the drug-running side of things.

"They were going well until a moment ago," he said through his teeth, hoping no one else would hear him.

"Well, life is full of surprises and tonight, no doubt, will be full of them," Ilhami said as a server placed a plate and silverware on the table in front of him. "Thank you very much." He took the wine glass from the server and reached across the table to grab the bottle. He filled his glass then openly pulled his flask from his pocket. He added a liberal dose of blood to it and held it up. "To The Syndicate, may it keep Crete safe from those who would want to destroy it."

Takis raised his glass, he had learned over the past week to defy Ilhami was like stabbing himself in the head with an ice pick over and over again. The other members' mouths dropped open, but they still raised their glasses. Ilhami took a long sip then looked around at the still startled faces. "What were we talking about before I arrived?" he asked, looking around the table and out the window across from him. He swore he saw someone out there, but he could not register a heartbeat outside of the house.

"We were talking about our children. Do you have any?" Evangelos's wife asked, taking a bite of her food.

"Children? No, Allah, did not grant me the greatest gift yet. Maybe someday." He looked at his empty plate then back around the table.

"Takis, you are unusually quiet this evening how are your little ones?" Agapios asked, and it made Ilhami wonder where Miguel was. Every time he tried to get close to Agapios, Miguel seemed to be there to stop him from starting a slave bond.

"Yes, well they just left for England and the boarding school we talked about." His wife murmured, not sounding happy that her children were so far away from her.

"Boarding school? Why would you do such a thing?" Serafeim asked, giving him a knowing look.

"I think it will be beneficial for them to learn about other cultures and languages. We will see how it goes. If they like it they can continue, if they don't I will let them come home." Takis stared at his plate, not wanting to make eye contact with any of them.

"If you are all finished eating I think the men will retire to the study for cognac and cigars. I just received a shipment from Cuba," Leonidas said, standing and offering his hand to his wife.

"Ladies, I would love to show you my roses, they are almost in full bloom," she said, taking his hand, and standing. Everyone stood and followed one of the two hosts out of the room.

When the men were safely away from the prying ears of their wives they turned on Ilhami. "What do you think you are doing? Showing up at my house when my wife is home?"

"I told you, I am going to be the new head of The Syndicate. I should be included in all meetings." Ilhami crossed his arms over his chest.

"Do you have the fifteen million euro buy in?" Serafeim asked, lighting his cigar.

"Not yet." Ilhami took a cigar from the box and lit it.

"Have you avenged Theron?" Leonidas asked, moving to stand near the door by his desk.

"No, I am still trying to find the murderer." The lie came easily. He had no desire to find the one who killed Theron and his vampires. He was just happy Theron was dead.

"Then why do you think you are part of us? What have you done to prove your worth other than murder innocent people in a horrible and brutal way and steal from us?" Serafeim asked, moving to the other door.

"You mean at Thekla? None of them were innocent, they set me up. They all deserved to die." Even though the exits were blocked he wasn't worried. They were nothing but humans, but what was that? He moved to get a better view of the window. It looked like someone running toward the house.

"The patrons of the bar had nothing to do with what the owner set up for you. Word has gotten around that you are investigating everyone's books on behalf of The Syndicate and causing many of them to go out of business."

"They were stealing from you. I was helping you. Every single place I went they kept at least three sets of books, the real one, the one they showed you, and the one they showed the government."

"Then where is the money you collected from them?" Agapios asked, turning red in the face.

"In my bank account, I was merely holding it for you. I was going to give it to you as a gift." Ilhami took a step toward Agapios, trying to make eye contact.

"We have a surprise for you," Serafeim said, changing the subject, and opening the door by the desk.

Ilhami took a step backwards when Theron came through the door followed by a female he did not recognize. Theron was alive? He wanted nothing more than to be the one to kill him. His heart shattered when Lolita told him Theron was killed, now he had a chance to avenge his family, but first he needed to come up with a plan. He moved to escape through the front door, but the door opened before he could get there, and Vince and Miguel entered the room. Vince was the bastard who had held his father down while Theron tortured him.

"Ilhami, didn't we tell you we would let you live as long as you never set foot on Crete again?" Vince asked, closing the door behind him.

Ilhami tried to say yes, but his throat was suddenly too dry, and no sound came out. He backed up and put his back against the wall next to the door. He had to escape, but how? Theron was standing in front of the window, a female vampire was in front of the door by the desk, Vince and Miguel were standing in front of the door to the rest of the house.

"Gentlemen, it is good to see you again." Theron said, standing with his hands behind his back.

"How are you alive? Where have you been?" Ilhami asked.

"All that matters is that I am alive, and I am not happy about what you have been trying to do to my island." Theron took a step forward and Ilhami tried to take a step back, but he was already against the wall.

"I took the island while you were gone. It is not yours anymore." Ilhami wasn't going to give up without a fight.

"How did you take it? You turned one of The Syndicate into a slave, burned down a bar and pissed off everyone else. You are being charged with the death of twenty civilians. How do you plead?"

"Not guilty," he said, pulling his Colt from behind his back and taking aim at Theron. He pulled the trigger as Vince tackled him to the ground, forcing him to drop the gun. He looked up between Vince's arms hoping to have hit one of the vampires in the room, but he had missed everyone.

"We find you guilty," Serafeim said, stepping into his line of sight. "Theron what do you sentence him to?"

"Death by the Brazen Bull seems appropriate after what he did to the civilians in Thekla." Theron walked over to where Ilhami lay on the floor. "Do you still have one?" he asked Leonidas.

"Of course, my wife loves it, she thinks it's lawn art. I will have it moved to the field, we don't want to upset the women." Leonidas said, leaving the room. Vince pulled Ilhami up and pinned his arms behind his back.

"You will all rot in hell for this," Ilhami vowed struggling to get away to no avail.

"Then we will meet you there," Theron said, leading the way to the side door.

"Lolita will kill you for doing this to me," Ilhami said, still struggling.

"Lolita has had me on her list for longer than you know," Theron said, looking over his shoulder. He hoped Vince's strength held up. If Ilhami got away now, he would kill everyone in The Syndicate.

"I was her second in command. She is depending on me to keep Crete open to her. When she finds out what you did, she will come at you with her army."

"Army? What army? Last I heard she was hiding out, afraid of what 'The One' would do to her," Vince said from behind him. "She could not even take care of the human herself, instead she hired a mercenary to do it for her and even he failed." Speaking the words so nonchalantly was like stabbing himself in the eye. He needed to find Katie.

"You have no idea what she is planning, do you?" Ilhami laughed, stopping abruptly to try and trip Vince. Helen grabbed one of his arms and Miguel grabbed his other before forcing him forward.

"She has been planning on taking over the world for decades, but she has done nothing yet. Why would she start now?" Miguel asked, dragging him forward.

"That is where you are wrong. She started to build her vampire army before she turned me. You have no chance of beating her, her numbers are too great."

Katie had told Vince months ago she thought Lolita was building an army. They had not worried about it much, since it would take decades for her to build her forces big enough to overtake Europe, but if she started building it before she turned Ilhami, something had to be done.

Vince put his worry aside as they entered a field with torches placed in a circle around the bronze bull making it shine like a demon sent from Tartarus. Each member of The Syndicate stood at a torch except for Serafeim who held the door on the side of the bull open while their bodyguards, and lesser men stood by to watch what happened when you crossed The Syndicate.

The four vampires took Ilhami directly to the opening and loaded him into the belly of the beast. He tried to break free of them but there was no escape. Serafeim closed the door and locked it once he was inside. Ilhami started to scream for help, but the bull was built to change screams to bellows. If someone heard the noises nearby they would think there was a bull having a bad night.

"For the crimes you committed on my island I sentence you to death by the Brazen Bull. May the Goddess have mercy on you," Theron bellowed, and each member of The Syndicate took a torch, and as one, they laid them under the bull igniting the wood beneath it.

The men moved back to their original positions and the vampires stood with them as the bull began to bellow, cooking Ilhami just as he had cooked the civilians in the bar. After an hour the sound stopped, and Leonidas pulled out a bottle of ouzo. "And now let us celebrate our victory over The Turk."

When the celebration was done Vince, Theron, Helen, and Miguel retired to the small house they had begun to call home. They sat in the living room and looked at each other. "Now that your island is secure I need to find Katie," Vince said, looking around the room.

"What's your plan?" Theron asked, lacing his fingers together.

"I want to retrace her steps. See if anyone remembers her, see if I can find any clues to where she might be. Someone must know something. From what little there is to go on, she never used the plane ticket she bought, and she stopped using the credit cards I gave her the day after she left here."

"She could be anywhere by now. Maybe we need to draw her out," Helen offered, unbuttoning her suit jacket and leaning back on the couch.

"How?" Miguel asked, pulling his eyebrows together in thought.

"Well, we want to let the world know that Theron is still the head of The Cretan Syndicate. We should make an announcement," Helen said.

"We can't tell them I am the head of The Syndicate," Theron scoffed.

"That's not what I am saying. I say we let people know you survived the attack, just like you did with The Syndicate. The media will eat it up, if we get your name on TV, and the internet, Katie will hear it and she will come to us."

"It's not a bad plan. She trusts you, Theron. I would do it, but only vampires would care that I am alive. She will come back just to see you and if anyone else survived." Vince ran his fingers through his hair.

"I do need to make a statement, good idea Helen." Theron got up and paced back and forth between the unlit fireplace and the couches. "Are you still going to look for her?"

"Yes, if she does not see, or hear the news she may be someone's prisoner, and I have to find her."

"Very well, when are you going to leave?" Theron sat down across from Vince.

"Tomorrow, I already have a plane ticket."

"We need to move before we make this announcement. I don't want to look like a vagrant. Evangelos is going to let me rent a house from him until I can rebuild. Once we are settled there we can make the announcement. I might have to fake a limp." Theron chuckled.

"How long will it be?" Vince asked.

"Not long, a day, maybe two."

"Then we have a plan, we find Katie and make sure she's safe, then we find Lolita and Alex," Helen said, holding in a yawn.

"I have an idea about how we can find Lolita," Miguel said, rubbing his hands together with a tight smile on his face.

Chapter 38

Vince

"How may I help you sir?" The man behind the desk asked, looking up from his computer.

"I have a reservation under Charchalis." Vince gave the man his passport and credit card.

"Thank you," he said, taking them, and starting to type on the keyboard. "What brings you to Athens?"

"My sister is missing; I am trying to find her." Vince looked around the lobby, trying to imagine Katie staying there.

"Oh, I'm so sorry. When did she go missing?" the man asked, looking shocked by Vince's announcement.

"A few months ago, she stayed at this hotel for two nights. Maybe you have seen her?" Vince took the photo out of his pocket and showed to the man. "This is a few months old, her hair was longer the last time I saw her, and she had lost some weight."

The man adjusted his glasses and looked at the photo. "She does not look familiar to me. What is her name?"

"Mary Sims, it's her married name." Excitement surged through Vince, maybe her name would make the man remember.

He clicked a few buttons on the computer. "I was on holiday when she was here. You will want to talk to Ted, he covered for me while I was gone. He'll be here tomorrow night."

"Thank you for your help." Vince's voice was flat, he wanted information now, not the next day.

"Any time. Here is your key, your room is 419. That's the same room she stayed in, what are the chances?" The man handed over the key, and Vince went to the elevator frustrated that he would have to wait until the next night to find out if Ted knew anything.

He opened the door to his room imagining what Katie would have done when she arrived. Checked to make sure no was in the room with her, then lock everything up, shower would have been next. He checked the room out. It was nothing special, but he could smell her. He was probably imagining it, but he did not care. It was the most important smell in the world to him.

He sat down at the desk and pulled his computer out of his bag. He plugged it into the hotel's hard line internet and brought up his video chat program.

"You made it," Theron said from the screen.

"Yes, but unfortunately the man working the front desk wasn't working when Katie was here. I will have to wait until tomorrow night to talk to the man who checked Katie in."

"Well let's see if I can access their records, maybe they still have the security footage on file. Do you want to give me control of your computer?"

"I just did, it's all yours." Vince pushed away from the desk and stood. He untucked the white dress shirt he had on and loosened a few buttons. He went to the window and looked outside. He had a view of the parking lot and the mall across the street.

"I'm in," he heard Theron say on the computer.

He closed the curtains and went back over to the desk. He sat down and looked at the screen. "What am I looking at?" Vince asked. It looked like a spreadsheet with dates and times on it.

"It is the list of when keycards were used, the date and the time. Most hotels keep the data in case they are accused of stealing from a room while the guest is gone."

Vince scanned the document. He found the dates of Katie's

262

stay. It looked like she checked in late the night of the attack, she went into her room, and she must have had the 'do not disturb' sign on her door because it wasn't used again until the following evening when it had been used twice. Something must have happened. Alex must have found her. "Can you get the security video?"

"Working on it. They store it on a cloud account, I'm almost there."

Vince wished he could tell when she left the room, but there was no way to track the information. He drummed his fingers on the desk impatiently, he wanted to see what happened. Had Alex found her and followed her back? Did he kidnap her and have her in some prison where he could take advantage of her? It was taking everything he was made of not to go insane with worry.

"OK, I'm in." A video popped up on the screen. It showed a woman with a large hat on, walking through the lobby, and stopping at the front desk.

"That's her," Vince whispered. He slumped in his chair.

"How can you tell with that hat on?" Theron asked, sounding skeptical.

"The way she moves, I will never forget the way she moves," Vince almost whispered, as he stared at Katie's back, wishing she would turn around, so he could see her face.

"I'm going to fast forward to the next day, and see if she came in with anyone when she came back."

The video jumped; the empty lobby from the night before was now filled with men. Mean looking men. He studied the faces until his eyes settled on one. "Fuck, there is Alex, he has to have her." The last thing Vince wanted to watch was her getting accosted by these guys, but he had to know for sure.

He watched and waited. They started fifteen minutes before the card was used. A few people came and went in that time but none of them were Katie. "Is there another way into the hotel?" Vince asked; maybe there was a side door.

"Let me see what I can find." Theron mumbled not sounding happy.

Vince got up and paced around the room. He had a horrible feeling in his gut. Where could she be? Who had her?

"There is a side entrance right next to the stairwell, but I found the camera on her floor, it will tell us more than the lobby camera."

Vince ran back to his seat and watched as a skinny, short man got off the elevator and went to Katie's room. "Is that the right room?" Vince asked.

"Yes, the date and time stamp match up."

The man came out with Katie's bag and katana in his hands. He did not walk back to the elevator though, he went down the hall to the stairwell. Vince did not know what to say or do, a man with Katie's key went into her room took all her stuff and left.

"Vince?" Theron called. "Are you, all right?"

"No, where is she? More importantly, who was the man she gave her key card to?"

"I don't know. There are a couple of ways to look at what we just watched."

"Enlighten me please." Vince's thoughts were full of horrible things that could have happened to her.

"Alex could have kidnapped her, but I think she figured out that Alex found her, and she found a way to hide from him. She had this guy get her stuff, and now she's in a safe house of some sort. You know she would have done anything to get her katana back. She wouldn't have told him where it was if he was a bad guy."

Vince let out a breath. Theron was right, if someone had done something to her they would not have come back for her stuff and her katana. "You are right. Now I need to find this man. Can you get a close up of him and email it to me?"

"I will try. He didn't really pose for the camera."

"You will, damn it. Then start running a search with your facial recognition software." Vince pounded his fist on the table.

"Vince, calm down, at least you have a clue."

"Thank you for your help, Theron. I apologize for being short with you." Vince rested his elbows on the table and covered his face with his hands. "I am just worried about her."

"I am too. We'll find her. I wish we could have gotten a better picture of her for the software though."

"Why don't we look at the camera from the night she arrived in the hallway?"

"Good idea." Theron started clicking buttons on the keyboard.

The video showed the doors opening and Katie coming out with the oversized hat on her hand. She was blond? Where were her black eyes? Everything but the hair looked like Katie.

"Bingo," Theron shouted, hitting buttons again. The picture froze. "I am emailing you a copy now. It is much better than the one Miguel gave you. I have to hand it to her, she is not as dumb as she looks."

"What did you say?" Vince moved closer to the computer.

"She's in disguise, she died her hair and covered up her bruises to hide from Alex and his men. I am betting it worked for a while. I wonder how he found her."

"I am impressed with what she has done, but it does not help me find her." He was going to have to wait until the following night to look any further and there was no reason to monopolize Theron's time. "Thank you, Theron, I will call you tomorrow night with an update."

Chapter 39

Katie

I was sitting in my apartment on Thanksgiving Day watching the previous night's footage of Lolita and trying not to think about what my parents would being doing without me, when I received a text from Uni. I opened it only to find a link to a website. It looked like it was for a television station. I went back to my computer and typed in the website. It was a story about Crete.

"It was originally believed that there were no survivors of the terrorist attack on Crete in August, however the owner of the property that was attacked is alive and well. It appears he was flown out by a helicopter to receive treatment at a private hospital where he has been convalescing for the past three months.

"Many of the residents of Crete were excited to hear that Theron Antonis is alive. He is thought of as the patron saint of Crete." The woman droned on without me hearing anything else. I got up and went to my closet, pulled my suitcase out, and started throwing things into it. I had accumulated more than I realized. I sent a text to Uni. 'Do you have a suitcase I can have? I will pay you back for it.' I pulled everything out of my dresser and tried to decide what to take and what to leave. I went back to my computer, I had no idea what the weather in Crete would be like in the winter. It was cool compared to the summer, but a lot warmer than it was in Kevò. I started to make piles when Uni knocked on the door. "Come in," I called from the bedroom.

"You're going to Crete?" Uni asked, putting the suitcase on the floor beside the bed.

"Yes, I need them," I said, putting a sweater in the take pile, and a base-layer shirt in the stay pile. "I can't believe he's alive. I wonder if anyone else is." It was taking everything I had to stay calm. I was ready to run out the door and leave everything behind. Theron was alive.

"I'm so happy for you." She sat down on the bed. "You need to go talk to Tad before you leave. How are you going to leave anyway? You don't even have a car."

"I have no idea." I dropped the jeans in my hand. "Crap, and how am I going to get there with Alex breathing down my neck?"

"I'm planning on going into Athens to see my mom tomorrow, so you could hitch a ride with me. Then you have two options, you can risk the airport or the ferry. The ferry has way less cameras than the airport, but they don't run on schedule most of the time because of the weather."

I looked at my suitcase then Uni's, I couldn't take them both. I needed to travel light and after what happened on my last ferry ride it was hard enough to keep track of one bag. "The ferry will give me a better chance of not being discovered, but I'm not going to need your suitcase. I need to travel light, especially with Vinny. Two suitcases would be a pain in the ass."

"Good idea, now go see Tad, then pack. We can leave as early tomorrow as you want," Uni said, starting to fold the clothes on the bed. "I will sort everything for you."

"Thanks," I went into the living room, shoved my feet into my boots, and was out the door with my jacket half-on in less than a minute. I ran to Tad's office and banged on the door. It opened, and I almost ran across the room to see him. "Tad, I'm sorry to bother you but I just got the best news."

"Yes, I saw it too. Theron is alive. Do you think the rest of his vampires are as well?" Tad was sitting behind his desk looking at

268

his monitor.

"I have no idea. When the last bomb went off they all disappeared from my mind. I was sure they were all dead." I sat down and tried not to think about Vince.

"Are you here to tell me you are leaving?" Tad turned away from his monitor and leveled his eyes on me.

"Yes, I need to go see Theron, even if it is just to let him know I am alive."

"How are you going to get there?"

"Uni is going to give me a ride to Athens, then I am going to take the ferry; fewer cameras."

"Good, you have learned a lot in your time here."

"I have, and I have no idea how to thank you for letting me stay. I'm sorry I haven't been able to find out who the mole is."

"I think we will be able to figure it out. In thanks, you can vow to never tell your mother about me." He bowed his head in shame.

"I will never tell my mother of your location or that you live," I vowed.

"Thank you, Katie Hunter. If you ever wish to return, our doors will always be open." Tad stood and reached his hand out. I took it and we shook, then I went back to my apartment to finish packing.

Vinny was waiting for me when I came in. "Vinny, you need to get your toys, so we can take them with us." I had no idea how he was going to do traveling, but there was no way I was going to leave him. He was the only reason I got out of bed some mornings. He cocked his head to the side like he didn't understand what I was talking about. I went around the room gathering his balls and chew-toys up and took them into the bedroom. My suitcase was open and packed. There was just enough room for Vinny's toys and dog food. Uni was sitting on the bed playing a game on her phone.

"Uni, you didn't have to pack for me. I was going to do it myself. I need to keep busy or I will start walking to Athens tonight." I thumbed through the folded clothes, the girl knew me well. She had everything I would need, and nothing I couldn't replace when I got to Crete.

"Yes, I did because now we are going to dinner, then we are going to watch a movie. I want to spend some time with you before you run off." She looked up at me with tears in her eyes.

"I'm going to miss you." I sat down on the bed next to her.

"I'm going to be so bored without you." She flung herself into my arms, and I hugged her close to me.

"We will have to meet up for a girl's vacation some time." *If I beat Lolita*, I didn't add.

I wanted her to think I had this in the bag, that everything was going to be all right, but there were too many what ifs for me to believe it. If Theron would help me, if Vince was dead, if I could avoid Alex, and if I could get Lolita alone.

"Yes, we will. I'll start looking for places tomorrow." She pulled away and smiled. "Come on let's go eat."

She pulled me off the bed and we went to the cafeteria. "Where is everyone?" I asked, looking around the almost empty room. It was seven in the evening, usually it was the busiest time to eat.

"I don't know, maybe they are all on a mission or something." We grabbed trays and went through the buffet line. We filled our plates then sat down at our usual table.

"Do you think Vince is alive?" she asked, between bites of food.

"I want him to be, but I doubt it." My mom said she couldn't feel him, but that didn't mean he was dead. "I just hope Theron will still be willing to help me. Even if he won't, I need to see him and tell him I'm alive, that I escaped."

"I'm sure he will be excited to see you," Uni said, looking at her phone for the hundredth time since we sat down.

"Are you waiting for a text from your boyfriend or something?" I asked, taking a drink of my water.

"What? I don't have a boyfriend. My mom is supposed to let me know when she gets into Athens."

"I'm sure she's fine." I finished the last bit of food on my plate and sat back. "I'm going to miss it here." I looked around the room.

"We're going to miss you too." Uni said, playing with the little bit of food on her plate.

"What movie are we going to watch?" I asked, trying to keep my mind from thinking leaving at that moment.

"Oh, I haven't picked one yet. We'll pick one when we are done eating."

"Are you done?" I asked, as she pushed the food around with her fork. "My mom always said not to play with your food."

"Sorry," she forked up what was left on her plate and shoved it in her mouth just as her phone vibrated. She glanced at the message then cleared the screen. "Come on let's go to my place."

She was acting strange and I didn't know what to make of it. We dumped our trash and set the trays down on the table. I looked around the room, it was going to be weird not standing in line to get my food anymore.

"KK come on, let's go," Uni called from the open door. I turned, and walked out, wondering if I would ever be back.

We walked down Main Street toward her apartment I looked in all the windows trying to commit everything to memory. The lights in the bar were on and it looked there were a few people getting a drink. "Uni, why don't we go in and have a drink for old time's sake?"

She looked at me then her watch. "Hummm, OK."

I held the door open for her and we went inside going directly to the bar. The bartender looked up when we sat down. "What can I get you ladies?"

I looked at Uni and she looked at me. "It's your last night here, you choose."

I looked at the bottles behind the bar. "I think we need a shot of ouzo and a beer."

"I thought you were never going to touch the stuff again," Uni sounded excited to have more than just a beer.

"Well it's my last night. Might as well live it up a little." I grinned at her, holding up the shot glass the bartender put down. Uni grabbed her glass.

"To Karate Kid. May you defeat your enemies and live a long and drama free life." Uni clinked her glass against mine and we threw the shot back, cringing at the anise. I took my beer and gulped it.

"Thanks. I'm going to miss this place."

"Really? You have a crappy apartment and most of the people didn't start talking to you until a month ago."

"This place was exactly what I needed, when I needed it." I took another sip of my beer and Uni's phone buzzed.

"Did your mom make it?"

"What?" She looked up at me, her brows furrowed a second before she smiled. "Yeah, she's all settled in at her hotel."

"Are looking forward to see her?" I asked, as she took a swig of her beer.

"Yes, but she can be drama, I never know if she is going to be cool or hysterical."

"Why do you say that?" I asked, pulling my eyebrows together in confusion.

"She wears her emotions on her sleeve and I never know if she is going to blame me for whatever drama is going on in her life."

"Well, I hope you have a drama free visit then."

"Yeah, well we'll see. Are you done? Come on let's go watch the movie, I want to get an early start tomorrow." Uni chugged the rest of her beer.

"You are a fun, slave driver." I swallowed the rest of my beer, and we left the bar. Another place I doubted I would ever see again.

Uni's apartment was dark when she opened the door. "Don't you normally leave a light on when you go out at night?" I asked as she walked in. Vinny barked, and I pulled my katana out of its sheath. "Uni get out, something's wrong."

"Its fine I'm just trying to find the light switch." She called, and I heard her run into something.

"What do you think, Vinny?" I asked, looking down at the dog. He took a step back, barked again, then sat down. I heard Uni stumbling around inside, and I stepped into the doorway. The lights went on and everyone I knew in Kevó yelled, "Surprise!" Vinny barked, and I lowered my sword and laughed.

"What is this?" I asked, "Vinny come inside its cold out there." Vinny followed me in; I shut the door behind me, then sheathed my katana.

"Did you think we were going to let you leave without a going away party?" Vangel asked, handing me a beer.

"I thought you didn't care," I said, taking a sip of it.

"You made life in Kevó much more interesting," Barkley said, coming over and clinking his bottle against mine. "I for one am going to miss you."

"I'm going to miss you too." I gave him a hug.

"Hey what about me?" Hound came over and wrapped me in a bear hug. "Who are we going to watch play with their sword now?"

"I'm sure you will find something else to keep you busy." I was going to miss these people.

"Let's dance," Uni called, hitting a button on her phone, and music erupted through the apartment.

I spent the rest of the night drinking too much and talking too much. It was the best party I had been to since my college graduation. It gave me hope that maybe someday my life would go back to normal. Three months ago, I thought that I would be on my own for the rest of life, no matter how short or long it would be. It was nice to know that if I survived I would always have a place in Kevó.

Chapter 40

Vince

The next evening as soon as it was safe for Vince to venture out, he walked to the mall. He had a list of every store Katie had made a purchase, and followed it as if it was a map that would lead him to Katie. After a quick tour of the stores she went into he was at a loss. He sat down across from a computer store and put his head in his hands. Women were the only people he had seen in the stores and while employee turnover was high in retail, he could not see a man working in women's fashion.

He could have been a random guy walking down the street for all he knew. She could have paid him to get her stuff, then she could have hitchhiked away. She could be anywhere in the world by now thinking she was alone, with no one to help her. He stood ready to leave and start walking the street looking for anyone Katie would have asked for help from. He looked at the computer store, someone had to help her disappear and figure out how to access her money without anyone tracing it back to her, she would have needed a computer guy. He went into the store and walked up to the counter.

"Can I help you?" the man behind the counter asked.

"Yes, my sister is missing. She was last seen in the mall and I was wondering if you had seen her." Vince pulled the photo of Katie out his pocket and showed it to the man.

"No, I do not think I have seen her. When did she go missing?" he asked, taking the picture from Vince, and bringing it closer to his face.

"Three months ago."

"Then I didn't see her, I started here last month. If you come back tomorrow one of the other employees might have seen her. Demetri has worked here for years; he would be the one to remember her."

"Thank you." Vince turned and left the store. He walked quickly to the exit and out into the night. He ran his hands through his hair. *Katie, where are you?* He sent his thought out into the night. He walked in circles around the mall, each circle larger than the last until he found himself standing in front of the hotel. It was the last place she had been seen before she disappeared off the face of the earth. There was no way she could have done it on her own. The question was, had Alex found her and taken her to Lolita or did she befriend someone else? He went inside ready to give up for the night. Halfway across the lobby his phone began buzzed in his pocket.

"Yes?" he asked annoyed.

"The news that I survived is out," Theron said, on the other side of the phone line. "If she has access to any television, or the internet, she will see it."

"Thank you for doing this, Theron." Vince got into the elevator and hit the button for his floor.

"Did you find anything out at the mall?"

"No, no one remembers her. Half of the people I talked to had not worked there three months ago." The elevator stopped, and the doors opened. He walked down the hall to his room. "I do not know what to do next."

"All you can do is wait. Come back here tomorrow night. I have alerts set up. If she is on her way back here we will know, and you can meet her." Theron sounded tired.

"You sound like you need to rest. If you hear anything let me know. In the meantime, I will make arrangements to come back tomorrow night."

"You need to rest too. You aren't going to be any good to anyone if you don't recover."

Vince's mind would not let him relax. He knew he needed to rest but without knowing if Katie was safe there would be little rest for him. "Call me if you hear anything."

"I will."

Vince hit the end button on his phone and unlocked the door to his room. He looked around the room and wondered what Katie was doing. Was she safe? Warm and out of harm's way? Or was she trapped in a dungeon freezing and starving? He undressed and lay on the bed to stare at the ceiling. The sun was almost up and there was nothing he could do but try to sleep.

Chapter 41

Katie

I woke up the next morning with a hangover that reminded me of my college days. It felt like a cat had defecated in my mouth and my head was pounding. I looked around, I was in my room. I didn't even remember getting home. I sat up remembering that we were leaving soon. I was going to find Theron and maybe the rest of my vampire friends. I grabbed my head as the throbbing increased and Vinny whined at me.

My body wanted me to go back to sleep and recover but my mind was ready to go. I forced myself out of bed and went into the living room to feed Vinny. With him happily eating his food, I went into the bathroom and got in the shower. When I was out, I dressed in black jeans and a black turtle neck. I put my harness on and adjusted the katana on my back, then attached the ankle sheath and knife, Vangel had given me, to my leg and pushed the leg of my jeans over it. I zipped up my suitcase and did one last walk through the apartment. I left most of my super warm clothes in a pile on the bed. I was sure Uni would take what she wanted and find a good home for the rest of it. I put my suitcase by the door and sent a text to Uni. ***Are you ready to go?***

I took Vinny outside to do his business, and willed Uni to text me back. My phone buzzed in my pocket. ***Bringing the car around. Meet me on Main Street.***

I left Vinny to finish sniffing around and went back inside to get my suitcase. I took one last look at the apartment that had been my haven, before hanging the key on the hook and closing the door. It was time to move on.

"Come on Vinny, let's blow this joint." I pulled my suitcase behind me and stopped when we reached Main Street. Uni was leaning against her cherry-red Mini Cooper with a cup of coffee in her hand. "You look about as good as I feel," I said, putting my suitcase in the open hatch.

"You don't look so hot yourself." She tried to smile, but it faded quickly. "You ready to go?"

"Yeah, let's do this." I opened the passenger door and pulled the seat forward. "Come on Vinny we have new adventures awaiting us. Vinny sniffed the car then jumped into the back seat. I pushed the seat back and got in while Uni started the car. I looked around one last time as we drove through the small village that had become a home to me and said a silent goodbye.

"Did you have fun last night?" Uni asked, once we were out of town.

"I think so, I don't know if I remember everything that happened. How much ouzo did I drink?" I pulled my floppy hat from between my legs and put it on.

"About half a bottle I think. The guys kept making you do shots with them. I think you told everyone that you love them three times. At least you didn't offer to have anyone's baby."

I grimaced. "Just the impression I want to leave them with."

"I think everyone liked watching you cut loose for a change. You are always too serious. Don't worry about it." Uni sounded upbeat, but she had something on her mind.

"Are you feeling all right? I can drive if you want."

"Yeah, I'm just tired, I can drive. I'm not looking forward to hanging out with my mom." She came to the end of the dirt road and turned left. "It's going to be a long week."

"I'm sorry." I would have given anything to be on the way to my mom's house. It would mean that my enemies were dead, and I could have my life back.

"I know you miss your mom, and I miss mine too. I just have a bad feeling about this visit is all. Hey, turn the radio on. I need something to keep me awake."

We listened to music until my stomach started to rumble. "Hey, can we stop somewhere and get something to eat? I'm starving."

"Yeah, there is a place coming up we can stop at," Uni said, looking at her watch. "I could use some food too."

She pulled off the road in front of a small café and parked the car. "You will have to leave Vinny in the car. They don't allow dogs in here."

I turned back to Vinny who was taking up the entire backseat. "Vinny, you stay and be a good boy," I said, before getting out, and following Uni into the restaurant.

We were seated quickly and we both ordered coffee and bottled waters. "How far from Athens are we?" I asked, after taking a sip of coffee.

"About halfway depending on traffic. We should make it to the port in plenty of time," Uni said, dumping sugar into her coffee.

"Good, it looks like there's a storm on the way and I don't want to be stuck in Athens waiting for the ferries to go out again."

"If they shut them down you can always take a plane." Uni winked at me.

"I don't know if I could get through the airport without showing up on a camera and I'm sure Alex has all the airport cameras tagged." I blew out a breath. I wanted to be in Crete already. I wasn't sure how I was going to find Theron once I got there, but I would have time on the boat to come up with a plan.

"What will you have?" the server asked, with her notebook ready.

We ordered our food and waited impatiently for it to come out. Uni took my hat and put it on her head. I put my head down and looked around for a camera. "What are you doing? Give me back my hat." I reached up and pulled it off her head.

"I just wanted to try it on. There aren't any cameras in here." She pouted, hitting a button on her phone, and putting it in her pocket.

"I don't want to take any chances. When was the last time you were here?" I asked, looking around. I didn't see any cameras, but it didn't mean they weren't there.

"Last month, I almost always stop here going or coming. There were no cameras here then and I'm sure there aren't any now." She looked around the room, verifying she was right.

Our food came a few minutes later and I forgot about the hat and thought about filling my stomach. We ate quickly then got back on the road.

When we got back to cell phone service I looked up the ferry schedule and verified it was running on time. Traffic was light, and we made it to the port in record time. I got out of the car and pulled the seat back for Vinny. "I need to take him for a walk really quick. Can you wait until he has peed to leave?"

"Yeah go for it," Uni said, leaning her seat back and closing her door.

I took Vinny on a quick walk, then we went back to Uni. I knocked on the window and she jumped. I laughed, "Do you want to open the back, so I can get my stuff?"

"You scared the crap out of me," she said, opening the door, and getting out.

"That's what you get for staying up too late." I followed her to the back of the car and pulled my suitcase and computer bag out. "Well I guess this is it." I slung my computer bag over my head, so it would hang across my back.

"Life is going to be so boring without you." She wrapped her arms around me and hugged me like she was never going to see me again.

"I'm sure you'll find something to keep you busy." I hugged

her back then took a few steps away.

She bent down and wrapped her arms around Vinny. "You take good care of her, OK, Vinny?" He looked up at me like he was miserable. I laughed, and the ferry blew its horn.

"OK, we have to go. Take care of yourself, OK?" I said, taking Vinny's leash in one hand, and the handle to my suitcase in the other.

"I will, but you have to take care of each other too." She stood and wiped a finger under her eyes.

"Come on Vinny we are going on a boat ride." We turned, leaving Uni behind, and boarded the ferry to take us back to Crete.

Chapter 42

Alex

Alex sat at his computer as he did most days waiting for Katie-Mary, whatever her real name was, to pop up on his screen. There were false positives almost every day, and every day he would double-check them just to make sure it wasn't not Katie. He had no idea where the bitch had gone, and he was running out of time. He clicked through the search programs with the news droning on in the background.

"Theron Antonis is alive," was all he registered as he turned his head toward the television.

"No, I killed him, he should be dead with the rest of his vampires." Alex yelled at the screen. How could Theron be alive? Alex watched as the tunnel collapsed on him, there was no way he could have survived. Lolita was going to be pissed. He needed to go to Crete, find Theron and kill him. Alex couldn't let him live.

He ran up the steps to his room and threw everything he needed into a bag. He came back down the stairs and logged into a travel website. He was about to make flight reservations when his computer pinged on a possible Katie-Mary sighting. He automatically clicked over thinking it was going to be another false positive, the mouse hovered over the ignore button as he looked at the face. The hair was wrong but dang if Katie wasn't looking right into the camera lens. Forgetting about the airline tickets he clicked on the camera to see where she was. It was just outside of Athens in a small town. "Finally found you bitch, now I just have to follow you and I bet you are going back to Crete to see if you boyfriend is still alive." He clicked back over to the travel website. She had obviously figured how he had found her in Athens months ago. Now she was trying to avoid cameras, she would take the ferry not a plane. He checked the ferry schedule. There was a ferry leaving just after three, going directly to Crete. He was going to take a gamble that she would be on the boat. He booked his ticket and started packing up the house.

Alex got to the port early, he wanted to make sure he had everything ready to go. As soon as he found Katie he wanted to disable her, and get her off the boat. If she made it to Crete, she would go running to Theron and make his job that much harder.

He put his bag in the lifeboat on the third deck. Lowering it to the water while they were underway would be risky, but he didn't have any other choice. If he failed, who knew what Lolita would do to him. When he had everything in place, he found a quiet spot to sit and wait. He would not start looking for Katie until they were underway. He wasn't going to give her a chance to escape this time. He smiled to himself and ran his fingers over the Taser in his pocket.

Chapter 43

Katie

Vinny and I went up to the top enclosed deck and found a seat on the aisle where my back would be against the wall. I felt like had done a good job avoiding the cameras on the dock and around the ferry, but I couldn't let myself relax. I was probably just nervous about finding Theron when arrived.

How was I going to find him? I didn't think he would be at the ruins of his compound. I thought about renting a car and using my vamp-sense to find him. There couldn't be that many vampires on the island and if I found one, they would probably know where I could find Theron. It wasn't the best plan, but it wasn't like I could pick up my phone and call him. I lost his number when I ran over my old phone before I left Crete the last time.

The ferry pushed off the dock and we were finally on our way. I rubbed Vinny behind the ears. "Everything is going to be all right." He lay down in front of me, but his ears were still perked up, making sure no one came too close.

It felt like someone was watching me. I had been sitting in the same spot for two hours and I could feel someone's eyes on me. I looked around, but the almost empty ferry had few clues. I was getting stir crazy and I needed to move around. Vinny was feeling it too. He was still lying down, but his head was up, and he was constantly looking around.

I stood and stretched. "Come on Vinny let's go for a walk. I swung my computer bag over my shoulder and pulled the handle up on my suitcase. We walked to the end of the upper deck then down past the concession stand and around. Vinny started to bark and lunge toward the door to the stairs

287

when we walked past them, and I pulled him back. "Vinny, what's your problem? There's nothing to be scared about." I pulled him back and looked down the stairwell to apologize for my misbehaving dog, only to find it empty. I heard footsteps going down the stairs and I shrugged. "Well you scared away whoever it was, I hope you're proud of yourself."

We went back to the front of the boat and looked at the angry sea. The wind had picked up and the storm clouds were starting to roll in. I hoped we made it to Crete before the water got too rough. Vinny barked, bringing me out of my thoughts and I turned around my hand automatically going to the sword on my back, but there was no one there, and Vinny was whining, pulling against his leash. "OK, let's check it out." I let him lead me back to the stairwell and we went down to the next deck. When we got to the door he scratched and pawed at it until I opened it. We went through the door, ending up outside in freezing wind and frozen rain. I slipped and almost fell as he dragged me around the deck with his nose to the ground. We were at the door to go back inside when something zapped me. My muscles locked, I felt my hand let go of my suitcase and computer bag then everything went black. I could hear Vinny attacking someone then yelping. I fell on something hard and everything just faded away.

"Where have you been?" My mother yelled at me from across the room of her temple. I swayed on my feet and tried to focus on her. What had happened?

"I have been hiding and trying to find Lolita." I moved over to a pillar and leaned against it.

"Don't ever do that again. I thought you were dead." She was in front of me in a second, pulling me into her arms.

"Are you going back to Delos?" she asked, pulling away enough to see my face.

288

"Not yet. I am going back to Crete. Theron is alive, I need to see if he will still help me." My mind finally caught up with what was going on. I had been on my way back to Crete then I lost consciousness. Vinny was attacking someone then he yelped. "Mom, something is wrong I need to wake up."

"No, you need to tell me what is going on." She shook me, and I started rocking back and forth.

"I will tell you when I know. Right now, I need to wake up or I may never wake up." I pulled away from her, my head still rocking. *Wake up*, I told myself, *Wake up*.

Chapter 44

Vince

Hours later his phone vibrated from it place on the desk where it was charging. He jumped to his feet and ran to the phone. "Did you find her?" Vince asked Theron.

"Our plan worked. She is one her way back to Athens. I'm guessing she is on the ferry back to Crete."

"Why wouldn't she fly?" Vince asked, opening his computer, and bringing up a travel website.

"Because of cameras. The only reason we found her was because the woman she is traveling with stole her hat while they had breakfast and posted a video of her online."

"How does she look?" Vince tried to keep his voice even, but he could not help the tightness in his throat.

"Her hair looks horrible, but other than that she looks good Vince. She looks happy and healthy. I am emailing you the still shot right now."

"Thank the Goddess," Vince murmured as he opened his email program, and the attachment Theron sent him. There she was. Her blue eyes looking just as bright as he remembered. Her bi-colored hair was longer than the last time he had seen her, but she was still beautiful. "What do we do now?"

"I think you need to plan on flying back, then you will have time to meet her at the port."

"Have you been able to tag Alex yet?" Vince knew the man would not stop looking for Katie.

"No, but I have alerts set up all over the world if he steps a foot outside we will know where he is."

"OK, I will make the flight arrangements. What time does the ferry leave?" Vince pulled up a list of flights to Crete.

"It leaves at three and gets in at nine, if the weather holds."

"OK, I can be there by eight that should give me plenty of time to get to the port and meet her." He was so excited he could hardly stand it. It was going to be a long wait until nightfall.

"If anything changes I will let you know." Theron ended the call, and Vince began to pace around the room.

Katie was coming back to him. She still had no idea that he was alive, but all that would change the moment he found her. Then he would make her his. He sat down at the desk and finished making his flight reservation. She thought he was dead though. What if she moved on to someone else? What if he was too late finding her and she found love with another? He would not handle rejection from her very well, but the prophecy said she had to have a protector. He had worried for some time if that was all he would ever be to her. A bodyguard who worshiped her from afar.

He needed to stop thinking about it. He pulled out his phone and listened to the last voice message she left him. If it had been on an old answering machine with a tape, he would have worn it out already. "I love you," her voice said, and he closed his eyes savoring the thought that she loved him, just as he loved her. They would be together again if it was the last thing he did.

He had hours before he needed to leave but he pulled his suitcase out and packed. He wanted to be out the door as soon as the sun went down. He called the front desk and arranged for a taxi to pick him up at dusk then he paced and watched the clock.

Two hours later his phone vibrated. He hit the answer button. "What's wrong?" he asked Theron, the only reason he would call was if there was a problem.

"Alex just boarded the same ferry we think Katie is taking," Theron said through the phone.

"Fuck, what can I do?" Vince asked, running his hand through his hair.

"Nothing but wait. I'm going to have a party waiting at the dock for him, but in the meantime, all we can do is keep track of it."

Vince turned the television on to the weather channel. "The storm looks like it is moving quicker than they thought. Do you think the ferry will make it to Crete?"

"Yes, it won't turn back unless it's closer to Athens than Crete. Just get here and everything will be fine." Theron ended the call, and Vince paced back and forth. He still had hours to wait and knowing Alex was on the same boat with Katie was driving him mad. Katie could easily beat Alex in a one on one fight if it was fair, but Vince doubted Alex would fight fair.

Five minutes before the sun went down he took his bags and went to the lobby. The taxi was waiting outside to take him to the airport as soon as the sun was down. He stood out of the way of the windows tapping his foot on the tile floor, wishing the sun would vanish already. As soon as it did he was out the door and in the taxi heading toward the airport. He fingers tapped a nervous beat on his leg as the cab driver drove through the slow-moving traffic and Vince wished he could have left before rush hour had begun.

The vibrating of his phone made his blood turn to ice. "What happened?"

"I don't know for sure, but a life boat was stolen from the ferry and is out in the middle of the Sea of Crete somewhere. Search and Rescue are already in route, but they don't know who stole it or how many people are inside."

"Get me a boat, and an idea of where to start looking," Vince said into the phone, before telling the taxi driver to take him to the marina.

"I will call you back as soon as everything is set up." Theron ended the call.

Thirty minutes later Vince paid the taxi driver and stood at the dock in the soaking, freezing rain wondering how he was going to find Katie. His phone buzzed, and he dug it out of his pocket. "Tell me you have a boat."

"Yes, it is in slip 10F, the keys are under the cushion on the seat behind the cabin, but I have some bad news."

"What?" Vince asked, walking quickly to the dock marked F.

"They found the life raft. It was capsized, and no one was found." Theron's voice was tight with concern as the words left his mouth.

"She is not dead. Give me a clue, what was the closest island to them when they left the ferry." Vince walked onto the dock and looked at the numbers until he came to the tenth slip. He jumped on board and started looking for the keys with one hand while he kept his phone to his ear with the other.

"Milos, would have been the closest, but the boat was found miles away from there." Theron did not sound confident that Katie would be found alive.

"That is where I am heading. If you hear anything text me."

"I will and just in case, I am going to the port to meet the ferry."

"Thank you, Theron." Vince hit the end button on the phone and got the boat ready to head out.

Chapter 45

Katie

The rocking hadn't just been a dream, I was in a low-ceilinged room and I was rocking back and forth. No wonder it felt like the ground was moving, I was in a boat. I tried to bring my arms in front of me to push myself into a sitting position, but they were zip-tied behind me. I tried to remember what happened on the ferry but there was nothing but the sound of Vinny growling, then yelping. I looked around the room I was in. There wasn't much. A bench on both sides of the long wall and a few water tight boxes. I need to find a way to get the zip-tie off. My katana was still on my back, but I couldn't reach it. I rubbed my ankles together and blew out a relieved breath. My knife was still in the ankle sheath.

I wedge one foot behind the other and took my shoe off then my sock. I used my toes to get a grip on the knife and after five minutes I managed to pull the knife out of the sheath. I dropped the knife in the middle of the floor then sat so I could reach it with my zip-tied wrists. I leaned back and wiggled around until my fingers could grab the handle. I turned it and somehow got it between my back and the ties. I ran the sharp edge over the plastic over and over again using the bench for leverage. The tie finally broke and I brought my arms around and rubbed my wrists. I stretched my fingers and rolled my wrists to get the stiffness out of them. I looked out the port hole and saw nothing but water and rain. I had no idea where I was or who had taken me. I wanted to open the door and race out with my katana raised but there was a good chance who ever took me had a gun, or whatever they used to drop me on the ferry. I went to the waterproof boxes and quietly started to go through them.

There was a flare gun on top of a bunch of freeze dried food and bottled water in the first box. I put the flare gun in the waist band of my pants then moved on to the next box. It was full of blankets and life jackets. I pulled a life jacket out and put it on. I went through the box on the bottom but there was nothing useful in it. I was on some kind of a small boat somewhere in the Mediterranean, in the middle of winter, and who ever had put me here had only one thing in mind. Taking me to Lolita.

It was time to meet whoever had kidnapped me. I pulled the flare gun out of my pants, cocked it, and made my way to the hatch door. I tested the handle, it wasn't locked. I closed my eyes and found my breath. Whoever it was would not take me alive.

Calmly, I opened the hatch, aimed the flare gun at the man's chest, I could not make out his face through the rain, but it didn't matter, and fired. I saw his eyes go wide a split second before he dove for the deck. The flare missed him and flew into the rainy night before getting caught in a wave and going from red to nothing.

I pulled the knife out of my pocket and stepped onto the deck. The man jumped to his feet and came at me as fast as the rocking boat would allow, but stopped just out of range when he saw the knife. "Put the knife down Mary. No one's going to help you out of this situation, just accept your fate and be a good girl," he shouted, and I should have known all along. It was Alex. *Why was he calling me Mary?*

"Fuck you Alex, I will die before I let you take me to Lolita." I gripped the knife tighter, looking for a way to push him overboard or stab him.

"Whatever works," he said, lunging at me, going for the knife.

I ducked under his arm and sliced through his rain jacket along his side, then turned around to see him coming back toward me. His bloodshot eyes were open too wide, and his nostrils flared. He bent his knees and prepared to body slam me into the deck of the boat. Just before he reached me I brought my foot up and kicked out aiming for his balls. My foot connected, and he went down curling into a ball on the deck of the boat. A high-pitched mewing coming from his throat.

I kicked him hard in the face, then pulled his head up to make sure he was unconscious. When I confirmed that he was, I went to the helm to make sure we weren't going around in circles. The automatic pilot was set to return to Athens, but I could see an island with lights closer than Athens, since I saw nothing but water in that direction. I started hitting buttons on the screen with one hand and hanging onto the railing with the other. I reprogramed the controls to take me to the island I could see just on the edge of the horizon. I had just hit enter when Alex grabbed me around the waist and pulled me backwards.

"First your stupid dog bites the shit out of me then you cut me and kick me in the balls." He yelled in my ear, holding a knife at my throat. "Why won't you die bitch?"

I elbowed him in the side, making sure to dig my elbow into the cut I made with the knife and stomped on his foot. He dropped the knife as the boat hit a wave and we were jerked from our footing. I came back down landing hard on my feet, and pain shot up my legs to my knees, but I kept my eyes on him. "Because you are too much of a pussy to kill me," I yelled back at him.

I bent my knees and reached for my katana but let go as a huge wave rolled toward the broad side of the boat. "Fuck," I yelled, pointing to the wave.

"I'm not going to fall for that old trick," Alex said, coming back at me. I had come to grips with my mortality. It would be better to drown in the sea, than to be taken to Lolita. As soon as he was within range I punched him in the face as hard as I could and jumped over the side of the boat before the huge wave crashed on top of it.

I dove as deep as the life jacket would allow me to go before I began to float to the surface. When my head came out of the water I looked at the choppy sea before exhaling and pulling another breath in. I turned in a circle looking for the boat, but it was nowhere. The boat and Alex were gone.

I needed to swim toward the island I had programed the GPS for, it was my only chance. I turned in a circle again trying to find the lights, but I was too low in the water to see them. I started to swim with the swells hoping they would lead me to land before I died of hypothermia. I started to slowly kick my feet back and forth while lying on my back, trying to keep moving forward but not exert too much effort. I was going to need all the energy I had to stay alive. I stared up at the raging sky while the rain pelted me. I looked at my watch to see what time it was, but the screen was cracked the display was blank.

I don't know how long I kicked before I became too tired to go on, but the storm was no longer overhead, and the stars were out. The sea had calmed, but only a little, at least the waves had stopped breaking over me. I had no idea where I was, or if I was headed toward an island, Africa, or back to Athens. No matter where I was going, I knew I needed to keep moving. I thought about my mom, and wondered if she had enough power to help me. If I died out there at least Lolita would never get the chance to take advantage of my powers, and Vince would be waiting for me in the afterlife. I closed my eyes, I just needed to rest for a little while, then I would start swimming again.

"Please help her Poseidon," I heard my mother say. I was dreaming, but when I blinked my eyes I saw nothing but darkness, all I could do was listen.

"Why?" a voice that sounded like waves crashing against a brick wall asked.

"She is my daughter. Please I cannot lose her like this,"

Asteria said.

"She is the one you sent the prophecy about?"

"Yes, please without her I am nothing." My mother sounded like she was sobbing.

"What have you done for me in return for hiding you from Zeus?" He didn't sound like he wanted anything to do with my mother.

"Please," I whispered. "I am not ready to die. Not like this." My teeth chattered so badly I doubted he could understand what I was saying.

"How would you rather die?" His voice boomed in my direction.

"In battle, or after a long life, surrounded by my family." I didn't know what else to say. I just really didn't want to die, even if it meant Vince would meet me there. I had more to do in this life.

"Yes. Please help her, otherwise we will both die," my mother said, sounding like she was on the verge of tears.

"Very well, but there may be a time when I come to you for a favor."

"Thank you," my mother and I said at the same time.

Something was rubbing against my back, it was cold and hard. I opened my eyes and looked at the stars above me. They weren't swaying with the water like they had been before I closed them, but I was still in the water; I could feel it lapping at my body. I tried to kick my feet, but they kept connecting with the ground. *Why couldn't I keep swimming? Wait*, I thought. *Was I kicking sand?* I looked around, I was on shore. I had no idea how I had gotten there but I was back on land. I rolled over and water flooded my mouth. I spit it out and crawled out of the shallow water I had been lying in. At least I wasn't cold anymore. I tried to stand up, but I had no strength. I made it to my knees then I fell over. I rolled over and stared at the stars. It wasn't too bad, I could just lay here until the sun came up, then maybe I would have some strength to find help.

Chapter 46

Alex

Alex knew he was dreaming. He knew he had been floating in the ocean after the lifeboat capsized, he was lucky there was a flotation device on the side of the boat that flew off when it capsized.

Instead of floating in the sea though, he found himself on top of a mountain with a gold palace at its peak. He looked around wondering where he was, he had never seen anything like it before.

"Welcome home," a baritone voice said from behind him.

Alex jumped and turned to see a large man standing a few feet away. He had to be at least six-foot-eight, three-hundred pounds of muscle, wearing a toga and a gold-leafed crown. Alex took an involuntary step back.

"What are you talking about?" Alex asked, bringing his eyebrows together in confusion. "I'm from America."

"Yes, but I am your father, so you are also part Olympian." The man crossed his arms over his chest, and smiled, showing his too white teeth.

"Who are you?" Alex had no idea what was going on in this dream, but this wasn't his father. His father was the head of a drug cartel in Mexico.

"Zeus, who else would I be? You know where we are right?" His eyes narrowed, and his cheeks puffed out in frustration.

"And you're my father?" Alex laughed and looked around. If the man before him was Zeus, then he must be on Mount Olympus. This was the craziest dream he had ever had.

"Yes, your mother was a nice woman. I'm sorry you lost her at such a young age."

"My father would have killed her if she slept with someone else."

"What do you think happened to her? I am sorry about that."

"You bastard." Alex wanted to punch the man but there was no way he could take him, dream or not. "What do you want then?"

"I want you to kill all of the vampires, and 'The One'. If you do this I guarantee you will get to spend the afterlife here on Mount Olympus, you will never want for anything again."

"Kill all of the vampires, and all I would get is a place to stay when I'm dead? I think I'll pass."

"If you do not, then I won't save you from your current predicament. You will drown, and live in Hades."

Alex thought about it for a moment. He wasn't ready for his life to be over, if this guy wanted him to kill vampires what was the harm? They were becoming a bigger thorn in his side every day. "I will go after the vampires, but I have no idea who 'The One' is."

"Asteria's daughter, you must find her and kill her."

"How am I going to find her? Is she a vampire too?" Alex had no idea where to start looking for 'The One.'"

"No, she has not yet been turned, but she will be with or near them. They are drawn to her."

"Are you talking about Mary?" She was the only one he could think of who liked to hang out with vampires.

"I do not know her name, but she has powers similar to vampires."

Alex thought about how fast Mary was and how strangely she acted around them. It had to be her. "Done deal. I have been trying to kill her for months."

"Good, I will help you get to shore, as long as my brother does not see me," Zeus said.

Alex closed his eyes for a moment and when he opened them

302

he was lying on a rocky shore with the cool winter sun beating down on him. His side hurt where Mary had cut him and the punctures where the dog bit him stung.

He had no idea what the dream meant, maybe it was his subconscious telling him the way to take care of all his problems was to kill Lolita and Mary.

He had other concerns then, though. Where was he? He got to his feet and looked around. It wasn't much of a beach, it was barely ten feet long and surrounded by rocks that shot almost straight up for twenty feet. He pulled the ripcord off his watch that would send a distress signal to a search and rescue company he paid for times like this. They would start a search for him immediately. He guessed that he would be on his own for at least a day or two, depending on where he was in the world

He was thirsty and hungry, survival 101. He scaled the rocks until he came to a small ledge with a depression perfect to catch rain water. After the storm the night before, he thought it would be fresh. He dipped his hand into the water and brought it to his mouth. It was fresh water, but it tasted horrible. He needed to start a fire, find something to hold water in, and boil it before he drank any more of it. The last thing he needed was to get sick.

He went back to the beach and began his hunt for supplies. The pollution of the oceans was a blessing for someone shipwrecked. He found a few small water bottles, fishing line, and rope combing the beach. He climbed the rocks until he was on top of the mountain and surrounded by low brush. He made a small fire pit, used the rope, and a small branch to make a hand drill. After an hour he had a fire with his water bottle slowing boiling the water he took from the depressions in the rocks.

After he drank the first bottle of water he refilled it and started to sterilize a second bottle before he laid down for a nap. He didn't dream, just slept. When he woke up he was starving. He drank more water and went in search of food. He found nothing edible on the island. He was going to have to catch a fish if he wanted to eat. He found lots of fishing line, but no hooks. He waded out into the water and found some crustaceans he could cook and eat. With all his basic needs met and the sun starting to set, he sat down by his fire and wondered how long it would be before he was rescued.

Chapter 47

Vince

The sea was horrible, Vince could only be thankful that the boat had an enclosed wheelhouse. He pushed through the waves as quickly as he could, hoping Katie had put on a life jacket. The storm started to lessen as he moved closer to Milos. He turned the spotlight on and started looking for anything that looked out of place. Specifically, a woman floating in the water, but he found nothing.

When he finally reached Milos, he circled it. He had no idea if Katie would end up on the island or not, but it was his best chance. He saw nothing out of the ordinary and had no choice but to pull into the Marina and dock the boat. After leaving the boat in the marina he started walking around the shore. The storm had washed a lot of trash and seaweed onto the shore and he went through every pile he found. It was cold and wet, but he did not care, he would not get hypothermia like Katie would.

He pulled his phone out of his pocket and dialed Theron. "Have you found her?"

"No not yet, but when I do I am going to need to get her someplace dry and warm. It is freezing out here."

"I'm on it. Keep looking and I will text you with a place you can spend the day and keep Katie dry and warm."

Vince ended the call and kept looking. He was half way around the island when he saw an orange life jacket near the shore. He ran faster than he ever had before and dropped to his knees.

She was cold, so cold, but she was breathing. He picked her up and started walking toward the road. "Katie," Vince looked down at her. "You are so cold. Are you, all right?"

"Am I in heaven or Hades?" she asked, reaching up and caressing his cheek, her hand was too cold.

"Neither, you are on Milos."

"I missed you so much Vince. I had a plan to kill Lolita, but now I'm dead. At least I get to be with you."

Her lips were blue, and her skin was ice. He wondered whether he should just take her to the hospital, but he thought about the media circus that would ensue and decided he could take care of her. He pulled out his phone and called Theron back. He put the phone on speaker and put it in his pocket, so he could carry her and talk at the same time.

"Hush, you are not dead you have hypothermia. Let's get you inside and warmed up. Then you are going to tell me what happened." He pulled her close to him. She smelled like the ocean but underneath the salt water, she smelled like she always did to him, and he could not help but smile.

"Did you find her?" Theron asked as soon as he answered the phone, concern lacing his voice.

"Yes, I need you to tell me how to get to the house and fast. She has hypothermia and I need to get her warm." Vince ran to the nearest street.

"Why don't you take her to a hospital?"

"I will explain later. Tell me where I am going. Hurry Theron." Vince did not have time to explain.

"I have the location of your phone. You aren't far, go south on the road you are on for a about a mile."

Vince ran for the first half-mile then realized he was just making Katie colder than she already was, but there was no choice, if he did not get her warm and dry soon she would die. He would not let that happen.

"OK, when you come to the next street turn right like you are going back to the beach." Vince took the corner wide, still running as fast as he could. "After you pass the next block it will be the third house on the left. The key is under the mat."

Vince counted the driveways then turned and headed for the front door of the house. He set Katie down on the ground while he removed the key and unlocked the door. He picked her up and went inside while Theron continued to speak. "It is Zoi's house, so the windows are all tinted and no one should bother you."

"Thank you, Theron," he said, as he ran through the house looking for a bedroom.

"Go take care of our girl. If you need anything call me." The call ended, and Vince set Katie down on the bed.

He pulled a knife out of his pocket and started to cut her clothes off. He did not care if she had to go around naked for the next twenty-four hours if it meant she would live.

"Hey, I'm awake, you only undress me when I'm unconscious," she said, laughing hysterically. "Hey, did you know I have a dog? I named him after you because I missed you so much. He was on the ferry. I hope someone takes good care of him."

He had no idea what she was talking about, he was more concerned with getting her warm. After he wrapped her up like a burrito with the blankets from the bed, he went into the bathroom and looked for anything else that would help her warm up slowly. If it was a vampire's house, there was a chance there would be a hot pad or something to keep blood warm. He went through every cabinet and storage area in the place only to find nothing. He checked on her every five minutes and while she did not get any worse, he wasn't seeing much improvement. He walked by the laundry room and stopped. There was a dryer. He took an extra blanket from the linen closet and put it in the dryer for ten minutes. When he pulled it out it was warm but not hot. He took it into the bedroom and wrapped it around her.

"Vince, are you alive or am I dead?" she asked, as her teeth started

307

to chatter. He let out a breath it was a good sign. She was starting to warm up.

"We are both alive, love. Sleep, we will talk in the morning."

Katie mumbled something else then started to shake. Vince lay down next to her and held her in his arms until she stopped shaking and started snoring. Relieved that she was out of danger Vince got up, he had things to do before the sun came up.

Chapter 48

Theron

Theron sat in the car and waited, knowing Katie wasn't going to be on the boat. He was sure Alex had found a way to get her on to the lifeboat and leave. He just hoped Vince would be able to find her before it was too late. The storm was horrible and unless she had a life jacket on she would never make it. There was no way to know if the Coast Guard would be able to find her. She might be 'The One,' but he doubted Poseidon cared.

People were filing out of the ferry, cars were being unloaded, and two of his humans were waiting with a sign with Katie's name on it. He wondered what happened to her things. He knew she hated to lose her belongings, maybe he should go and see if he could find them.

A flame red Mini Cooper pulled off the ferry and Theron smiled a real smile. Such a fun car for such a small engine. The Cooper did not speed away as the other cars did but parked next to his BMW. A tall woman with pink hair and blue eyes got out with a large dog on a leash. She walked along the people holding signs and stopped at his men. Confused, he rolled his window down to listen.

"You are waiting for Katie Hunter?" she asked. Unable to stand still, she bounced from one foot to the other. She looked like she was too young to be driving let alone speaking with such authority.

"Yes, who are you?" Vasilis asked.

"I'm a friend of hers. She won't be getting off the boat."

"Why not?"

"She was kidnapped by Alex. He tasered her, stole a lifeboat, and went out into the storm."

Theron got of the car and approached the woman. "And you did nothing to stop it?" he asked, putting his hand on his hips, and looking at the dog.

"I tried, but I slipped and fell on the deck. When I got to my feet, he was lowering the lifeboat into the water. Who are you?"

The dog who had been looking around sat down in front of Theron. "I am Theron, a friend of hers. Were you traveling together?"

"Yeah, of course we were." Her eyes darted from side to side. Theron didn't need to hear her heart rate pick up to know she was lying. "Look I have her bags and her dog." She looked down at the dog and rubbed him behind the ears.

"When did she get a dog?" Theron didn't trust this human; she was lying and couldn't hold still.

"She found him in the back of a trash truck. She wanted to find Vinny a good home, but no one would take him, so she kept him."

"Vinny?" She was telling the truth now. Katie must have believed Vince was dead if she named a dog after him.

"Yes, Vinny, look we have to go look for her. She could be dead, or dying, and that asshole will not play nice with her."

Theron's phone buzzed in his pocket and he pulled it out. It was Vince. He turned his back on her to talked to him. He had found Katie, and was trying to save her. When Theron was done talking to Vince, he turned back to the girl.

"Katie has been found, she is fighting through hypothermia, but she's alive." He needed to find out how much this human knew. He didn't think Katie would tell her about who she was or the existence of vampires, but he needed to make sure. "Get in your car and follow me," he said, trying to compel her.

"Why would I do that? I don't know you from Adam." She

took a step back and pulled on Vinny's leash, but the dog did not move from Theron's feet.

Theron had no idea what to do, the last thing he needed was another human he could not compel. "Please, Vince will bring Katie to my house when she is well enough. If you want to return her things and give her back her dog, you will come and stay at my house."

She looked at him for a long second as if deliberating whether she could trust him or not. "OK, but the dog stays with me. Come on Vinny, we will get you back to KK before you know it."

"Let's get back to the house," Theron said to his men, and got into the backseat of the car. The two humans he was thinking about changing got into the front. "Make sure she stays behind us. I don't trust her."

"Yes sir," Vasilis said, turning in his seat to watch out the back window.

When they reached the house, the woman got out of the car and went to the trunk letting the dog run around in the landscaping outside the house. She pulled two suitcases out of the trunk and walked toward the front door before stopping and waiting for Theron. "Vinny are you done?" she called, and the dog came running over to her.

Theron stopped by Yannis. "Get a picture of her. I want to run it through the facial recognition program. I want to know everything about her."

"Yes sir." He pulled his phone out and quickly snapped a profile photo of the girl. "I will get a full face when the opportunity arises."

"Good, get her inside and feed her." Theron walked to the door, opened it, and held it open for her.

"Thank you." She and Vinny went inside, and the dog started to sniff around.

"Is the dog house broken?" Theron didn't want any of Evangelos's furniture to be ruined by dog pee.

"Yes, he is. Don't worry he is a very well-behaved dog. Katie had nothing to do but train him for like a month." She stood in the doorway with her hands on her hips.

"Yannis will show you to your room. I will take Katie's bag to hers. What is your name by the way?" Theron asked.

"You can call me Jean." She stood a little straighter; she was telling the truth.

"Thank you for not lying to me. Yannis will help you with whatever you need." Theron turned, and started walking down the hall leading to the master suite.

"When is Katie going to be here?" Jean called.

"I do not know, but at the soonest tomorrow night. I wouldn't be surprised, however, if it was longer." Theron said, without looking back.

He went to the master suite and put Katie's suitcase on the bed. He should have kept the master suite for himself, but if Katie and Vince's reunion went like he thought it would, they were going to need the bigger bed. Plus, it was on the opposite side of the house from the other bedrooms, so the rest of the occupants would not have to listen to their sexcapades. Her things dropped off, he went back to his new office and sat down at the desk.

Theron opened his computer and started his search for Alex. he wasn't sure if he survived or not, but if he did, he wanted to know. The man had destroyed his home and almost the entire island, it could not go unpunished. He wanted to find Lolita too, but Alex was on the top of his list. From what he knew of the man he would not give up trying to kill Katie. Removing him from the game was going to be just as important as removing Lolita.

A knock at the door interrupted his search but it was to be expected on a day like today. "Come." He closed the lid on his computer as Yannis came in.

"I just emailed you the photos of Jean." He stopped in front of Theron's desk and put his hands behind his back.

"Good, what is she doing now?" Theron leaned back in his

chair, pushed his palms together, and rested his chin on his fingers.

"She is eating dinner and taking care of the dog. Vasilis is with her."

"I do not want her left alone, unless she is in her room. When she is, I want a guard on her door."

"Is she a prisoner?"

"No, but I don't trust her. Until I find out more about her I want to keep an eye on her. That will be all."

Yannis turned and left the office closing the door behind him.

Theron opened his computer and accessed his email program. He saved the photos of Jean, then uploaded them into his facial recognition program. It would take hours to find a match, so he locked his screen and got up to check on Helen.

He walked down the hall to her room and knocked lightly on the door. "Come," she called, and he went inside.

Helen was laying on her bed fully clothed. She still wasn't up to one hundred percent and needed to rest a few times a night. She put on a brave face, but she was still weak, and he wondered how long it would take her to fully recover from the attack. He moved to the chair beside her bed and sat.

"How are you feeling?" Theron asked, taking her hand in his.

"I am sick of being tired all the time. It is taking me too long to recover. Why is it you and Vince bounced back so quickly?"

"We are quite a few years older than you Helen. It is expected that it will take you longer." He shook his head.

"Is Katie safe? Did Vince find her?"

"Yes, Vince found her on Milos, she is battling hypothermia right now, but Vince is confident that she will be fine."

"When do you think they will show up here?" she laughed.

"I will give them a week, before I start hounding him to get back here so we can plan. Maybe sooner depending on our new guests."

"What? Who is here?" Helen sat up and inhaled deeply. "Do I smell a dog?"

"Yes, it seems Katie saved it wherever she was hiding, and now she has a dog named Vinny."

"You're kidding?" Helen laughed. "Vince is going to love that."

"I know, I hope I'm there when Katie tells him. He is going to be pissed."

"Who else is here though?" Helen moved, so her back rested against the headboard.

"A friend of Katie's, she had Katie's bag and the dog when she got off the ferry." Theron frowned and looked down at his hand in Helen's.

"Is it a man?" Helen asked, not understanding the frown.

"No, it's a woman, well more a girl than a woman."

"Why the frown then?"

"There is something about her I don't trust, and compulsion does not work on her."

"Well, I am sure you will figure out who she is in no time. What is her name?" Helen asked, looking pleased to have another woman around. It had been a boy's club for too long.

"She told me it was Jean, but I think it was only a half truth." He pulled his hand away. "I need to get back to work. Can I get you anything?"

"No, I am going to get up in a few minutes. I just needed to lay down for a little while. I have work to do too."

"Take it easy, Rome wasn't built in a day and rebuilding the compound will take longer than that." He got up and went to the door. "I think we need to have a party when Katie and Vince get back. We need to celebrate being alive and mourn our losses."

"I will organize it after I sort a few things out." Helen leaned back and closed her eyes.

"Take all the time you need." Theron left, closing the door quietly behind him.

"Vinny," he heard Jean yell from the other side of the house.

"Vinny where did you go?"

Great, Theron thought, *now there is a dog running loose in the house.* He inhaled, he knew where the dog was. He went to the master bedroom door and found it partly open. He pushed it wide and found the dog not only in the room but on the bed with his head resting on Katie's suitcase.

"Jean, the dog is in here." He called from the open door. He walked over to Vinny and made eye contact. "Dogs are not allowed on the bed. Get down." The dog merely perked an ear up and looked away with a low whine. "I said get *down*." Theron put emphasis on the last word. The dog ignored him. He took the suitcase and pulled it from under his head. The dog perked up for a second then put his head back on the bed when Theron put the suitcase on the floor. "Look you stupid dog, I know you miss her, I do too. She will be here in a few days, but I need you to get off the bed before you make a mess of it." Theron grabbed Vinny's collar and tugged on it. Vinny growled.

"What did you do to him?" Jean's voice filled the room as she stomped over and sat down on the bed next to Vinny.

"Nothing, I was just trying to get him off the bed. This is not my house, if he damages anything I will have to pay to replace it and believe me nothing in this house comes cheap." Theron took a step away from the dog. In his youth dogs were not allowed in the house. They had a job and if they did not do it they were killed. This new century and its kindness to animals amazed him.

"Katie always let him sleep on the bed. I'm sure he is in here because you put her suitcase in here. Come on Vinny, you are going to hang out with me until KK gets back." The dog jumped off the bed and stood next to Jean.

"Why does he like you so much? He doesn't listen to a word I have to say." Theron ran his fingers through his hair. Why did he care? He had much more important things to worry about.

Chapter 49

Vince

Vince went back to the Marina, to get his suitcase then stopped at a store to pick up a few groceries. Katie was going to be hungry when she woke up. He ate from the clerk behind the counter then hurried back to the house, worried about Katie.

After he returned and was satisfied that Katie was sleeping soundly he brought a chair in from the other room and sat it next to the bed before sitting and calling Theron.

"Is she going to be all right?" Theron asked, answering on the first ring.

"I think so, I have done all I could. She is dry and as warm as I want her to be. I wanted to put her in a hot bath, but it would kill her."

"Warm her up slowly and she will be fine. I was able to locate her suitcase and her dog."

"She said she had a dog." Vince looked over at her; were her lips a little bit less blue now? He could not tell.

"Yes, and he is jumping all over the furniture. I am ready to kill him."

"Any sign of Alex?"

"No, he wasn't on the boat when it arrived, and her friend is not going to leave until she makes sure Katie is safe."

"Sounds like you have your hands full." Vince wanted to laugh, but looking at Katie he could not.

"I do, but her friend wants to know why you didn't take her to the hospital and I would like to know as well."

"She was wearing a life jacket with the boat's name on it Theron. If I took her in wearing it, they would know what happened to her. There would be no way to keep it quiet and we both know she does not need that kind of attention."

Theron relayed Vince's words to Katie's friend. "We understand." He sounded annoyed.

"She sounds stubborn, just like you. I will let you go have fun with that."

"You have no idea. I have to go, but please let me know if there is any change in Katie's condition."

"I will, thank you again." Vince ended the call and looked over to Katie. Her lips were definitely losing their blue color. He climbed into bed behind her and rested his arm on her waist. He had dreamed of sharing a bed with Katie since the first time he saw her, and now he was. It wasn't how he wanted it, but they were both alive and she would survive. He buried his face as close to her as he could and fell into a dreamless sleep.

Chapter 50

Katie

I woke up the next day with a vampire's arms around me. I was a little concerned about who it was. All I remembered was escaping Alex and swimming for what felt like ever. Then dreaming of my mom talking to Poseidon? After that everything was hazy. I thought I dreamt of Vince too, but I wasn't sure, and it didn't answer my question of whose arm was around me.

My bladder was full, but I didn't want to wake up whoever was in bed with me. I looked around not recognizing anything about the room. The man behind me shifted and pulled me closer. *Crap*, I thought to myself, how was I going to get out of bed without waking him. I slowly began to pull away from him moving his arm slowly until I was out from under it. I slid off the bed and almost fell when my feet hit the floor.

I whirled around to make sure I didn't wake him up. Wait it was Vangel? No, it was a vampire. It was my vampire. I had been sleeping in Vince's arms. He wasn't dead. I looked at the side profile of the man I loved. Tears of joy blurred my vision. I held in the sob that wanted to rip from my chest. As much as I wanted to jump on him, kiss him and tell him I loved him, I needed to pee.

I staggered to a door with my head rocking, it was trying to convince me I was still in the sea. I opened the door as quietly as I could and closed it behind me. I groaned, I could not remember the last time my legs were so sore. After I took care of business I turned the shower on.

I got in and stood there for a second before I doubled over and sobbed, the love of my life wasn't dead, I wasn't dead, and we were finally going to be together. I couldn't help the tears that came. I couldn't remember the last time I was so happy. When I had cried myself out I scrubbed the salt and sand from my body, I think ten pounds of sand came out of my hair. I was almost done when I heard Vince shout my name. "I'm in the shower," I yelled back, turning the water off. I grabbed a towel and started to dry off when the door opened, and Vince walked in looking distressed.

"Katie, are you OK?" He stood in the middle of the room staring at me as if he was reassuring himself that he wasn't hallucinating.

"Yeah, I think so. My legs are sore, I have some scrapes and taser marks from where that dickhead Alex hit, me but other than that I'm fine. What about you?"

"I am fine now that I found you." He moved too fast for me to follow. One moment he was standing in the doorway and the next his arms were around me and his face was buried in my neck.

"I thought you were dead." The tears I thought were gone came back. He really was alive.

"I know, I'm sorry. I'm so sorry I left you to fend for yourself."

"Wait, what do you mean left me?"

Did he fake his death to get away from me?

"Theron, Helen and I were buried in the tunnels, knocked unconscious. It took me six weeks to wake up. Then I could not find you."

"It doesn't sound like you left me on purpose, Vince. I thought you were dead, then Alex figured out my alias, and I had to disappear for a while."

"I am supposed to protect you. I failed to keep you safe."

"I wasn't on my own. I had Vinny for most of it." I squeezed him back, still dumbstruck that he was alive. "How many of Theron's

320

vampires survived? Who found you?"

Vince blew out a breath. "Miguel only found Theron, Helen, and me."

"What?" I yelled, ready to push out of his arms. "Why would Miguel save you? I thought he hated you."

"Miguel was staying on the island you could see from the beach at Theron's. Alex and his men met there before they attacked the compound. He called and left Theron a message the night of your test to warn us. Theron never checked his messages after everything with Ben.

"Miguel watched everything happen from a cave on the island that day. There was nothing he could do until night fell. He started searching for survivors as soon as he got there. He did not find us for days. When he did we were all unconscious, he had to hand feed us blood. When I woke up I was weak. I had to eat every night to regain my strength. Miguel took care of all of us during that time."

"He saved you all?" My voice came out in a whisper. Maybe he had changed, I thought to myself. "I still can't forgive him for what he did to me."

"I am not asking you to. I will never forgive him for what he did to you either. If I would have been able to move when I woke up I would have killed him."

"Where is he now? Is he trying to find me too?"

"No, we sent him to Lolita as a spy. He is feeding us information, so we can come up with a plan to kill her."

"You think we can trust him?" I didn't know how to take this. The 'evil one' was on our side? "What if Lolita sent him to the island to spy on us?"

"He saved us Katie, we owe him the respect he deserves. Believe me, it took a while for me to trust him again." He kissed the top of my head.

"I won't have to see him until we meet Lolita?" I asked, thinking I would like to put it off for the rest of my life.

"Yes, he is fitting in very well with her. He has been there for a week. Tell me what happened with Alex. I was terrified you were dead when I found you on the beach."

After I finished telling him about what happened to me he pulled me into a tight hug. "You are lucky to be alive."

He pulled away from me and looked into my eyes for a moment before his mouth met mine. How many times in the past three months had I dreamed of kissing him again? His lips were just as I remembered them, soft and smooth, tasting of everything Vince. I ran my fingers through his hair, it still felt like silk. His tongue forced its way through my lips as he bent down, wrapped his arms under my butt, lifting me up and sat me on the counter. Without breaking the kiss, he pulled the towel away and ran his hands up and down my side, grazing the side of my breasts each time. I arched into him as he pulled me closer settling himself between my spread legs.

You have no idea how much I have missed you, he thought to me while cupping my breast in one hand. I moaned and leaned back to give him better access.

"I was so lost without you. I didn't know how to go on. I still can't believe you're here with me," I said as he kissed down my neck, across my collar bone, then settled on my nipple. He nipped and sucked until I was withering beneath him. "Vince, I need you."

He pulled his head up and looked at me. "Patience, do you know how long I have been dreaming about this moment? I intend to savor it." He switched to the other nipple and stared to pull and suck it.

My core was on fire, throbbing, and aching for friction. I closed my eyes and relished the attention he was paying to my breasts before the junction of my thighs could no longer be ignored. I ran my hands through his hair, grabbed a handful, and pulled him away. "You can play with my boobs later, right now I need something else."

His eyes flashed red and a devilish grin pulled at his lips before he sank to his knees before me. I gasped as he buried his face in my moist center. I moaned as he licked and sucked on my nub forcing it to the surface. His fangs scraped against my flesh and panic of being bitten rose but faded almost as soon as it came. Vince would never bite me. My mind was torn from the thought as a finger caressed my channel before entering me and began to move in and out. He pulled me closer and closer to the climax I never thought I would never get to experience.

"Come for me," he said releasing me for a moment, before he continued adding another finger to the first one rapidly moving inside me.

I grabbed his hair and pushed him harder into my core before the blinding pleasure washed over me and my body convulsed around his fingers. My mind floated blissfully in the aftershock of the orgasm. I expected him to stop and take me to bed but he continued, and my pleasure continued to multiply until I could no longer stand it.

"Vince stop, please I need you inside me." I moaned, trying to push him away. If he didn't stop soon I was going to pass out.

He finally pulled away giving me a rare smile before he threw me over his shoulder, walked out of the bathroom and threw me onto the bed. I moved to the center of it and held out my hand to him. He took it and moved between my thighs. *You look like a goddess right now,* he thought pushing a strand of hair out of my face.

"Please, I have dreamed of this for so long. Please make love to me." I put my hands on his hips and tried to move him where I needed him to be, but the stubborn vampire wouldn't budge.

"All in good time," he whispered before taking my lips with his. His hands found my breasts again and he kneaded them before finding my nipples and gently pinching them.

I moaned in response and arched my back into him. I broke the kiss unable to concentrate on his lips while he was making my nipples sing. "Please," I moaned. I needed him like I had never needed anyone in my life. I reached between us and found his cock. I wrapped my fingers around it, surprised when I couldn't get my hand all the way around and ran my hand up and down its length.

Are you ready for me? He reared back forcing me to let go of him.

I have never been more ready, I thought back to him. He positioned himself between my legs and pushed forward sheathing himself deep inside me with one smooth stroke. I gasped at how tight the fit was.

Are you, all right? He thought to me, freezing.

"Yes, after the attack I never thought we would get to be together," I moaned out. He started to move in an out, and I matched him stroke for stroke. I was never going to get enough of him.

I have never felt anything more amazing than this. His eyes locked on my mine. *You are the most amazing person I have ever known.*

The pressure started building again, and the idea that he was alive, let alone making passionate love to me had my emotions spinning out of control. *I missed you so much.* I wanted to say more but he increased his pace and put pressure on just the right spot. I moaned, I was so close.

Wait for me, he thought speeding up even more.

I'm trying. He bent his head and kissed me as the pressure exploded. I screamed my pleasure into his mouth. My eyesight dimmed as the pleasure went on and on until he groaned coming deep inside me before he collapsed onto my chest. I floated down from my climax and wrapped my arms around the vampire I could not help but love.

"Am I too heavy? Do you want me to move?" he asked, lifting his head up.

"No, just stay where you are for a little while longer." I sniffed my nose, while tears of joy ran down my face.

"What's wrong? Did I hurt you?" he asked, looking concerned about the tears.

"Vince, I thought you were dead. I thought I was going to be on my own for the rest of my life. I never thought we would be together again." I hugged him to me tighter and more tears spilled out. "I've never been better."

"I still can't believe I found you. When I saw that the last time you had used your credit card was the day after the attack, I thought Alex or Lolita had captured you. I was ready to kill everyone I came across." He moved to my side and pulled me to him, wrapping his arms around me. I rested my head on his chest, content for the first time in months.

"I've dreamed of you holding me every night. I'm sorry I didn't come back and look for you."

He squeezed me tighter. "You thought I was dead, there would not have been anything for you to find if that was true. It was much more important to get away from Alex than to find me."

"I hope he drowned, the bastard."

"Tell me where you have been," Vince said, running his hand up and down my side, before tracing my tattoo.

I explained everything to him. Figuring out Alex was using the cameras to find me, then my alias. Ramstein and everyone in Kevò, who taught me and helped me. I told him about Tad, leaving out that he was the first vampire and about Mordor.

"You are smarter than I gave you credit for. I'm proud of you." He squeezed me again.

"Are you going to tell me what happened to you? What about Theron and Helen, are they all right? What happened to the rest of Theron's vampires?"

Once Vince filled me in on everything that had happened in Crete I was starving. I wiggled out of his arms and stood looking around for my clothes. I found a pile and picked up what was left of my jeans. "You didn't?" I held up one leg of my pants.

"Hey, you were awake, you don't remember?" He sat up and looked at me.

"No, I don't." I narrowed my eyes at him.

"You told me I was doing it wrong because you were awake." He laughed.

"Just so we are clear, you are still a creepy vampire who likes to cut clothes off me when I'm unconscious or delirious. And now I have nothing to wear." I looked around the room and spotted a suitcase. "Is this yours?"

"Yes, I went to get it from the boat last night after I knew you were out of danger. What are you doing?" Vince moved to get out of bed but relaxed when I pulled out a pair of boxer shorts, and the T-shirt I had given him with Yoda on it.

"How did this survive?" I asked, holding it up, and remembering how excited I was to give it to him.

"It didn't. Miguel bought it for me having no idea that you had bought me one."

Part of me wanted to drop it back in the suitcase knowing where it came from, but the look in Vince's eye told me that he loved the shirt because I bought it for him first. I pulled it over my head then pulled on the boxers.

"Why are you getting dressed? Come back to bed." Vince pulled a pillow under his head and lay on his side with the sheet pulled up to his belly button. *Damn he was fine*, I thought to myself.

"Bathroom, then I need food. I haven't eaten since lunch yesterday." I backed toward the bathroom door. "Don't disappear on me while I'm in there."

"I won't," he chuckled and lay back on the bed.

When I came out of the bathroom, Vince wasn't in bed, and the door to the living room was open. I walked down the hall, realizing I didn't even know where I was.

I found him in the kitchen, doing what he did best, cooking for me. "I thought you weren't going to disappear," I said, coming up behind him, and wrapping my arms around his waist.

"I didn't, I walked into the kitchen." He rested his hand on mine then turned around to face me. "Hi."

"Hi." He bent his head down and kissed me. "Now, out of the kitchen until breakfast is ready."

I moved to the bar overlooking the kitchen. "What are we going to do now?" I asked.

"Your suitcase, your dog, and your friend are at Theron's in Crete, so eventually we need to go back over there."

"What friend?" I asked, confused.

Epilogue
Lolita

Lolita looked down at the courtyard below. Her soldiers were coming along nicely, Pier and the other generals were putting them through their paces. They were finally starting to look like an army for a change. They looked hungry though. It was becoming harder and harder to keep them fed from her current location. Someone walking toward her interrupted her thought.

She turned when the door opened, and Greta came out. "There is someone here to see you, Mistress."

"Who is it?" Very few people knew where she was living.

"He said to tell you it was your brother." Greta shrank back a step when Lolita cringed. How had he found her?

"Very well, take him into my office, then alert the girls, I will be with him shortly." Lolita turned back to watch her soldiers and wondered why Miguel was there.

She knew he had been looking for Katie when she last saw him, but she doubted he would be able to find her. Did he finally understand that they did not need the human? She let out a sigh and went inside to find out.

Miguel was standing in front of her bookcase reading the titles of the books with his hands behind his back. He looked the same as the last time she saw him except not quite as upset. "Miguel," she said getting his attention.

"Lolita, thank you for seeing me." He turned, letting his hands hang loosely at his sides in case she attacked him no doubt. They had not parted peacefully last time.

"Of course, I knew you would be back. What can I do for you?" She walked behind her desk and sat down.

"I want to help you." His voice sounded convincing, but the tightness in his shoulders made her not want to believe him.

"You don't sound like it. Why are you really here?" She drummed her fingers on the desk, keeping her eyes glued to him.

"Katie's gone. Vince must have brainwashed her before he was killed. When the dust settled, and he was dead, I thought she would try and find me, but she never did." Miguel sat down in the chair across from her desk and folded his hands together settling them on his lap. "I'm tired of being on the wrong side of this battle. I want her out of the way and I want to help you."

"Why should I believe you after how you reacted when I told you what I did to father?" Lolita could normally see though Miguel's lies, but as farfetched as his story was, she wanted to believe him.

"Because I understand where you are coming from now. If she is 'The One', she is going to kill me for what I did to her and I don't want to die. Let's find her and kill her, then take over Europe."

"Then I'm glad to have you." She stood, came around the desk, and hugged him. "Let me show you around." She walked to the door of the study. She would find out the truth soon enough.

"Thank you," Miguel stood and followed her through the door. "You chose a great spot for you headquarters; everyone is terrified of this island."

"It is one of the reasons I bought it. Its sordid past makes it a fitting location to rule from." She led him down the hallway to the stairs then down to the basement.

"This is where I keep my prisoners," she said, waving her arm at the closed cell doors. "It's dark so they will not burn, and it is deep enough I do not have to listen to them scream."

"Good idea," Miguel murmured.

"This is my new torture room. What do you think?" she asked, as they entered a room about twenty by twenty.

"It looks like it will be useful," Miguel looked around at the various devices of torture: a rack, an iron maiden, there was even a bare bedspring attached to a car battery.

"Don't worry Miguel. I don't intend on using any of this on you." Lolita walked around the room, caressing the different machines here and there. "I do need you to prove your loyalty to me though."

"What do you want me to do?" Miguel asked.

"I need you to help me build my army. I am growing weak from changing too many too close together. Find a good candidate and turn them so they may join our forces. I always need new blood for the army." They left the room and Lolita closed the door. "Come, I will show you the rest of the property," she said, not waiting for an answer.

She had done nothing with the landscaping or the outward appearance, but when they entered what was the main dormitory of the sanitarium he looked surprised. It had been completely renovated. The walls were white, and the tile floors were clean. They walked the halls and stuck their heads into a few rooms. They were all filled with vampires. Some were training in hand-to-hand combat, some were eating out of blood bags, while others were sleeping. "How long have you been working on this?" Miguel asked.

"Since before the first world war." Lolita looked at her nails then back at her troops.

"Why didn't you tell me about this?" Miguel looked shocked by the number of soldiers she had.

"You were too wrapped up in the prophecy. I'm only showing it to you now because you let it go." She turned around and went back outside.

"Would you like something to eat?" she asked, walking down a hallway to a locked door.

"If it is not too much trouble." Miguel waited while she pulled a set of keys from a concealed pocket in her dress, unlocked the door, then opened it, indicating Miguel should enter first.

He walked through the door and down a corridor. The end of it opened into a sitting room. "Ladies, I have a surprise for you," Lolita called from behind him.

A few seconds later ten beautiful women filed out of a door on the right side of the room. "Take your pick they all taste amazing." Lolita said, sitting on the sofa, and leaning back.

Miguel looked at the women and chose one with black hair and pale eyes. She led him to her bedroom leaving Lolita alone with the rest of her female donors. Lolita smiled to herself, of course he would take the one that looked the most like Katie. He might say he was over her, but based on his pick he would always have a soft spot for the girl.

Lolita dismissed the rest of the women and sat back to wait for him. All the of girls had been injected with truth serum a few minutes before they arrived. She was going to find out exactly what he was really doing there.

Miguel came out of the room fifteen minutes later looking almost drunk. "Thank you, Lolo, she tasted wonderful. What are you feeding them?"

"Just a cocktail of sorts. Have a seat, Miguelito." Lolita patted the spot next to her on the sofa. He ambled over before collapsing next to her. "Why don't you tell me why you're really here?"

"Because I missed you. Do you know where I spent the summer? On a fucking deserted island. I was living in a cave," he was almost sobbing as he continued. "Do you have any idea how dirty and boring living in a cave is?"

"Why were you living in a cave?"

"Because I was waiting for Katie to come around. I thought Vince or her would come to me to find you, but they never did. I just wanted to be near her." Lolita thought he looked like he was about to start crying.

"Do you really want to rule by my side?" she asked, putting a calming hand on this thigh.

"I would rather rule on my own, but you and I have always had fun together so why not?"

"I missed you little brother, now we will be together forever. We will rule the world side by side." She leaned over and rested her head against his. She had her brother back and there would be no more talk of the prophecy. She almost had everything she wanted.

Dear Reader,

Thank you for reading, <u>Hunted by Vampires</u>. I hope you enjoyed this phase of Katie's journey into the world of vampires.

If you liked this story, please tell a friend, and leave a review on **Amazon** or **Goodreads**.

Look for the next book in the series later in 2018.

Happy reading!

Joy.

Visit Joy's website at: **www.joymosby.com** or follow her on social media: **https://www.facebook.com/joymosby81625**
Twitter: **@joy_mosby**

Acknowledgements

This book would not have been possible without the help of so many people.

First a huge thank you goes out to my husband, who puts up with my moods. (This is going to be the best book ever or great now I have to start over). I could not do what I am doing without your love and support. Love you.

Leah and Amy, my own personal cheerleaders and beta readers. Your enthusiasm and support make me want to continue.

Mom and Dad, I would not be where I am today if you had not gotten me tested for dyslexia.

Anelia, your covers have helped me more than you will know. Thank you for the Facebook ads you made, and helping through the re-sizing fiasco.

The biggest THANK YOU goes out to my readers. Without you this would be a pretty boring job.

About the Author

I love to write about the Heroines Journey in the paranormal universe, because writing about everyday life is boring for me (hence I am horrible at blogging). I love taking a character who thinks she is weak and show her how strong she really is.

I live on forty acres in Northwest Colorado with two dogs (Ajax and Achilles), a few barn cats (Two-Face, Skeletor, and Silvester) and my amazing husband. I love not having any neighbors, being outside in the summer and inside in the winter. I have traveled to many places in the world, but I have many more places to visit before I am done.

When I am not staring at the monitor writing, I am staring at my Kindle reading, or spending time with my husband and animals.

Check out my website: Joymosby.com to find out about new releases and join my mailing list. I am not very good at updating it but bear with me I am working on it.

CPSIA information can be obtained
at www.ICGtesting.com
Printed in the USA
BVHW041721210319
543354BV00018B/180/P